THE CONSTANT MAN

THE CONSTANT MAN

Peter Steiner

SEVERN HOUSE

First world edition published in Great Britain and the USA in 2021
by Severn House, an imprint of Canongate Books Ltd,
14 High Street, Edinburgh EH1 1TE.

Trade paperback edition first published in Great Britain and the USA in 2022
by Severn House, an imprint of Canongate Books Ltd.

severnhouse.com

British Library Cataloguing-in-Publication Data
A CIP catalogue record for this title is available from the British Library.

ISBN-13: 978-0-7278-9074-0 (cased)
ISBN-13: 978-1-78029-782-8 (trade paper)
ISBN-13: 978-1-4483-0520-9 (e-book)

All Severn House titles are printed on acid-free paper.

MIX
Paper from
responsible sources
FSC
www.fsc.org   FSC® C013056

Typeset by Palimpsest Book Production Ltd.,
Falkirk, Stirlingshire, Scotland.
Printed and bound in Great Britain by
TJ Books Limited, Padstow, Cornwall.

PART ONE

Willi

In the Munich police department Willi Geismeier had been known either as a pain in the ass or a brilliant detective, depending on who you asked. He had been a thorn in the side of his superiors, flouting regulations, doing investigations in his own way, but always following the facts no matter where they led. That was the problem. More and more often these days the facts led where you didn't want a detective to go.

'Maybe you're just not cut out to be a detective, Geismeier.' Willi had heard that over and over again. And maybe it was true. The trouble was he loved the work and he was good at it. And he loved justice, both the idea of it and the fact of it. Hans Bergemann always said Willi was obsessed with justice.

Willi's discovery and pursuit of the perpetrator of multiple murders and rapes had led him directly to a high-ranking Nazi official, a man named Otto Bruck. And once Otto Bruck, one of Hitler's favorites, came to harm, Willi had no choice but to disappear. The police, the SS, the Gestapo were all looking for him, and he'd gotten out of his apartment in the nick of time, thanks to Bergemann and to Lola. After a couple of nights in various safe houses, Willi left Munich. But he left reluctantly. He did not like to leave Lola to fend for herself, even for a short time. But both she and Bergemann had argued he was in imminent danger if he stayed, and if he was in danger, he placed them in danger too. So Willi hid out in the Bavarian Forest near the Austrian and Czech borders, in a hut belonging to Eberhardt von Hohenstein, an old schoolfriend.

Then came the attack on Lola.

Once a week Lola Zeff went to supper at her mother and father's house. Afterwards – sometimes it was after midnight – she took the streetcar home, changing at Karolinenplatz and then getting off at Rennstraße, from where it was a five-minute walk to her apartment. That night it was raining and a strong wind was blowing as she got off at Rennstraße. She had to turn toward the wind to open her umbrella so that it wouldn't turn inside out. As she turned, a man

standing right there – maybe the noise of the departing streetcar
had allowed him to get so close – lunged at her. His hand and arm
ripped through the umbrella half open in front of her. And because
she let go and the wind caught it, the man was momentarily caught
by the umbrella, his arm tangled in the spokes. Lola screamed and
fell backwards, hitting her head, and the man ran off, his arm still
caught in the umbrella. She got up and ran in the opposite direction.
She found a night watchman, making his rounds, just outside a
factory. Lola told him she had been attacked, and he took her inside
and called the police.

'You're injured, Fräulein,' he said, pointing to his own head. She
touched her head and her hand came away bloody. She sat down
heavily in the watchman's chair. He folded up a spare shirt he kept
in his locker and made a compress for her to hold against the wound
and stanch the bleeding until the ambulance arrived. He gave her a
sip of the brandy he kept in his desk. 'For emergencies,' he said.

Willi learned from Hans Bergemann about the attack and rushed
back to Munich, cursing himself for having left. He had already
acquired the necessary false documents – identity card, passport,
residency permit – and had begun to arrange for a life in Munich
as Karl Juncker. He thought he could safely stay in Munich. 'I think
our Führer has bigger fish to fry,' he said. Bergemann did not agree
and counseled Willi to leave again as soon as Lola was better.
'Munich is small and closely watched. You'll have no room to
maneuver here. You're well known in the wrong circles. New
eyeglasses or not.' He looked Willi up and down.

The 'disguise' was laughable. Willi wore his hair shorter now.
He had a new mustache that remotely resembled the Führer's, except
that Willi's was grey and, despite his best efforts, a little unkempt.
He had exchanged his wire-rimmed eyeglasses for some with round
black frames and tinted lenses. Bergemann just shook his head in
exasperation.

Bergemann reminded him he was no longer a policeman, and
there was nothing he could do, even if he stayed, to find Lola's
attacker. 'I didn't come back for that,' said Willi. But, said Willi,
now that Bergemann mentioned it, the police were having no luck
finding the attacker, and, as far as he could tell, hadn't made much
of an effort.

Bergemann, himself a detective, couldn't disagree. The
policemen on the case had taken Lola's statement. They had done

a perfunctory investigation, had then determined there were no clues to be found, and nothing more was to be done. Lola was alive, they said, and an assault charge was the best they could hope for if they ever found the man, which, they said again, was unlikely. They pointed out that, despite a serious gash on her forehead and a concussion, Lola had recovered completely. After three days in the hospital, she had been able to return home, and after a few more days, she was able to go back to work and resume her normal life.

Willi couldn't resist investigating, even though it was dangerous for him to do so. He interviewed the night watchman and had a look at the spot where the attack had happened. But just as the police had said, there were no witnesses and no physical evidence. Even the umbrella was gone. He questioned Lola extensively, asking her everything he could think of about her assailant until she told him to stop.

'You're not a detective any more, Willi,' she said. 'I understand why you're doing this, and I appreciate it. But you're putting both of us in danger.' Willi said she was probably right. But he did not promise to stop looking into it.

Lola's parents, Klara and Klaus Zeff, had been the cook and caretaker at the Geismeier home when Willi was growing up. Willi and Lola had been playmates and constant companions as children. But when they were twelve Lola was apprenticed to a seamstress in Aschaffenburg, while Willi was sent off to boarding school at Schloß Barzelhof in the Bavarian Forest, and that was the last they saw of one another.

Lola eventually left her apprenticeship to work as a private nurse for an elderly invalid. She had the night shift, moving her patient from his wheelchair to his bed, changing the dressings on his arms and legs, and spooning soup into his mouth. When he died, the war had started and Lola found work in a military hospital not far from the western front. She could hear the dull thump of the shelling, which usually meant that ambulances would be arriving within minutes.

The hospital work involved mopping up blood and swabbing out wounds, while the boys were held down screaming in pain. But Lola loved caring for the soldiers and found she was good at it. She fed them, read them their letters from home, and held their hands when they wept. Once the war ended, Lola came back to Munich. Work was hard to find, but she eventually got a job as a maid in the Hotel zur Kaiserkrone, one of Munich's great hotels.

Lola had flaming red hair and an electric smile, and Herr Kuzinski, the hotel manager, was attracted to her and pursued her with flowers and gifts. Lola was not interested and said so. To her surprise, instead of firing her, Herr Kuzinski offered her a position behind the bar. He could see, he said, that the tact and diplomacy she had shown in refusing him made her perfect for the bar. She didn't know whether he was joking or not. But he said men would drink more if she was serving them. And he could continue to hope, couldn't he?

The Kaiserkrone was a magnificent Belle Epoque structure with towers and gables, high gilt ceilings and crystal chandeliers. Its bar – the Mahogany Room – was splendid too, with its long, polished mahogany bar, Persian rugs, easy chairs and tapestry-covered walls. The hotel's floorshow sparkled, its orchestra was first rate and played all the latest hits from America. It was where connections were made, deals were struck and, increasingly, political schemes were hatched.

Herr Kuzinski's assessment of Lola proved to be astute. She was personable, smart, and responsible. She had real managerial talent, and after a few months he put her in charge of the bar. She negotiated with the liquor salesmen, ordered stock, arranged for deliveries, and supervised the bartenders and servers. That they were eventually all women was her idea.

The men at the bar – sometimes they were three or four deep – seemed to drink more with women serving them. And they talked more too, trying to impress the pretty young things. They liked to joke, especially with Lola, who was no longer all that young, but who was still pretty and clever and could give as good as she got.

It had been twenty years or more since Lola had seen Willi. And she had only heard his name from her parents when they talked about old times. But now she heard it in the Mahogany Room.

'How do you think we ought to deal with traitors, Lola?' A drunken SS-Obersturmführer – a lieutenant – leaned across the bar and tried to take her hand. The Kaiserkrone had become a favorite hangout for the SS.

She laughed and batted his hand away.

'Come on, Lolachen,' he said. 'I mean a real bad guy, a traitor cop.'

'Send him to me,' said Lola. 'I like bad guys.'

The lieutenant gave a sort of whinnying laugh.

'Hey, Lieutenant,' said one of his SS companions. 'You're giving away confidensher . . . confidensher . . . Shit, man, I can't even say it!' He guffawed too and slapped the Obersturmführer's shoulder.

The Obersturmführer whinnied again. 'Confidenshal,' he said.

'He means a shecret,' said a third SS man to Lola, as he picked up the bottle in front of him and drank from it. 'A big, fat shecret.'

Lola smiled at them and removed the empties from the bar – this was their fourth bottle of French champagne. As she turned away she heard one of them say the name 'Geismeier.' She couldn't hear what else they were saying, but then she heard 'Geismeier' again.

'Shhhh!' said the Obersturmführer with his finger against his lips. 'Confidensher!' and the three of them laughed all over again.

That night Lola visited her parents. It was late and her visit was unexpected, but they were pleased to see her. Her mother served her *Gulaschsuppe*, then poppyseed dumplings with plum sauce for dessert. 'Have you seen or heard anything about Willi Geismeier?' Lola asked.

'Why do you ask?' her father said.

'Is he still with the police?' said Lola.

'I don't think so,' her father said. 'But it's funny you should ask. He stopped by this week.'

'Really?' said Lola.

'Somehow he heard I was sick. He came to visit me. It was a complete surprise. It was really nice of him.'

'That's the way Willi is,' said her mother.

Lola managed to piece together enough information from her parents to find Willi's old precinct. When she went there and inquired after Willi Geismeier, the desk sergeant took her to see Detective Sergeant Gruber, the head of the detective squad.

Gruber stood up as she came into his office. He bowed slightly and gave her his hand. 'How can I help you, Frau . . .?'

'Zeff. Lola Zeff. I'm looking for Willi Geismeier.'

Gruber was surprised. He hadn't heard Willi's name for a long time either. 'Really?' he said, sounding a little too interested. 'May I ask why?' Just the mention of Willi's name got Gruber's back up. He despised Willi. Willi had outsmarted Gruber again and again and had thwarted him at every turn. Gruber was nominally in charge of the squad, but while Willi had been there, Gruber often found himself doing what Willi wanted instead of the other way around. Which made Gruber all the more eager to get his hands on Willi and put him away.

'We were neighbors when we were young,' said Lola. 'We were friends back then.'

Gruber found it hard to believe that anyone had ever been friends with Willi Geismeier. 'He's no longer with the Munich police,' he said.

'Did he retire?'

'I'm afraid I can't help you with that, Frau Zeff. But do you know where we might find him?'

'No, I don't. That's why I'm asking.'

'Nothing at all?'

'No. Nothing'

'I'll tell you what. Leave your information with the desk sergeant, Frau Zeff. And if we hear anything at all from Herr Geismeier, we'll let you know.'

'I will,' she said. She stopped at the front desk on her way out.

Gruber stepped out of his office. 'Bergemann,' he said, 'did you hear any of that?'

'Yes, Sergeant, I did. Do you want me to follow her?'

Bergemann caught up to Lola as she boarded a streetcar and got on behind her. He got off when she did and stopped her as she was about to go into the Kaiserkrone. He explained that he was a detective and had once been a friend of Willi's.

'Can you take me to him?' she said.

'Willi Geismeier is a wanted man, Frau Zeff. Why are you interested in his whereabouts?'

'Do you know where he is?'

'No, I don't.'

'Could you give him greetings from Lola Zeff?'

'Because you're old friends?' said Bergemann.

'I thought it might be nice to see him after all this time, that's all.'

'And he would remember you?'

'Yes, I think he would.' Lola wondered at Bergemann's reticence, and he wondered at hers. But this was the kind of cat-and-mouse game one had to play these days. Lola could not trust Bergemann to be who he claimed to be. But neither could Bergemann trust Lola; who could say what her interest might be? So whatever arrangements could be made would necessarily be convoluted. Lola regretted now having left her information with the desk sergeant.

Bergemann was now walking a thin and dangerous line. Long

ago he had joined the Nazi Party, but more for social than political reasons. He had liked the singing and the folklorish aspects of it. He was smart but intellectually lazy, going along to get along. And he might have remained the detective he was – lazy and ineffectual – if Willi Geismeier had not gotten hold of him and shown him what it meant to be a good and conscientious policeman. These days it meant that Bergemann solved cases and, at the same time, did what he could to help and protect Willi, his mentor and friend.

Bergemann had adopted some aspects of Willi's methodology, and more importantly he had adopted his rigor. He was not as brilliant as Willi, but he made up for it in persistence. And, to his credit, he was not as uncompromising as Willi. He had remained in the Party and in the SA, not out of conviction, but as a useful cover. His storm trooper uniform, which he put on when it was helpful, got him in doors and loosened tongues that might otherwise not have been available to him. He now found satisfaction in his work, and in his double life too.

Bergemann's wife Louise was as grateful to Willi as Hans was, maybe more so, because Willi had given her a new husband. The new Bergemann, a sincere and disciplined man, had replaced the old lazy, indifferent Bergemann. She would have sworn the two Hans Bergemanns not only *acted* different, they *looked* different. The new Hans was more alert, more in the moment. His face was enlivened, not slack, and he was always in motion. And he was more loving than he had been. Louise believed she owed Willi her newfound happiness. Willi denied it. 'That's all up to you two,' he said. Willi didn't always realize the part he played in other people's lives.

The morning was frosty, but it was the first day of March, and Willi could feel the warmth of the sun on his hands and face. He sat in a cafe watching the street. The linden trees looked like they were dead, but soon they would have buds, then leaves. Then the birds would come. Willi had not seen Lola for twenty years – or was it even longer – but he recognized her as soon as she turned the corner. There was her red hair, of course, but also her light step. She went into the small grocery across the street. He waited ten minutes to be certain she hadn't been followed, paid for his coffee, and crossed the street.

Willi looked stern and Lola cocked her head slightly and brushed a red curl back from her forehead as they shook hands. She smiled. She rose on her toes and kissed his cheek. To anyone watching, they might have been neighbors or colleagues, not friends who hadn't seen one another in a very long time. As they looked into each other's eyes, each of them was rearranging the furnishing of his own existence, to make room for this well known, even beloved, but entirely unexpected stranger.

Willi looked around. 'Let's walk, shall we?' he said, taking Lola's arm. As they walked, Lola told him what she had overheard at work. Willi asked her for details, and she told him everything she remembered the drunken SS men saying. 'It sounded like they were coming for you. I had to warn you,' she said.

'I am very grateful,' he said.

'*Are* they coming for you?' she said.

'It's likely,' he said. Willi had already received other indications, and had been clearing out of his apartment.

'Can I help you?' she said.

'No,' said Willi. That sounded too hard. 'You already have,' he said. 'But we shouldn't meet again. I don't want you involved.' Willi felt a lump in his throat as he said it, so he said it again. He was having trouble navigating these waters. 'I've always . . . been fond of you, Lola, but I can't have you involved in my life.'

'How have you been getting along, Willi?' she said. 'And thank you for stopping by Mutti and Papa's.'

'I had heard he was sick, and I'm glad he's better. Don't change the subject, Lola. Please. My life is a dangerous place. Especially right now.'

'I'm getting that sense,' she said. 'Are you married?'

'No,' said Willi. 'Lola, you're not listening to me.'

'Oh, yes, I am, Willi. *You're* the one not listening: If I hadn't overheard your name – hadn't learned that the SS and the police are interested in you, and that they may know your whereabouts—'

'I'm not your responsibility, Lola—'

'You're my friend, Willi; that's an even bigger responsibility.'

And so, a few nights later, when the SS battered his door in, Willi and all his belongings were gone. The apartment had been stripped of every stick of furniture, every belonging. Only a lone teakettle had been left on the stove. The SS men circled around it as though it were explosive.

A furious manhunt followed. The SS went to all the sites they thought Willi frequented. It turned out that they knew very little about the man, despite his more than fifteen years on the force. 'He's like a goddamned ghost,' said Obersturmbannführer Tannenwald. Even when they thought they were getting close, Willi would be several steps ahead of them.

Schloß Barzelhof

Willi was born into privilege. His grandfather had invented and manufactured the seamless ceramic pipe used in the reconstruction of Munich's sewer system. The family lived in a villa he had built in Bogenhausen, on the outskirts of Munich. Willi had spent an idyllic childhood there, playing in the great walled garden, being pampered and cared for by his loving parents and grandparents.

In 1905, when Willi was twelve and seemed to be drifting through school, he was sent off to Schloß Barzelhof, a military boarding school in a castle in the Bavarian Forest near Passau. Many of the instructors at Barzelhof had served in the Imperial German Army.

Every day at five o'clock, the boys – there were about forty of them – were awakened. After washing up, they went off for an hour of running and calisthenics. After that they had a cold shower, put on their uniforms and marched to breakfast. Then came chapel, then classes – Latin, Greek, mathematics, history, geography, and German. At four they marched to the large gloomy common room where they did their assignments until supper at six.

After supper they returned to the common room for more study overseen by faculty proctors. There was no talking allowed. The long study tables were illuminated by gas lights. A fire crackled in the enormous fireplace. At eight thirty they went up to the dormitory where each boy had a cot and a footlocker for his belongings.

A strict code of conduct and an exaggerated sense of honor and duty prevailed at Schloß Barzelhof. It was no different from many other military boarding schools in that regard. And, like other such schools, it had its own way of doing things, what was spoken of as 'the Barzelhof culture.' This included certain harmless rituals, like the Polar Bear Swim on the first day of spring. The ice that remained along the edge of the river would be broken up and removed, and boys and teachers alike peeled off their clothes and jumped in. And just as quickly they scrambled out, shrieking and laughing and slapping their sides against the stabbing cold.

Barzelhof culture also included – unofficially, of course – hazing, particularly for those boys who were seen as not fitting in. The faculty did not participate in this abuse, but they did not discourage it either. Many of them had taken part in such torments themselves when they had been in school, either at Barzelhof or at some other institution. They believed in it, thought it toughened the boys up, made men of them.

Eberhardt von Hohenstein and Erich Lobe were a year ahead of Willi. They liked Willi well enough and set about teaching him the Barzelhof ropes – which teachers let you get away with stuff and which didn't, how to sneak out of the dormitory if you were given detention, that sort of thing. Eberhardt's father was a diplomat stationed in the United States, and before that he had been stationed in Singapore and South Africa. Eberhardt could tell wonderful stories about places Willi could only dream of.

Willi was skinny and awkward, but he was a fast runner and an excellent soccer player, so Eberhardt and Erich asked him to join their soccer team. Willi was pleased and flattered. And he made a good addition to the team, passing the ball skillfully, dribbling downfield at full speed, and scoring against other teams with relative ease.

Andrea Welke was one of the boys who didn't fit in. He was small and had a dark complexion, and because a serious case of rheumatic fever had left his heart weakened, he was excused from all physical activity, a fact that did not sit well with the rest of the boys or, for that matter, with some of the teachers. One of the teachers, a particularly bitter and unpleasant former cavalry officer, liked to pick on Welke, and some of the other boys followed suit. He would get jostled marching between classes, or someone would unscrew the salt shaker so Andrea would dump a shaker full of salt on his meal. Eberhardt and Erich decided to have a little fun with Welke and they invited Willi to join them.

'Andrea,' said Erich, 'have you seen the comet?'

'What comet?' said Andrea.

'Schiller's comet. You can see it tonight. It's amazing. Right, Eberhardt?'

'Spectacular,' said Eberhardt. 'Really.' He winked at Willi.

'We'll wait until lights out and then sneak out,' said Erich.

'I don't know,' said Andrea. He didn't like the idea. They might get caught and then they'd be in trouble. At the same time, he didn't want to miss out on the chance to be friends with Erich and Eberhardt whom everyone admired. He looked at Willi for reassurance.

'It'll be fun, Andrea,' said Willi. 'Come on.'

After lights out the four boys crept downstairs and out of the castle. It was a very dark night. They made their way single file through the woods.

After a short while, Andrea became fearful and said, 'I want to go back.'

'It's just a little further,' said Erich. 'Just up there at the edge of the woods we'll see the comet.'

'No, I'm going back,' said Andrea.

'Why?' said Eberhardt. 'Are you scared?'

'There's no comet,' said Andrea. 'Is there?'

'Yes, there is,' said Erich.

'I'm going back,' said Andrea. He turned around.

'No, you're not,' said Eberhardt. 'Keep going.' He pushed Andrea, who fell. 'Get up,' said Eberhardt. Andrea didn't move. 'Get up, you little cunt.' He kicked Andrea.

Willi had known the comet was a ruse to get Andrea out of the building, but he hadn't thought about what Eberhardt and Erich might want to do with him. 'Come on, guys,' said Willi. 'Let's go back.'

Eberhardt and Erich turned on Willi. 'What, Geismeier, are you a cunt too?'

'Get up, Welke,' said Eberhardt. But Andrea stayed on the ground. He was breathing heavily and making odd moaning sounds.

Now Eberhardt and Erich started getting nervous. 'What the hell's wrong with you, Welke?' said Eberhardt. 'Get the hell up.'

'He's faking,' said Erich.

'No, he isn't,' said Willi.

'Shut up, Geismeier.'

'Leave him alone,' said Willi.

'Shut up, you goddamn weasel,' said Erich. He put his fist in Willi's face. The two boys stared at one another. Finally Erich realized Willi wasn't going to back down. 'Let's go, Eberhardt,' he said. 'These two girls want to be alone.'

'Yeah, right,' said Eberhardt with a laugh. He spat in Willi's direction as they left.

Willi helped Andrea stand and then supported him as they made their way back to the building. The duty officer was waiting for them inside the front door.

The next morning Willi was summoned to the commandant's office. Erich and Eberhardt had reported seeing Geismeier and Welke sneak out of the building. They didn't know where they had gone, but they were sure they were up to no good.

Willi stood at attention. The commandant was angry. 'You're in serious trouble, Geismeier. This is a serious infraction of the Barzelhof code of honor.'

Willi told about the Schiller comet and about luring Welke out to the woods. The commandant wanted to know whose idea it was. Willi said it had been the three of them: Erich, Eberhardt, and him.

'I don't believe you, Geismeier,' said the commandant. 'Von Hohenstein and Lobe both saw you go and they reported it. I want the truth, Geismeier, and I want it now.'

'They were with us, sir.'

'I said no lies, Geismeier.'

'I'm not lying, sir,' said Willi.

'One more chance, Geismeier. Tell me what you and Welke were up to. We don't tolerate lies at Barzelhof, Geismeier.'

'I'm telling you the truth, sir.'

The commandant had faced situations like this before – boys experimenting with one another, their first tentative sexual explorations, and this had to be nipped in the bud. 'There's no room for deviancy at Barzelhof, Geismeier. We're all men here, not fairies. We won't stand for deviancy of any sort.' The commandant had read a book about human psychology once, and deviancy was the one concept that had stayed with him. He had expanded the concept to mean any behavior he regarded as unmanly.

'Do you know what deviancy is, Geismeier? I might have suspected Welke of deviant behavior, Geismeier. But you surprise me.'

'That's not what happened,' said Willi. 'Erich and Eberhardt are lying.'

'I won't stand for that, Geismeier. That is an unfounded accusation. They're both trustworthy men. They're Barzelhof men.' Which meant that their fathers and grandfathers had gone through Barzelhof. 'Enough of the lies and false accusations. I want the truth.'

Tears of anger sprang into Willi's eyes. 'I'm telling the truth. I'm not lying!' he said. 'They're lying.'

Willi had gone along with the prank at first, so he had been part of it. He had known Andrea was sickly, and that he was picked on because he was different. And Willi had been slow and tentative in his defense of Andrea, even once he was in distress. But then he had tried to defend the boy, and had helped him home. So that was something, wasn't it? That was the right thing to do, wasn't it? And yet the commandant, the one man responsible for discipline and fairness at the school, was accepting the obviously untrue accusations of two bullies because they were 'Barzelhof men.'

Andrea's and Willi's parents received letters from the commandant explaining the obligations of a Schloß Barzelhof education. 'Becoming a Barzelhof Man is a High Achievement,' he wrote. The commandant favored upper case letters when he wanted to emphasize the importance of certain ideas. 'But, like all Worthwhile Achievements, it is not Something Everyone Can Achieve. It demands Much but offers Much in Return.' Andrea and Willi, being guilty of serious violations of the school's code of honor, were evidently not cut out to be Barzelhof men. Arrangements should be made to fetch them home as soon as possible. 'We wish your son Well in his Future Endeavors, and Hope he will have Learned from his Failures here at Schloß Barzelhof.'

After that night's adventure, Andrea had been taken to a clinic in Passau. His mother arrived in a coach two days later to take him home. Willi continued with the daily Barzelhof routine for the next several days, but was not permitted to wear the Barzelhof uniform. And the other boys were under orders to shun him, which they did.

Willi gazed from the train window watching the colorless March landscape slip by – the farms with smoke spiraling up from the chimneys, the fields with strips of snow between stubble where last summer's crops had been, the impenetrable black shadows of the evergreen forest, and before long the gloomy mills and industrial buildings of Munich. Willi and his father spoke very little during the ride. Willi's father tried to embrace his son, but Willi did not want to be embraced. He did not want to be comforted. Nothing had changed between them, but Willi's father could see that something momentous had happened to Willi. He hoped Willi had not been damaged by the experience.

Willi had by no means been damaged. In fact, it was as though a veil had lifted from in front of Willi's eyes, and understanding had flooded in. Willi understood the commandant's motivation and his failure. He understood that in the adult world, the world he was soon to enter, truth, fairness, honesty, things adults talked on and on about, were often less important than other trivial things, like manliness, tribal loyalty, popularity. He could not have articulated this until much later, but Willi recognized then and there where he stood in the world and what he had to do. For instance, he would have known even then that he had no choice now but to try to find out who had attacked and hurt Lola, and then bring him to justice.

As he grew up, he became a student of human psychology and a lover of justice. The first time Willi read a Shakespeare play – he was in university and it was *Julius Caesar* – it took him back to Schloß Barzelhof. The commandant, Andrea Welke, Eberhardt von Hohenstein, all the others, they were all there. Shakespeare's understanding of their complicated and contradictory motives was profound and exact. Willi found in Shakespeare an exhaustive catalogue of human behavior.

He decided to learn English so he could read the plays in their original language. He found a professor who was willing to indulge his interest, and who could guide him. He charted the plays' structures, scrutinized the make-up and motivation of the characters, and discovered what drove them, both their inner dynamics, and their interactions which made up, to his way of thinking, a kind of metaphysical clockwork. He even spent a year in England, just so he could continue his studies where Shakespeare had lived and worked.

To everyone's surprise, after these years of study Willi joined the Munich police force. He saw something Shakespearean in police work, something he did not find in the academic world or in the manufacture of seamless ceramic pipe. After the slapdash and, to his mind, inferior training he got at the police academy, Willi saw no reason not to apply the methods that had unlocked the secrets of Shakespearean drama for him to the study of criminal behavior. Willi examined the setting and circumstances of every case that came his way, as though it were a play, as though its dynamics were a clue to how it had unfolded. He found the seeds of the tragedy or comedy (some crimes were comic) tucked in obscure corners of the larger drama. He searched out and examined the actions and motives of even the minor characters, believing that their apparently incidental activity could well have influenced the trajectory of the principals. After all, Rosencrantz and Guildenstern had moved Hamlet; three old hags had influenced Macbeth. Predicting Macbeth's downfall had, in a sense, led to his downfall. And Richard the Third bounced off one secondary character after the other, thinking all the while he was a free agent.

Willi did not hesitate to focus on peripheral characters, those who might be connected by only the slimmest of threads to whatever case he was working on and might appear, to themselves at least, not to be connected to it at all. He interviewed the patrolmen first called to the scene at what everyone took to be excessive length. He questioned the civilians who had first called in the crime and then questioned others connected to them, but not necessarily connected to the crime in any discernible way. Sometimes his method even required that he interview his own superiors: Willi was, after all, a character in this drama himself.

'Damn it, Geismeier, this is ridiculous. Focus on the case.'

'I am,' he said. Higher-ups did not understand and did not like being questioned by a lowly police detective, but they could hardly refuse. Not given the fact that year after year Willi accumulated one of the best case-closure rates in the entire Munich police department.

Eventually Willi was known throughout the department. And as the police department became more and more political, Willi began to be accused of investigating the police themselves. Willi denied this, but in fact it was true. Willi was hopelessly addicted – and addicted was not too strong a word – to justice. He had no choice but to follow every lead where it took him, and make certain, to the extent that he was able, that every injustice was brought to light.

As Hitler rose in influence and power, the Munich police department was increasingly populated by Nazis and Nazi sympathizers. And crimes Willi found himself investigating increasingly involved police and political figures, not just as peripheral characters or witnesses, but often enough as perpetrators. And, because Munich was Hitler's spiritual home, the place where his movement had been born, increasingly some of these police criminals were uncomfortably close to the Führer himself. Again and again, Willi insisted he was not political. It was just that politics was where his investigations sometimes took him.

Even now, when Willi was no longer a detective, he did not –

could not – stop thinking about such matters. For instance, he could not let go of the fact that the police had been so quick to drop their investigation of the attack on Lola. Willi knew too little so far to even suspect that the attack had a political aspect. At the same time, though, Lola *had* warned him of the SS's interest in him. This made her his accomplice. It made her warning a treasonous act. That might, in itself, have made her a target for attack.

The First Kiss

Gerd Fegelein was a former cat burglar who had retired once he could no longer shinny up and down drainpipes as he once had, or navigate steep slate roofs when they were slick with rain. It was Willi who had informed Fegelein of his retirement on a snowy New Year's Eve several years back. Fegelein had come through a third-floor apartment window onto a small wrought-iron balcony, had lowered himself to the balcony below, but had slipped on the icy iron rail and dropped hard into the alley, where Willi was waiting.

Fegelein was crestfallen when he saw Willi there. His shoulders slumped. They had never met, but he knew Willi by reputation. Willi had caught countless villains who had eluded the police for years, so it was not exactly a disgrace to be caught by him. But Fegelein had his own reputation as uncatchable to maintain. And yet here he was: caught. He might still have outrun Willi, but when he tried to get up, he found that his ankle was badly sprained, and he crumpled back to the ground in pain. So he did the only thing he could think to do, and that was to offer Willi his hand. Willi took it. 'Herr Fegelein,' he said.

'Herr Geismeier,' said Fegelein, 'will you help me?'

This sudden and immediate accord was not as strange as it might seem. While the two men had been on opposite sides of the law for most of their careers, the law had gradually shifted until now they found themselves in the same boat: both enemies of the Third Reich.

Willi was well known among Munich's villains as an effective and honest cop, and now he was known among Munich's Nazis as an impediment to the advancement of Hitler's agenda, particularly as it applied to the criminal justice system. Fegelein was known mainly as a cat burglar, but also to some as a devoted Marxist. Like Willi, he had fought in the trenches during the war, and then afterwards had battled fascists as part of a red militia when Munich's future was up in the air. And if that were not enough to doom him, he was also a Jew. So how could Willi arrest Fegelein when doing so would deliver him to the hands of the SS and likely mean his death? Willi walked to a nearby taxi stand, summoned a cab and helped Fegelein to his home.

After that night, Fegelein disappeared. He waited weeks, then months, and in time the police lost interest in him. Now, years later, he owned and ran a bicycle shop out of the back of an industrial building in Lerchenau, far from Munich's center. The small sign in the window read: LERCHENAU BICYCLES, SALES AND REPAIRS

The shop was dingy and dimly lit and filled with an assortment of salvaged bicycles in various stages of repair. They were stacked against the walls around the front room. A few almost new and reconditioned bicycles were for sale and dangled from hooks screwed into the ceiling. The back room was a workshop with all the requisite work stands, benches, and spare parts. Willi, no longer a detective and looking for some other trade, had recently taken up bicycle repair at Fegelein's urging and, thanks to his thorough and meticulous nature, had become good at it – so good, in fact, that he, under the pseudonym Karl Juncker, had been retained as the team mechanic by the Bavarian Wheelmen, a professional racing team.

As a thief, Fegelein had been a big proponent of bicycle travel in the city. A well-tuned bicycle was part of the reason he had been so uncatchable. A bicycle was fast, maneuverable, and portable. A bicycle could go where cars couldn't, and there were no papers or license plates to lead the police back to you.

Until recently the shop had been exactly what the sign said it was. But thanks to the shifting social and political situation and to the circumstances of his new partner and part-time repairman, Lerchenau Bicycles came to be known among other misfits and enemies of the Reich as a sort of message center and rendezvous point where you could go for information or other forms of assistance.

If one knew enough to slide a heavy workbench out from the back wall and then lift a wooden trapdoor, you could descend a rickety staircase and find yourself in the building's basement, a large, low and secret space beneath heavy floor joists. Fegelein hadn't even known there was a basement when he had opened his shop. It is doubtful the landlord knew, since the stairs had been blocked off and boarded up for many years.

The basement was mostly empty when Fegelein discovered it, but with time it filled up. First he installed a bed and some other rudimentary furniture and used the space as a safe house for those who needed it. Willi had sheltered there the night of the teakettle. Next came various machines, tools and materials Fegelein had salvaged from all over, things which he thought might eventually come in handy. 'Eventually,' he said, 'will come soon enough.'

By the time the war began in September of 1939, the basement had a small engraving studio and print shop that, on relatively short notice, could turn out an excellent passport and other convincing personal papers. It remained a safe house, and eventually became a stopping point for fleeing Jews, downed English and American pilots, and members of the resistance. Lives that were saved and lives that were lost passed through that basement.

After two nights in the Lerchenau basement, Willi had moved on to other hideouts. The Horvaths had an unused maid's room in the attic of their building. Detective Hans Bergemann had access to a vacant garage across the alley from his apartment. From there he went to the cabin in the Bavarian Forest.

Once he was back in Munich, he registered as Karl Juncker with the local police as every new resident was required to do and made Tullemannstraße 54 his home. He kept his things there, his beloved Shakespeare volumes, his clothes, his bits of furniture. More and more, though, he stayed with Lola.

Lola's small apartment had originally been a workshop belonging to a leather goods shop on Lindwurmstraße, a busy shopping street across town from Tullemannstraße. The door between the shop and workshop had been closed off years earlier when the workshop had been converted to an apartment. The apartment's entrance was in the building's courtyard. Next to the leather shop was a liquor store, with a large storeroom with two rear doors, one that opened into Lola's courtyard and one that opened into the courtyard next door. And there was a profusion of doors around Lola's courtyard leading off in various directions.

Willi investigated this labyrinthine arrangement and found it extremely satisfactory. He found two stairways to different roofs – the older part of the building had four stories and a steep slate roof; the newer addition had six stories with a flat roof and connections to adjoining roofs. He also found inside passages to two different alleys and meandering hallways of apartments, closets, and storage rooms.

Lola's apartment was a single room of twenty-five square meters. There was a sink and a small gas stove in the kitchen alcove and a table and three upright chairs. The window beside the entry door faced south and actually got several hours of sun a day. Lola kept a few flowerpots with geraniums and forget-me-nots outside. The previous summer she had managed to grow a tomato plant and a cucumber, whose vine had climbed the green trellis nailed to her wall, giving the place the incongruent appearance of a country cottage.

Lola had hung a curtain across the middle of the room to separate the toilet and bedroom with its dresser, mirror, and bed from the rest of the apartment. The flush toilet had been added after the war and was enclosed in what looked like a wooden cupboard.

It was late evening the first time Willi stayed with Lola. He had a small canvas rucksack on his back. Lola was worried; she had expected him for supper. He apologized and explained he had been followed by a car. The driver had suddenly swerved to a stop in front of him, and two men had jumped out – thieves maybe, more likely Gestapo. Willi, still on the bike, swerved around them. The men jumped back in their car and gave chase. But Fegelein was right: in old Munich's narrow, winding streets a car was no match for a bicycle. He took to the sidewalk, went through an alley too narrow for a car, and lost them.

'I don't think they knew who I was. They go after anyone and everyone these days. Anyone on the street after dark is prey for thieves or a suspect for the Gestapo. Anyway, I lost them, and here I am.' Lola suspected Willi had been investigating her attack, and she didn't like it. She knew he had somehow gotten his hands on the police report, and had been trying to find out what he could about the investigating officers, whether they were political and whether they were competent. But she threw her arms around him anyway and kissed him on the mouth.

Willi and Lola were on the wrong side of forty. They had each experienced love and disappointment more than a few times, and neither had given the other much thought over the years, except perhaps to wonder now and then what had become of Willi, or where was Lola these days, and to hope that they were doing well and having a good life. On those few occasions when Willi had visited Lola's parents, after her father was sick, for instance, he had asked about her, but only in the most general terms. He hadn't known whether she was married or had children, and he hadn't asked. And Lola too knew nothing about Willi, until she had set out to warn him about what she had heard at the bar in the Mahogany Room. As Lola said, their old friendship led her to want to help Willi. And Willi could have said, although he didn't, that their old friendship led him to allow her to help.

They were both surprised by the kiss and where it led. Willi lay on Lola's bed later, his head resting on his arms. He watched Lola's silhouette on the curtain as she washed herself at the sink. She stooped and rose and turned, raising her arms and legs. *She's dancing, a strange, exotic, wonderful dance*, he thought, as he fell asleep.

Operation Hummingbird

T he Black Parrot Cabaret dance floor was filled with gyrating, sweaty dancers. The orchestra was playing an uptempo version of '42nd Street.' Storm trooper Lieutenant Walter Kempf was wriggling his hands into the pants of a pretty boy named Bobby, when the hard steel of a Luger on his neck stopped him cold.

An hour later Walter found himself being marched into a walled courtyard with other men who had been rounded up in the city. Some wore brown uniforms; others were in suits or pajamas or whatever they had been wearing when they were arrested. Walter wore a tuxedo. The men were lined up in front of a brick wall. They weren't the first; you could smell the spent gunpowder in the air.

Walter shouted his last words, 'Heil Hitler!' just as the command 'Fire!' came. The bodies were dragged away, and the next group of men was lined up and shot. It went on that way through much of the night.

In the early morning as the rising sun was burning away the

fog, a half dozen black cars sped into Bad Wiessee, a picturesque village halfway to the Austrian border. Adolf Hitler stepped from the lead car while SS men spilled out of the others and ran into the Hanslbauer Hotel.

Ernst Röhm and his comrades were mostly sleeping after a night of carousing. They were torn from their beds and dragged into the garden where most were shot. For the Führer their homosexuality was yet another abomination that made this action, Operation Hummingbird, necessary.

Röhm was taken back to Munich. 'I've been with the Führer longer than any of you,' he shouted. 'If I'm to be killed, let Adolf do it himself.' Instead he was offered a pistol. When he refused to do the right thing, it was done for him. All over Germany Hitler's enemies were being arrested and executed.

Hitler had decided it was time to rein in his storm troopers. These thugs and brawlers had played a big part in bringing him to power, but there were too many of them now, and they were out of control. What is more, Ernst Röhm, the head storm trooper, had been pushing for a 'second revolution.'

'The Party needs to take on the capitalists,' he said. 'To do more for working people. After all, we're National *Socialists*, aren't we?' His followers cheered. But Hitler needed the capitalists – he needed their money so there wouldn't be any socialism.

Röhm also wanted to get the regular army under his control. 'The damned generals,' he reminded Hitler, 'they're always getting in our way. They hate you. We need to come down hard on them.'

'I know, Ernst,' said the Führer.

'They're treacherous, arrogant shitheads, Adi. You've never trusted them. Believe me, they're plotting your downfall.' He and Hitler had been friends since the very beginning, so he could talk to the Führer that way.

'Ernst, I said I *know*! But you can't seem to understand that I need the generals on my side. If they wanted to, they could turn things against me in a minute.'

'You've heard what they call you, haven't you? "The Bohemian corporal?"'

'Damn it, Ernst, that's *enough*!' Röhm never knew when to shut up.

Adolf Hitler had been chancellor for barely a year. His hold on power was shaky. If he was going to survive, now was the moment to consolidate his power. Having the army high command behind him was essential. Unfortunately for Röhm, he was not.

Operation Hummingbird was a stunning success. Several thousands of Hitler's enemies, great and small, were done away with in one night. And amazingly, Paul von Hindenburg, Germany's doddering president, who had been contemptuous of Hitler, now showered him with praise and thanked him for his courage and decisiveness in this murderous undertaking. Even General von Blomberg, Hitler's defense minister, grateful that his rival Röhm was out of the picture, congratulated the Führer and swore his allegiance and the army's.

Willi heard about the killings on the BBC and then from Bergemann. Willi might have been a target if they had known where to find him. Bergemann was shaken. This was how those who got in Hitler's way were going to be dealt with from now on.

The killings were on the front pages of newspapers all over Germany. Margarete Horvath lowered the paper she had been reading and turned to her husband. 'What does it mean, Benno? How is this even possible here in Germany?'

Benno Horvath stood gazing out the tall window at Munich, the city he loved but no longer understood. In the small park across the street the magnolias were in bloom. He listened to the sound of children laughing as they chased one another about. Red, white, and black Nazi flags fluttered in the summer breeze. The sun was warm on his face and the same breeze that riffled the flags lifted the curtains beside him. For a moment he had the sensation that it was he and not the curtains moving, as though he were drifting out into a new, more dangerous world. 'I think, Gretl, it means that everything has changed.'

'How could this happen, Benno? How could Hindenburg go along with this violence? How could he congratulate that terrible man? If all those people were traitors, why weren't they arrested and brought to trial, the way things are supposed to happen in Germany? And General von Blomberg falling in line like that? It's unbelievable. It's just unbelievable.'

'What was it Hitler said, Gretl? Read it to me again.'

'Let's see, where . . .' She scanned down the page. 'Here it is. *Speaking before the Reichstag, the chancellor said, "If anyone reproaches me and asks why I did not resort to the regular courts of justice, then all I can say is this: In this hour I was responsible for the fate of the German people, and therefore I became the supreme judge of the German people. Everyone must know for all future time that if he raises his hand against the German state, then his lot is certain death".'*

'My God. Think of it, Gretl. He proclaims himself the law, and Hindenburg and the army get behind him. Who could ever have imagined they would sell their souls so cheaply? They obviously have their own political reasons. I understand that. But they've just signed a pact with the devil.'

'But how could it happen?' she said again. 'Did we do this? Did we let this happen?'

'I think we did,' said Benno. 'If we didn't bring it about, at least we stood by and let it happen. We watched as lies took the place of truth. And we stood by and let power take the place of justice. We were content . . .'

'No, Benno! No! We were never content!' said Margarete. 'I wasn't content. I don't accept that.'

'But, Gretl, look here. As a people we let it come to this. We saw it coming, didn't we? We talked about it. We've known for a long time who Hitler is. And if we didn't know, we should have.'

'But could we have stopped it? How could we have stopped it?'

'I don't know,' said Benno. 'Maybe we couldn't have. There's something in people. A man like Hitler, he can find the vein of evil in people, and mine it. He follows his basest instincts, and when he does, we give ourselves permission to do the same. He tells us his malevolence is strength, and we believe him because it is convenient, and we follow his lead.'

'Remember what Goethe said about the Germans?' said Margarete.

Benno knew exactly the quote she meant. *'I have often felt a bitter sadness when I think of the German people; we are so estimable as individuals and so dreadful in the collective.* But, you know, Gretl, I don't think it's just us Germans. I think every people on earth gets their chance at collective evil. And history tells us very few can resist.'

And It Didn't Stop There

Willi went for an early supper with Margarete and Benno Horvath. They met at a small Gasthaus some distance from their homes where they would be unknown. Benno was an old friend of Willi's father. Before his retirement he had been a senior police official and had become young Willi's mentor when Willi had decided to become a policeman.

Willi got to the Gasthaus early and leaned his bicycle against a small maple tree at the curb where he could see it. The edges of the tree's leaves were showing the first fall colors. It was only five thirty and he was the only customer. He chose a corner table beside the door leading to the kitchen. 'A beer, please,' he said. The waitress brought it. She was young and pretty.

Willi stood as the Horvaths came in. It had been several months since he had last seen them, and they had both aged in that time. Benno seemed less steady on his feet, and Margarete was thinner. She had white, almost translucent skin, the lightest azure eyes, a cloud of silver hair, and the erect posture of a dancer. A pale blue vein ran across her temple. She had an ethereal, almost otherworldly quality, as though she already had one foot in the great beyond.

Summer was almost over, but the evening was warm. Margarete wore a light sweater and a scarf around her shoulders. She kissed Willi's cheek. 'Willi!' she whispered, as though his name were a secret, which in fact it was. Benno kissed him too, then grasped his hand.

Benno held the chair for Margarete. You could see from his face how he adored her, and it seemed to Willi for an instant that he should warn Benno. Even showing love so openly seemed like a dangerous thing to do these days. Willi sat on the bench against the wall.

'Lola says hello,' said Willi.

'She's recovered?' said Margarete.

'She has mostly,' said Willi. 'She's doing well.'

'They haven't caught the man?' said Benno.

'They haven't really tried,' said Willi.

'Why not? Is it somehow political?' Benno said.

'Maybe,' said Willi. 'But, if it is, I haven't figured out how. The cops on the case have good reputations. They're supposedly conscientious and thorough investigators, so someone must have taken them off the case.'

'Leave it alone, Willi,' said Benno.

'That's what Lola says.'

'I'm glad she's recovered,' said Margarete. 'You both deserve to be happy.'

Willi was a little afraid to name his happiness, as if doing so might cause it to disappear.

They studied the menu, ordered their food, and then sat for a long time in silence.

'What's new?' said Willi finally, an ordinary question in ordinary times, but not any more.

'Nothing,' said Benno, and then described all the ways that wasn't true. Seven hundred Protestant pastors had just that week been arrested by the Gestapo for refusing to integrate their Confessional Church into the Nazified Evangelical church. Another Munich newspaper, the *Courier*, had been forced out of existence by the Propaganda Ministry. Otto Bierbaum, its publisher, was a Jew, and so had been forced to give up control. The paper had closed the following week.

Almost the only professors remaining in universities these days were those who had sworn allegiance to the Führer. The new rector of the University of Berlin, a storm trooper and veterinarian by trade, instituted courses in Racial Science. The new director of the Dresden Institute of Physics had proclaimed, 'Modern physics is an instrument of World Jewry for the destruction of Nordic Science. True physics is the creation of the German spirit. In fact, all European science is the fruit of Aryan thought.' Meanwhile Germany's great thinkers, artists, scientists – Einstein, Thomas Mann, dozens of them, hundreds of them – were long gone, scattered to the four winds and erased from the pages of German culture.

'And it didn't stop there,' said Benno.

'We were at the theater,' said Margarete. She didn't want to talk about politics. 'Kleist. *The Broken Jug*. Wonderful. We laughed and laughed.' They stopped talking when the food arrived.

'I'll see what I can find out about the investigation,' said Benno, taking up the topic of Lola's attack again.

'Don't,' said Willi. 'I don't think you'd find anything, and it's not worth the risk. I may ask Bergemann to look into it, although . . .' Hans Bergemann's connection to Willi was necessarily more and more tenuous, and his access to information was more and more limited, so looking into it wouldn't be easy for him either. The police were ruled by the SS now. A culture of suspicion prevailed. Just seeking information could signify treachery.

'It's like an infection, isn't it?' said Benno. 'And not just at police headquarters. Suspicion is a virus that has infected the whole society. The very words we speak are dangerous. You have to think of all possible meanings before you say anything out loud. And you have to pay attention to how you look, *where* you look, how you stand or sit or pick up a mug of beer. Nothing is beyond suspicion.'

At that moment, as if to underscore Benno's point, the door opened and a young couple came in and took a table by the front door. They cast a vague unfocused look in the Horvaths' direction, then sat down and never looked their way again. And the Horvaths never looked in their direction either. They were strangers to one another, and the safest thing for everyone was to keep it that way.

Tullemannstraße 54

*D*eutsche Reichspost regulations required that all mail deliveries be placed inside locked mailboxes. No exceptions were allowed. And Trude Heinemann always delivered the mail in accordance with the *Reichspost* requirements. She could get in trouble if she didn't.

A keyring hung from a long chain at her side. She drew it up, found the right key, opened the metal panel above the boxes, and slid the letters in. She had more than forty buildings on her route, with over five hundred and fifty individual mailboxes. So her work required efficiency and dispatch.

Heinz Schleiffer was the fly in the ointment. Heinz Schleiffer waited by the door of 54 Tullemannstraße each morning – outside when the weather was nice, inside when it wasn't – for the mail to arrive. Heinz lived in the small apartment off the lobby of number 54, a brick and concrete block structure of five stories and of no discernible style. Most of the building's thirty-six apartments were inhabited by working-class tenants. There were two staircases leading up from the lobby, with landings on each floor. Each landing had a porcelain sink for the use of the tenants. The landlords had promised to install running water in each apartment by year's end, but there was no sign that they actually intended to do it. So a few tenants had run pipes and put in sinks at their own expense.

A highly polished metal sign with the word 'Guardian' was attached to Heinz's front door. Heinz took his duties as guardian very seriously. 'My job,' he had said to Trude the first time she encountered him there, wearing the well pressed, if ill fitting, brown uniform of the SA. 'My *duty*' – he corrected himself – 'is to a greater authority than the *Reichspost*.'

'Heil Hitler,' said Heinz, and saluted as Trude mounted the three steps to number 54.

'Heil Hitler,' she said. You were required to greet others that way. A few people said nothing or said 'Heitler' or something like that, something that sounded like Heil Hitler. But they were tempting fate. Trude's teenage son Dieter had told her that he had once said 'Ein Liter!' (one liter) and given a snappy salute to the leader of the Hitler Youth at school. Trude was horrified. She shook her finger at him. 'Don't ever do that again,' she said. 'People end up in Dachau for less. You're playing with fire.'

Dieter just laughed. 'That idiot Herbert?' he said. 'He's an asshole.'

Now Heinz, standing with his legs apart and his arms folded across his narrow chest, held out his hand. 'Give it here,' he said. He blocked her way every day now and had made it clear he would not budge until he inspected the mail. She handed him the small stack of letters for the building and waited while he leafed through them, making sure every letter belonged at 54.

'There are more important things at stake than efficient postal delivery,' he said.

That's easy for you to say, thought Trude. *You never get any mail.* And it was true: no one had ever written to Heinz Schleiffer, at least not since Trude had been delivering the mail.

'Wait,' said Heinz. 'What's this?' He held up a letter toward Trude.

'Herr Karl Juncker, Tullemannstraße 54,' she read the name on the envelope. 'What about it?'

'The return address,' said Heinz, '*and* the postage stamp?'

Trude leaned in and looked more closely. 'What about it?' she said again.

'American,' said Heinz. 'I'll deliver this one in person.'

'You can't,' said Trude.

'*I'll* deliver this one,' said Heinz again. He handed her the other letters and stepped aside so Trude could unlock the panel and drop the other mail in the boxes.

Trude did not move. 'Postal regulations . . . *Reich* postal regulations require that I deposit the mail in the appropriate boxes.'

Heinz took a small step toward Trude and examined her as though he hadn't quite seen her until now. She could smell the alcohol on his breath. 'I see,' he said. His voice was suddenly quite calm, and the beginnings of a smile flickered around the corners of his mouth. 'Let's ask Ortsgruppenleiter Mecklinger at SA headquarters what he thinks of postal regulations when the security of the Reich is at stake, shall we?'

'The security of . . .?'

'I'm talking about official Party business' – he pretended to read her name tag – 'Frau Heinemann. Suffice it to say that there is official interest in this Karl Juncker, and I have my orders to investigate.' This was a lie. 'So, if it is your intention to impede an investigation, by all means, take the letter. Of course, I'll have to report your obstruction of a legitimate and important investigation, and we will see where it goes from there.' He handed the rest of the letters back to her. She stood looking at him. 'Well, what are you waiting for?'

Trude sighed, stepped forward and unlocked the panel above the mailboxes. She dropped the letters into the various boxes as quickly as she could and closed the panel.

'Heil Hitler,' said Heinz with a smart salute.

'Heil Hitler,' said Trude. She wanted nothing more than to get out of there.

Heinz Schleiffer

After the Great War had ended, Tullemannstraße 54 had been mostly vacant and without a guardian for several years. Without anyone in residence who could see to the maintenance, the building had slid into decline, until it had come under new ownership and Heinz Schleiffer had been engaged to fill the guardian slot. Heinz drove a beer truck afternoons and evenings, which gave him a flexible enough schedule to assume the duties of building guardian. This office required him to make small repairs – he was a handy carpenter and passable with plumbing and electricity – and perform regular maintenance: unlocking the entry door in the morning and locking it in the evening, sweeping the stairs, cleaning the lobby floor, washing the front windows, and, of course, polishing the brass plaque on the door of his lodgings. In exchange for fulfilling these duties – and he was assiduous in their fulfillment, you had to give him that – he got the use of the apartment rent free.

His guardian duties did not require that he be a storm trooper or that he wear the uniform. Nor did they include harassing the mail lady or investigating his neighbors. But the Führer had inspired in Heinz, as he had in many others, a newfound love of a particular sort of authority. The Führer's own abusive ways were liberating. He gave people like Heinz, people who felt that they had been abused or mistreated or cheated or taken advantage of – whether they actually had or not – license to become abusive to others.

Heinz had first heard Hitler speak five years earlier when word had started spreading about him and his movement. Hitler promised that when he came to power, the little people, the forgotten ones, people just like Heinz, would have their day in the sun. 'The socialist government has sold you out, has sold Germany out. But we will give you back your country.'

Heinz was not political. He didn't even vote in those days, but he was moved by what he had heard.

Heinz was a little adrift and lonely. He wanted to be somebody, to be respected by other people. Hitler said that by joining their party you became part of a great German movement. That suited

Heinz; he wanted to be part of something larger than himself, especially if it meant getting back at all those shitheads who had messed up his life.

Heinz's wife had run off with another beer truck driver years earlier. There were two shitheads right there. His son Tomas was another. He had gone away to university and was now too big for his britches – studying art history, of all things. He came home to Munich less and less, and when he did, he stayed with his mother and rarely came to see Heinz.

'Stop whining,' said Jürgen, another driver. He had a wayward son too and thought he knew just what Heinz needed to do. 'Haul the little shit back to Munich and slap some sense into him.' They were drinking with their buddies at the *Stammtisch*, the table at the Three Crowns reserved for the neighborhood regulars.

'No, I can't do that,' said Heinz, pretending to be reasonable. 'He should have the chance to make something of himself.'

'Yeah?' Jürgen snorted. 'Well, you're his father. He needs to show you some respect and gratitude. I'd knock some sense into him.'

'How about Lechler's header on Sunday?'

Heinz was boring; his son was boring. So somebody brought up the spectacular last-minute goal by Lechler to win the match against Dresden.

'Well, face it,' said someone else. 'Dresden has no defense. They threw that match away.'

'Yeah, defense was always Dresden's problem.' The others nodded and muttered in agreement.

When talk turned to soccer or money or jobs, Heinz could never think of anything to say. He didn't like soccer and he had a boring job. And anyway, no matter what the subject, he was bad at banter. The more they drank, the livelier the others got, while Heinz went silent. He sat with his back against the tile oven, but the warmth did nothing for him.

What warmed Heinz Schleiffer was putting on the brown shirt and tie, the brown pants, the boots of the SA. He had become a storm trooper not long after he had joined the Party. The uniform was like an exoskeleton for Heinz, supporting his insubstantial flesh, making his blood run hot, giving him, in his own eyes at least, substance, strength, and authority. Hitler and the National Socialists meant to restore national pride and bring prosperity back to Germany.

And for there to be pride and prosperity there had to be order, and for there to be order, there had to be those who enforced the order. And that was where the SA and Heinz Schleiffer came in.

The purge, Operation Hummingbird, hadn't bothered Heinz one bit when he heard about it. Röhm and his buddies had been trouble for the Führer and that was all that mattered. And they were perverts to boot. Hard measures were called for. The SA, the storm troopers, had been purified, and the new SA would be better than ever. There were still millions of them. End of story.

Heinz had failed to keep order in his own family. He thought he should have beat up his wife when she was disobedient, and she might not have run off. And Jürgen was right: he should have summoned that little pissant of a son with his fancy ideas and slapped some sense into his silly head. But it was too late for that too.

Now he had the building to look after. He was the guardian, after all, and now that Hitler was on his way to total power, Tullemannstraße 54 needed tending to. As Heinz saw it, Tullemannstraße 54 was a small version of Germany itself, a microcosm, his son would have said. The pissant liked fancy words. The building had fallen into disrepair and disrepute, and it was Heinz's duty to restore and maintain order, to know, as best he could, everyone living there, to see that there were no malefactors among them, that everyone was living by the rules, living by German rules.

Heinz made it a point to know who came and went. He spoke to them, inquired about their well-being in a sufficiently friendly manner to learn what he could about them. He helped old Frau Schimmel carry her groceries up to her apartment and managed to learn that her husband had died forty years earlier as a result of wounds sustained fighting in the Franco-Prussian War. She lived on her war widow's pension. Or at least that was what she said. She invited Heinz in for a glass of schnapps and told him, with a little prompting, what she knew about the building's other inhabitants. And she knew quite a bit – who did what for a living, who feuded with their neighbor, that sort of thing.

She knew nothing about Karl Juncker, even though he lived across the hall from her. 'I never see the man,' she said. When he thought about it, Heinz realized that he hardly ever saw Juncker either. That was suspicious in itself. What was Juncker up to anyway?

Now, as a storm trooper, Heinz had a larger responsibility, not only to the building but also to the Reich. If Karl Juncker was getting letters from America, it was up to Heinz to find out why. 'Is he getting letters from America?' Frau Schimmel asked. She filled Heinz's glass. 'My, oh my,' she said.

All Heinz knew about Karl Juncker was that he kept to himself. He came and went on an irregular schedule. When he and Heinz met in the hall, which was not very often, Juncker walked right past without so much as a hello. He got his bicycle out of the bicycle room and rode it wherever it was that he went. Heinz had not been able to find out where that might be. Frau Schimmel said she didn't know. Juncker came and went at irregular hours. Did he have a job? What did he do every day? Now, with this letter from the United States, Heinz had the perfect opportunity to find out a little more about who he might be.

Heinz marched up the stairs to the second floor, planted himself in front of apartment 21, and rapped sharply on the door. He was about to knock again when Willi opened the door.

'Herr Juncker?' said Heinz, his arms folded across his chest, the letter held in front of him.

'Yes?' said Willi.

'Heil Hitler,' said Heinz.

'Heil Hitler,' said Willi. Heinz tried to look into the apartment, but Willi stepped into the hall and pulled the door closed behind him. 'What do you want?'

'I'm Heinz Schleiffer, the building guardian.'

'Yes. I know who you are.'

'This letter came for you, Herr Juncker.' Heinz waved it back and forth in front of his chest.

'Give it to me,' said Willi.

'It's from America,' said Heinz.

'Why wasn't it left in my mailbox?' Willi said.

'Because,' said Heinz, but he couldn't think of a good answer to that obvious question. And suddenly he realized that his decision to take the letter from the postwoman and deliver it himself might not have been such a good idea.

Willi was taller than Heinz, and muscular. His thick eyeglasses made his eyes look small and narrow and menacing. The fingers of his left hand stroked his chin as he studied Heinz. As he moved his hand from his chin, a small rosette in the buttonhole of his lapel became visible. Heinz had seen such rosettes before in the lapels of high Nazi officials.

'The postwoman . . . she . . . she dropped it in the wrong mailbox,' said Heinz. 'I wanted to . . . I'll make sure it doesn't happen again.'

'See that it doesn't, Herr Schleiffer,' said Willi. 'There are postal regulations, you know. Heil Hitler,' he said with a salute, stepped back into his apartment, and closed the door. Heinz stood there for another moment. He remembered to mutter Heil Hitler, but the door was already shut. *Jesus*, he thought. *What have I done now?*

Willi listened at the door to the noise of Heinz Schleiffer's boots clattering down the stairs. He wondered: was Schleiffer intimidated, or would he make inquiries about Karl Juncker? Did Schleiffer represent a danger, a nuisance, or no threat at all?

'What did he want?' Lola said.

'I think he was just snooping,' said Willi.

'That's not a surprise,' said Lola. 'It's only a surprise it took him this long to get here.'

'Did he see you arrive?' said Willi.

'I don't think so,' she said. 'Frau Schimmel did though.'

Willi laughed. 'Frau Schimmel sees everything.'

The First Report

'SA Mann Heinz Schleiffer to see you, Herr Ortsgruppenleiter.' Lorelei, the District Group Leader's secretary – and his lover until the night before – gave the 'Herr' a sneering emphasis. Ortsgruppenleiter Gerhard Mecklinger had promised Lorelei he would divorce his wife and marry her. But now he had called off their affair, saying he just couldn't leave Gudrun, his wife. He had called her Lorelei once too often, and she had given him an ultimatum.

Gerhard had recently been named District Group Leader, which was a big step up for him. It put him in charge of some hundred storm troopers. Gudrun reminded him that this, his big break, had come about entirely thanks to her being Heinrich Himmler's favorite niece. So the choice was Gerhard's: he could stay with her and rise

through the ranks to higher and higher office, thanks to Uncle
Heinrich. Or he could run off with that trollop Lorelei, in which
case Gudrun would see to it that he wound up in Dachau.

And now, with this mess on his mind, here came that asshole
Schleiffer once again. Every district had its troublemakers, but
Schleiffer was in a class by himself. Every week he showed up
to report an imaginary traitor. Gerhard had dutifully reported the
first infractions to his higher-ups, but soon heard back from them
in no uncertain terms that what he was reporting was nonsense,
the suspicions of a deranged mind. For instance, jumping onto a
moving streetcar was a little dangerous, but it was not treason.
A Reichsmark and fifteen pfennigs was a little high for a sausage
and a hard roll, but it was not a betrayal of the Fatherland or an
insult to the Führer. Schleiffer had even reported a homeless
beggar, as though her asking for a handout were an act of sabotage. It was up to the Ortsgruppenleiter, they said, to decide what
was a legitimate complaint and what wasn't and to put a stop to
this nonsense.

'Shall I show Herr Schleiffer in, Herr Ortsgruppenleiter?' said
Lorelei.

'Tell him I'm busy,' said Mecklinger and began shuffling the
papers that lay on the desk in front of him.

'He says he has an important matter to report,' said Lorelei. A
smile crept across her pretty red mouth. She clearly enjoyed delivering this unpleasant news. Mecklinger decided in that moment this
couldn't go on; he was going to have to fire her.

'Shall I show him in?' she said again. Without waiting for an
answer, Lorelei said, 'This way, Herr Schleiffer.'

'Close the door, Fräulein,' said the Ortsgruppenleiter as Lorelei
left the room. She slammed the door so hard that the glass rattled.

Heinz stood at attention, gazing at the huge portrait of Hitler
behind Ortsgruppenleiter Mecklinger. He saluted. 'Heil Hitler!' he
shouted.

'Heil Hitler, Schleiffer. What is it this time?'

'The Ortsgruppenleiter is well?'

'Yes, Schleiffer, very well, thank you. What is it? As you can
see, I'm very busy.'

'I'm sorry to disturb you, Herr Ortsgruppenleiter. But something
very important has occurred, and I think it is essential that you
know.'

'All right. Tell me,' said Mecklinger.

'Aren't you going to write it down, Herr Ortsgruppenleiter?'

Mecklinger picked up his pen. 'Tell me, Schleiffer.'

'I'm here to report a Herr Karl Juncker, residing in apartment twenty-one in my building, Tullemannstraße fifty-four. Herr Juncker received a letter from the United States a few days ago. And then, yesterday, he received a package from England.'

'A package?'

'A book, I think.'

Gerhard Mecklinger stopped writing and lay down his pen. 'Could you get straight to the point, Schleiffer? I'm a busy man.' He tapped the stacks of paper on his desk. 'What exactly is the important thing that you wish to report?'

'Herr Ortsgruppenleiter?'

'Wait. Are you seriously telling me that you are reporting someone for receiving mail from abroad?'

'Herr Ortsgruppenleiter, I don't think I need to remind you of the Führer's dire warnings against foreign elements at work trying hard to undermine Germany's economy and our well-being. There are English and American agents in our beloved Fatherland at this very moment seeking . . .'

'And you believe, Schleiffer, that this . . .' he looked at the name he had written . . . 'Karl Juncker is one such dangerous character, because he receives mail from abroad?'

'Why not?' Schleiffer said. He was not to be deterred. 'The evidence is circumstantial, I realize that. But I am certain, if I could get into his apartment, I would find evidence to prove my case.'

'You do not have a case, Schleiffer, and you are certainly not authorized to get into his apartment. You are not the Gestapo. Do you understand me? There is no case. You are wasting my time, Schleiffer, with your endless fantasies of wrongdoing.'

'Really? Well, Herr Ortsgruppenleiter, what if I told you this Karl Juncker is pretending to be a high Party official? Would you think my suspicions were a fantasy then?'

Schleiffer had decided to play his trump card, and in fact Mecklinger was momentarily taken aback. 'What are you talking about? Was he in uniform or what?'

'When I encountered him, he was wearing an official Party decoration.'

'What decoration?' Mecklinger had picked up his pen again.

'A red rosette, Herr Ortsgruppenleiter.'

'A red rosette?' He laid the pen down again. 'Was this a decoration that you recognized, Schleiffer?'

'No, Herr Ortsgruppenleiter. But . . .'

'And how do you know this is a Party decoration and not a military decoration or, for that matter, a civilian decoration? There are countless rosettes of every color, Schleiffer, red, black, white, blue, violet . . .'

'I assumed, Herr Ortsgruppenleiter . . .'

Mecklinger paused for a moment and thought. He rubbed his chin and nodded, as though he had reached a decision. 'You're right, Schleiffer . . . yes, I think you're right. Yes. We're going to look into it.'

'You will?' This was a sudden and surprising change. For the first time ever, one of Heinz Schleiffer's reports was being taken seriously. It would go up the chain of command and would be acted upon. 'You mean, Herr Ortsgruppenleiter, that it will be . . . investigated?'

'Absolutely,' said Mecklinger. It had finally dawned on him – he wondered why it had taken him so long – that the way to get rid of Schleiffer was to pretend to take his bizarre fantasies seriously, and to promise an investigation. True, there was always the chance that it might encourage him, that he might show up even more often with even more ridiculous charges. But, by the same token, maybe it would slow him down, make him more circumspect about which 'reports' he filed. Anyway, at the very least, it would get him out of the office for now.

'We will do a thorough investigation, Schleiffer.'

'And you will let me know how it turns out?' said Schleiffer, suddenly filled with pride and hope.

'Oh no, I'm afraid not, Schleiffer. No, no. You realize, this has to be investigated in secret and dealt with in secret, too. Any findings will be kept secret as well.' Mecklinger lowered his voice. 'You can see, Herr Schleiffer, that because there are foreign elements involved, in fact everywhere, as you say' – he gestured to the left and right – 'investigations of this sort are particularly sensitive. Which is why, Schleiffer, you must not speak of this matter to anyone.'

Mecklinger stood up and saluted. 'Thank you, Schleiffer, for coming forward with this information. Heil Hitler!'

Schleiffer was startled by the abrupt ending of their meeting, but he recovered quickly, snapped to attention, and saluted. 'Jawohl, Herr Ortsgruppenleiter! Heil Hitler!' Schleiffer spun on his heels and left the office.

Mecklinger took the piece of paper where he had written Karl Juncker's name and address. He looked at it for a moment before he crumpled it into a tight little ball and threw it into the trash. He smiled. He was pleased to have finally figured out how to deal with the Schleiffers of the world. He wondered whether in fact he might adapt the same technique – 'the Schleiffer method' he would call it – to other, more personal circumstances. He could pretend, for instance, to comply with Gudrun's demands and yet still have his way with Lorelei. 'Maybe. Just maybe it would work. But I'll have to be careful. *Really* careful. Gudrun must remain Gudrun and Lorelei must remain Lorelei.'

The Gestapo

Reinhard Pabst was a fourth-year university student when he became disillusioned with academic life. German literature had been his course of study. But Lessing, Goethe, Schiller, Heine, the heroes of his chosen field, seemed to him to be essentially celebrating self-indulgence. Professor Schultheiß had proved this in his course and in his writings. Their 'Enlightenment' had only led the world into bitter conflict and secular confusion, and eventually brought about the cultural degeneracy and spiritual wasteland that was Weimar Germany. What ultimate purpose could studying these degenerate writers have besides the glorification of the self and the denigration of man and God?

This, Reinhard's first epiphany, a 'spiritual revelation,' came about as he was reading a biography of Saint Ignatius of Loyola, the warrior who had become a Christian saint. Reinhard thought that the way to happiness might lie for him through abandoning his own troubling earthly longings and pursuits, laying his discontent and unhappiness aside, and substituting God-filled dreams and meditations, visions of holiness, of Christ and Biblical Truth. And, in fact, he discovered that when he tried to think better thoughts, his anguish left him, and he did momentarily feel better.

He joined the Jesuit novitiate and began a month-long retreat in silence and isolation that took him through Ignatius's Spiritual Exercises. Through this series of spiritual practices – prayer, meditation, contemplation – he sought, like other Jesuits before him, 'to conquer myself and to regulate my life in such a way that no decision is made under the influence of any inordinate attachment.' The trouble was his 'inordinate attachments' would not leave him. During that period of extreme aloneness, he slept little and was visited by strong and disturbing visions and voices.

Next, Reinhard engaged in a series of what was called apostolic experiments, spending time in a Jesuit ministry, serving the war injured, the sick, the needy and the forgotten. He ministered in shelters and soup kitchens, among the poor and downtrodden, wherever he was needed. After two years Reinhard took the vows of perpetual poverty, chastity and obedience. He promised to commit his life 'to serve God, the Church, and those to whom I am missioned for the greater glory of God.' He embarked on a study in theology and philosophy – reading Aristotle and Thomas Aquinas – while continuing his apostolic service.

It was during this philosophical study – he had strayed for some reason to the dark philosophers, Schopenhauer, Hobbes, Nietzsche – that he had his second epiphany, even more violent than the first. It came about as he sat in a tenement room by the bed of a prostitute suffering from tuberculosis. He read to her comforting words from the Bible about heaven and reunion with God, about the sufferings of Jesus. She didn't want his comfort or his God, for that matter. 'Go away. Who are you anyway?'

'I'm Brother Reinhard. Reinhard Pabst,' he said. He thought she was asking his name.

'Pabst? Pabst?' She laughed, because Pabst is German for pope. 'Pope Reinhard! Your Christian charity is crap. Go away, your Holiness.'

'Please,' said Reinhard. 'I only want to help you find comfort.'

'That's shit,' she said. 'You hypocritical Pope. You just want to make yourself feel righteous. Rot in hell.'

She turned to face the wall. Reinhard took her arm and tried to turn her back his way. She pulled her arm away abruptly. 'Stop it,' she said. He tugged at her arm again, and she turned toward him in a fury. 'Listen, Pope, hands off! I've been fucked by priests before. I was eight the first time. Are you going to fuck me too?' Then she laughed again until her laughter turned into coughing.

Despite the woman's wretched condition, or maybe because of it, Reinhard felt a violent anger welling up inside. What an idiot he was; what had he even been pretending to be with this charitable crap? In this violent and corrupt world, prayer and contemplation were worse than useless exercises. They were stupid, self-indulgent, narcissistic frivolities. Reinhard tore back the blanket, tore off the woman's tattered gown and forced himself between her legs. He clawed at her breasts, grunting and thrashing about like a wild beast, until he had stopped her laughter.

Doing violence to this defeated woman and at the same time doing violence to his own oaths of devotion to God and Jesus liberated Reinhard from his weak, ineffectual, tormented self. It felt good. *This* was power. Destruction was power. And through destruction lay the path to liberation and fulfillment. What a fool he had been! Good and evil were a false duality, ridiculous abstractions that had nothing to do with real existence. They were intellectual constructs designed to mask the total chaos, to somehow make the world seem orderly. Love was just another expression of fear and submission. Violence was the only true response in this chaotic world. Chaos could only be made orderly by brute force. The only true duality was power and powerlessness. It was fuck or be fucked, defeat or be defeated, kill or be killed.

Reinhard had just experienced an exhilaration unlike any he had ever experienced before. And so it was not surprising that he eventually sought to repeat the experience. When the irrepressible desire overcame him, he would attack another woman, and have the exhilaration all over again. True, the woman with the umbrella, that had gone awry. But there was always the risk that something would go wrong. However, the risk, the audacity, was part of the thrill.

There was nothing in Reinhard's upbringing that could have predicted his violent eruption of mind and spirit. He was the son of decent Catholics – his father was a government bureaucrat, his mother ran a small nursery school out of their home. Reinhard, an only child, had been a sweet boy, shy, a little bit fearful. He was not stupid, but neither was he gifted or bold. He was a mediocre student, confused and adrift. He had vague dreams, but he was not moved to do anything, was not moved by anything or anyone. He had been weak all his life. Pathetic really. Until now.

Reinhard believed that he had found the courage to see things as they really were. Adolf Hitler – not Jesus or Saint Ignatius – became his patron saint. Only Hitler embodied the *true* human spirit. Adolf Hitler was willfulness, lust, power in human form, and that was everything Reinhard had been lacking. He saw it now: power was as close as he would ever get to goodness, because power was the only thing that was *true*. Hitler and Hitler alone understood the necessity of dominance.

Reinhard did not want to be loved, he wanted to be feared. Being feared would bring him the freedom he had been missing; being feared would bring the fulfillment he sought. Invoking fear in others would be the irrefutable confirmation of the triumph of his power and his will. It would end his own fearfulness and timidity and finally bring focus and meaning to his life.

The SS and the Gestapo drew their members from all segments of society. And not a few had been doctors and lawyers and teachers and even members of the clergy. What went on in their minds to take them from the helping professions to the hating professions is essentially unknowable. In Reinhard's case it had to do with the void within. He was and always had been morally empty, devoid of purpose because he was devoid of humanity. He had a great barren desert at his center, where the hot, empty wind blew back and forth and never stopped. Just as it can be with anyone, the lawyer's or the doctor's or the teacher's or even the priest's conscience can be a feeble organ. In Reinhard's case, whatever conscience he had was too small and too weak to resist the siren call of fearsomeness, power and malignant and sadistic delight.

Reinhard Pabst had sufficient intelligence and training to allow him to construct an intellectual framework on which he could organize a justification for his malignancy. 'Look around, Reinhard,' said Hobbes, 'at the life of man, solitary, poor, nasty, brutish and short.' Nietzsche told him, 'Give up on God. He's dead. Your Christian love is nothing more than impotent hate.' The world Hitler was making was the one true reality, one that sprang from the tribal Germanic essence, from blood and soil, and from an unblinking appraisal of human existence. And most importantly it spoke to Reinhard's desire.

The SS were Hitler's knights, dressed in black and silver with the death's head on their hats. And the Gestapo, the secret state police, were of an even higher order. The Gestapo wore no uniforms. They could not be recognized until you felt their hand on your shoulder. Their charge was to pursue traitors, spies, saboteurs and those who committed criminal attacks on the Nazi Party and on Germany – that is, on the essential truth of power. And because their charge was almost a holy one, they did so without oversight by the courts or by anyone else, except the Führer himself. They could take any citizen into custody for any reason or no reason at all and dispose of them as they saw fit. Reinhard joined the SS where you swore an oath to live and die for the Führer. And, after his basic military training, he went to work for the Gestapo, an occupation that meshed nicely with his murderous inclination.

The Gestapo sent Reinhard to Berlin for several months of advanced training. He was attached to a security service unit and, because of his Jesuit experience, was sent to root out trouble in the theology department at Humboldt University. Because Reinhard was young and attractive, he mingled easily with the students and could join in their theological conversations.

Over beers they talked about scripture and doctrine, about the sacraments and Christian symbology. They all knew the risks, of course, and were circumspect when it came to talking about the political situation, or Hitler, or anything else having to do with the Third Reich. The trouble was that nearly everything these days had something to do with the Third Reich, every thought was measured against Hitler's thought and was either correct or treasonous. Reinhard was a patient and gifted interlocutor. He found that he could discern from discussions that had nothing to do with politics which of his new friends might harbor errant ideas, who might be a traitor to the Reich. After less than a week at the Humboldt University, he made his first arrest.

The Blood Flag

The *Reichsbahn*, the national railroad, had laid on special trains, and every one of them was filled to bursting with uniformed men. The atmosphere was festive, despite the heat of the day. Someone would start to sing, Horst Wessel or the Deutschland song or some other marching song, it didn't matter what, and by the second or third line everyone had joined in. Heinz Schleiffer knew all the words. His shirt was soaked, and sweat was running down his back, down his legs and into his boots. He didn't mind a bit.

In Nürnberg the train shuddered to a halt with a screech and a great sigh, spewing steam across the platform. The men spilled out of the train, out of the station and into the square. They fell into formation, hoisted their flags and standards, and marched off in the direction of the Zeppelin field. The parade, one group in black, the next in brown, seemed endless. Their flags fluttered overhead. Their marching and singing echoed off the ancient buildings back at them in a grand and joyous cacophony. Just to hear the power of it, to feel the company of those marching beside him, filled Heinz with happiness.

After an hour's march, the vast field opened up before them. They joined the other thousands streaming onto the grounds or already standing in formation. They found their assigned place not far from the Grandstand with its giant swastika and countless red, white, and black flags. The celebratory noise was deafening. Cries of 'Heil Hitler' rang out from every direction. And then everything went quiet.

Suddenly there he was, in front of a small procession coming toward them. One man was carrying the Blood Flag. They had carried that very flag during the Beer Hall Putsch twelve years earlier, where it had supposedly been soaked in the blood of the martyrs. For some reason it made Heinz think of the veil of Veronica, but he drove the thought from his mind. The Führer, standing right in front of him, solemnly touched the flag to the unit's guidon in the *Bluftahnenweihe*, the Blood Flag Baptism, consecrating the unit and with it Heinz himself. It was a sacred moment, one Heinz would never forget, no matter how long he lived.

Tens of thousands of men and boys – the Hitler Youth were there too – stood in the sun and waited. Finally Hitler stepped onto the podium, saluted, and everyone raised their arms and shouted, 'Heil Hitler! Heil Hitler! Heil Hitler! Heil Hitler! Heil Hitler! Heil Hitler!' It was as though they would never stop. Finally Hitler stepped to the microphone, his eyes cast down, his hands folded in front of him, and the entire mass of men fell silent.

He spoke softly, hesitantly at first, and the crowd strained forward so as not to miss a word. He welcomed this army of followers, and with the greatest humility professed his gratitude for their devotion. He had been called to leadership, he said, a role he had neither wanted nor sought, by the dire situation Germany had faced. He recalled the early years of the movement in which his vision for a reinvigorated Germany had crystalized and taken on the hardness of steel.

He was not a vain or arrogant man, he said, but he had felt called to this sacred task of renewal. It was his divine duty to do battle against a weak, decadent, and corrupted order. This order had been created, and was run, by socialists and democrats following their false gods of socialism and egalitarianism. He had come to destroy them, remove them from their thrones, and to solve the longstanding 'Jew problem.'

'Now,' he said, his voice rising, 'that which is old, decayed and evil perishes. And let it die! For new life will spring up. We have come together on this day to prove that we are more than a collection of individuals striving one against another, that none of us is too proud, none of us too high, none is too rich, and none too poor, to stand together before the face of the Lord and of the world in this indissoluble, sworn community. When was a leadership at any time faced with a heavier task than our German leadership?

'Consider, my comrades: how little we Germans have, compared with the wealth of other states, the wealth of other countries, the wealth of other peoples, with the possibilities they possess. Germany is crowded. We have one hundred and thirty-seven people per square kilometer. But we have no colonies, no raw materials, no foreign exchange, no capital. We no longer have any foreign credits. We carry heavy burdens, face only sacrifice, taxation, and low wages.

'What *do* we have, then? One thing only: we have our people, our German people. Either it is everything or it is nothing. It is the one thing we can count on. It is the one thing we can build on. Everything that we have created up to the present we owe solely to the people's goodness of heart, its capacity, its loyalty, its decency, its industry, its sense of order. And when I weigh all this in the balance, it seems to me to be more than all that the rest of the world can offer us.

'So this, I believe, can be our message to other peoples on this great day. You do not have to be afraid that we want anything of you. We are proud enough to confess that we already own a treasure, one you definitely could not give us: our people. I could, as Führer, think of no more glorious, no prouder task in this world than to serve this people. One might give me continents, but I would rather be the poorest citizen among this people. And with this people we must and shall succeed in achieving the tasks that are still to come.

'What we want lies clear before us: not war and not strife. Just as we have established peace within our own people, so we want nothing more than peace with the world. For we know that our great work can succeed only in a time of peace. But just as we have never sacrificed honor in our relations with the German people, so will we never surrender the honor of the German people in our dealings with the world.'

Heinz Schleiffer felt pride well up and fill his being. A feeling came over him, unlike any other he had ever known. He *belonged* somewhere. He belonged to something bigger than his beer truck or his pissant son. He belonged to something great and eternal, a great movement, a proud nation.

Many, maybe even most, ordinary Germans – listening to the speech on the radio, or even just going about their business – felt something like what Heinz felt. Their lives, their work, their families had significance again. They were once again part of a great culture and a great nation. The Nazis, whatever else you could say about them, had made life worth living again. Even the fact that while the Nürnberg celebration was going on, the Reichstag had adopted the new Race Laws stripping German Jews of their citizenship, while not unknown to Germany's ordinary citizens, did not get in the way of their happiness. After all, only the Jews were affected. Not them, not the *real* Germans.

We humans seem to have a natural inclination toward normalization. We get used to whatever conditions may come along. We can fit even dire circumstances into our daily lives, once we get used to them. It shouldn't be surprising therefore that, when tyranny and fear became the norm in Germany, when criminal behavior became acceptable, and simple humanity became dangerous, most ordinary Germans went on with their lives as though these changes and the curtailment of rights and freedom did not matter all that much. If people even knew about these changes, it was from the newspaper and not from their own experience. And what was in the paper might be a lie. The Führer said it was a lie. And even if it wasn't a lie, well, then at least it had happened somewhere else, in someone else's life.

Ordinary Germans could carry on with their lives despite 'Blood Flag Baptisms' and other such colorful nonsense. They told themselves and each other, 'Well, yes, all this has its ridiculous side, and, yes, its awful aspects too. I mean the race laws go too far. Yes, the Führer's methods are hard, even cruel. But maybe he has no choice, like he says; maybe he has to strike with an iron fist. Did you ever think of that, how hard his task has been?'

On March 2, 1936, Hitler ordered a small contingent of German troops to cross the Rhine River and occupy the demilitarized zone of the Rhineland. He did this, of course, in defiance of the Treaty of Versailles and against the advice of his generals. General von Blomberg was certain they would be forced by the French and English to beat a quick retreat.

Instead, nothing happened. The Germans retook their land without any opposition. 'There, you see? If he hadn't just marched into the Rhineland, if he hadn't started building up an army and navy again, even when the French and British fuss and fume about it, where would Germany be? Still in the doldrums, still a defeated third-rate power, that's where.' But thanks to the Führer, every red-blooded true German could feel pride again, could walk with his head held high.

Thanks to the Führer's bold military and industrial initiatives, Germany's prosperity was on the rise, its economy was getting stronger all the time, while the French and British and Americans were still struggling to come out of the Great Depression. In the German Reich food was plentiful and affordable again, hunger was banished. People had homes, they had jobs again and were paid a livable wage. They could enjoy life again too. How long it had been! They went to movies and concerts, visited nightclubs and cabarets, sang in choirs, exercised at the gym, played soccer with their friends, shopped, had neighbors in for dinner. And, at the same time, they were part of something larger than themselves.

Thanks to the Führer, and to no one else, you could have a satisfying life. 'Keep your mouth shut, your nose clean, and your head down, and you'll be fine. Life goes on. And we have to go on too, don't we? For the sake of our children, for the sake of our parents.'

The Second Report

Willi listened to Hitler's speeches when they were broadcast and read the newspaper accounts of the rallies. His and Lola's safety depended on their knowing what was going on. Something like the retaking of the Rhineland could embolden Hitler to accelerate his aggression. The new Nürnberg Race Laws could cause the police to modify their procedures and their focus and, by the same token, could cause Willi to curtail certain activities, to lie low, to avoid some contacts and risk others. A speech like the Nürnberg speech would almost certainly reinvigorate Hitler's followers. Especially someone like Heinz Schleiffer, who was part of the flotsam and jetsam, swept this way and that by the fascist tide.

Willi had continued to spend some time in Karl Juncker's apartment even after Schleiffer had appeared at his door, calculating, wrongly as it turned out, that Schleiffer would do nothing after their confrontation. As he watched Schleiffer in his freshly pressed uniform going off to catch the Nürnberg train, Willi had second thoughts.

Normally Schleiffer was content to harass the poor postwoman, or to drive the occasional homeless man from the building's entrance. But his sense of purpose had been reinvigorated by Nürnberg, just as Willi imagined it could be. Heinz determined to refocus his attention on the task at hand – Germany's greatness and the Party's power. Immediately on returning, he paid Ortsgruppenleiter Mecklinger another visit.

Lorelei, Mecklinger's secretary and lover, had been replaced by a solid, stern-faced middle-aged woman, Frau Irmgard Kinski. She had close-cropped hair and small, wire-rimmed glasses that magnified her grey eyes so that she resembled a large, pale fish. She wore a uniform – a brown man's shirt, a black tie and a long brown skirt. 'Do you have an appointment?' she barked. It did not sound like a question.

The Führer had spoken of all Germans having an appointment with destiny, and for a moment it occurred to Heinz to say that he had an appointment with destiny. Instead he said, 'I do not. But I have important information about a German traitor the Ortsgruppenleiter is going to want to hear.'

'Your name?' said Kinski.

'SA Mann Schleiffer!' he said and saluted.

Frau Kinski had much to recommend her. She was neither young nor beautiful, which pleased Gudrun Mecklinger – there was no chance her husband, Gerhard, would be tempted to begin a dalliance with her. And it pleased Gerhard for the very same reason. Gerhard had found Lorelei a secretarial position in police headquarters in Ettstraße, where the pay was better, for which she was of course grateful and wonderfully forgiving. Now he could rollick in her sweet arms without Gudrun being any the wiser.

Moreover, Frau Kinski could take dictation, was an efficient typist and an effective buffer between the Ortsgruppenleiter and unwanted visitors like Schleiffer. Her only deficit was her defective hearing. 'Herr Ortsgruppenleiter, there is an SA Mann Steiffel with information about a German traitor.' She had misheard Schleiffer's name and gave the word *traitor* a special honking emphasis. 'You will want to see him.' Mecklinger did *not* want to see anyone, but Frau Kinski really gave him no choice.

His face fell as Schleiffer entered the office. 'Heil Hitler, Herr Ortsgruppenleiter!' said Schleiffer, snapping his heels together and saluting.

Mecklinger stood up, his face turning red. 'Damn you, Schleiffer. How dare you give a false name to get in here!'

'What? No, Herr Ortsgruppenleiter. I didn't, I didn't, I swear . . .'

'I told you that we would investigate the case of . . . of . . . that you brought in earlier. And we are doing exactly as I promised. The investigation is proceeding as we speak. And unless you have genuine new evidence of treachery, I want you to leave immediately. NOW, GET OUT!'

'Herr Ortsgruppenleiter, it is my duty to report to you that Karl Juncker continues to receive mail from abroad, that he—'

'Get out, Schleiffer!'

'Herr Ortsgruppenleiter . . .'

'Out!'

Once Schleiffer had saluted, Heil-Hitlered, and fled, Mecklinger went out front. 'Frau Kinski,' he said, 'see that that man is never admitted again. Never. Is that understood?'

He went back and sat down at his desk. Whatever he had been doing before Schleiffer had arrived, now he had completely lost his train of thought. This Schleiffer; what an idiot; he had some nerve. But then Mecklinger remembered Frau Kinski's hearing problem. So it wasn't necessarily that Schleiffer had lied.

Well, it didn't matter; the man was a pest. But then the thought occurred to him: why *would* a German citizen be receiving regular mail from abroad? Most likely it was completely innocent. But what if it wasn't? That was how you had to think nowadays – suspect the worst. What if this person really *was* engaged in some treachery, and it was found out, as it certainly would be, given the thoroughness of the SS and the Gestapo? Gerhard would then be seen to have ignored repeated reports of treachery from one of his underlings. And in that case even Gudrun's Uncle Himmler wouldn't be able to save him. Mecklinger wrote the name 'Karl Juncker' on a note pad. He would call the information in to headquarters tomorrow.

Frau Schimmel

Willi had been staying with Lola during the months since the Nürnberg rally. The day he came back to Tullemannstraße, Frau Schimmel knocked at his door. 'May I come in, Herr Juncker?' she said.

Willi still only knew Frau Schimmel from passing her in the hall. They said hello to one another and occasionally exchanged a few pleasantries. She was, he could tell, watchful and observant. She had a way of being there when something happened. 'Come in,' he said. She used a cane with a silver head, but moved briskly and with a sense of purpose. She waited until Willi had closed the door and was facing her.

'I'll get right to it,' she said. 'While you were gone, you had visitors.' Willi said nothing. 'There were two of them,' she said. 'It was the afternoon of December nineteenth, around noon. They stayed about thirty minutes.'

'In my apartment?' he said.

'In your apartment,' she said. 'Herr Schleiffer let them in. I waited until they were leaving, then I came out and met them in the hall.'

'Frau Schimmel, you . . .'

'I had my shopping cart; I was on my way to get groceries. They said they were friends of yours. I nodded and said hello. They gave me names.' She opened her purse and drew out a slip of paper. 'Herr Weber and Herr Meier.' She laughed. 'Weber and Meier? Really?'

'Frau Schimmel, you astonish me,' said Willi. 'Won't you sit down?'

'A cup of tea would be nice,' she said, as though Willi had already offered one. She gave you the sense that she knew what you were going to say before you said it.

Willi brought the tea and cups on a tray along with a few cookies on a plate. Frau Schimmel was standing by the small dining table. 'Please,' said Willi, motioning toward a chair.

'You don't have any pictures,' said Frau Schimmel.

'What?'

'Pictures.' She motioned around the room. 'You don't have any pictures on the wall.'

'No,' he said. 'Frau Schimmel, would you . . .'

'They were in plain clothes, Herr Juncker. They wore hats; their hair was short on the sides. If I had to guess, I'd say your Herr Weber and Herr Meier were Gestapo.'

'Frau Schimmel . . .'

'You need some pictures on the wall, Herr Juncker. A few knick-knacks too. A vase maybe. Your apartment looks like nobody lives here.'

'Who are you, Frau Schimmel?'

'Who am I? I'm the old lady who lives across the hall, Herr Juncker. Who are *you*?' She smiled. 'No, Herr Juncker, I'm not really asking. I just thought you'd want to know about your visitors. Your tea is very good, by the way.'

'It's from England,' said Willi.

'I know,' she said.

They sipped for a while in silence.

'Frau Schimmel, may I ask you a question?' said Willi. 'Several questions, actually?'

'Of course,' she said, but did not pause to hear his questions. 'I don't get around as well as I used to,' she said, 'but as you're certainly already aware, I make it my business to know as much as I can about what goes on in the building. And elsewhere too, if I can. True, I know almost nothing about you, Herr Juncker, but that is as you want it, isn't it?

'I know a bit about Schleiffer, though, the little storm trooper and his Nazi nonsense. He visits me, you know, for information. I give him gossip and he spills the beans.' She laughed. 'He's quite a competent plumber, by the way, and he likes to talk as he works.

'But he doesn't like or trust you, Herr Juncker. That won't be news to you. He has reported you at least once to his *Obergruppennazi*. He more or less told me so, when he was asking me about you and your foreign mail. I think he has reported me as well, although for invented and inconsequential stuff.

'No, Herr Juncker, I don't tell him anything about you or anyone else. He is simply set off by suspicions that come to him apparently out of thin air. He believes, for instance, that several people in the building are Jews, when I am quite certain that I am the only one.'

'Frau Schimmel, you don't have to . . .'

'Herr Juncker, look at me.' Willi realized he had been avoiding her eyes, looking at the bare wall above and behind her instead. He lowered his gaze. Her eyes were dark and penetrating, and he could sense a fierce intelligence behind them. She had short, stylishly cut white hair, a small nose, a firmly set mouth with brightly painted lips, and a strong, rounded chin which she held high. 'First of all,' she said, 'I was a member of the KPD – the German Communist Party – and the Spartacus League during and after the war, in the teens and twenties. I was friends with Rosa Luxembourg. We were together during the November revolution. I loved her dearly. So you see that, besides being a Jew, well, the Third Reich has many reasons to want me dead.'

Willi's discomfort was plain to see.

'I'm eighty-two years old, Herr Juncker. My family is either dead or out of the country. I've been operated on three times for cancer, and the prognosis isn't good. So, you could say, I suppose that by talking to you as I am, I'm placing myself – and possibly you and others – in danger. However, I don't think that is the case. First of all, I know enough about you and your . . . circumstances to be reasonably sure that what I have told you about your visitors will be helpful to you. And I think of myself as having nothing to lose and also much to gain by what you probably regard as my "reckless" behavior.'

'Much to gain?' said Willi.

'Well, your friendship, for one thing. And Lola's too. She's lovely. I like her very much.'

Frau Schimmel stood up with the help of her stick. 'Herr Juncker, it has been a pleasure. I'm sure we will be in touch again.' She turned toward the door and then turned back toward Willi. She held out her hand. Willi took it, and she held on for a minute. 'You know, the Nazis know everything about me. They will have reams of paper with my name on them – not Bertha Schimmel. Still, they'll find me eventually – they're not *all* idiots. But I like the idea of going down fighting.' She turned again and took Willi's arm as they walked to the door.

'Hang a few pictures, Herr Juncker,' she said. 'Here and maybe over there. A potted plant or two would be good. Make the place a little homier.'

Willi was unnerved. That evening he stayed with Lola and told her about the visit. 'I don't know a thing about her, and she knows a great deal about me.'

'But she told you about the Gestapo visitors. Without her you wouldn't know that.'

'That's not reassuring,' he said. 'I don't need more people.' Having few social connections still seemed like the best thing for him and for others too. Lola looked at him with raised eyebrows. 'I didn't mean you,' he said. 'But Frau Schimmel was reckless.'

'Was she really?' said Lola. 'I mean, she told you what she saw and who she is, knowing that it won't go any further.'

'Why would she do that?' said Willi. 'And how does she know it won't go further?'

'Because she knows who you are, Willi. She figured out enough about you to know she can trust you.'

'I know. You're right,' said Willi. 'She figured me out.'

'Aha. That's what bothers you, isn't it? But she trusts you,' Lola said again, 'and I think she was saying you can trust her. I understand your caution, Willi, and your fear. But you can't let your situation turn you more suspicious than you have to be. I know, I know; I don't understand much about these things. But haven't you said yourself that too much caution can be as dangerous as too little?'

Willi still wasn't ready to lay this caution aside. 'She implicates me, doesn't she? Now I – we both – have knowledge that we didn't have before, things that it's dangerous for any of us to know.'

'Yes, but you also know things that it's good to know that you didn't know before. Herr Weber and Herr Meier, for instance. You know you have a friend across the hall. Knowing that could save your life.'

'Yes, but . . .'

'You like her, don't you?' said Lola, finally finding her way to the heart of the matter. 'Now there's someone else you care about who you have to worry about.'

Willi did not answer, but he looked up and met Lola's eyes. She saw she was right.

Detective Sergeant Hermann Gruber

Detective Sergeant Hermann and Mitzi Gruber had recently celebrated their wedding anniversary with an excellent dinner in a fancy restaurant. The Golden Pheasant was known for its *Tafelspitz,* and it had a good cellar of German and French wines. It should have been a happy occasion for them both. But Mitzi had become more and more anxious as the evening went on, as uniformed SS officers and their wives or girlfriends filled nearby tables. Hermann should have expected her reaction, given that the Golden Pheasant was known to be favored by Party members and officials. Maybe it *had* occurred to him. Maybe it was even part of a subconscious strategy.

Mitzi doesn't look Jewish, Hermann thought, *so what's her problem? She's pretty with her blond hair and upturned nose and high bosom.* But the fact remained that her mother, Anna Schwarz, née Flegenheim – who didn't look Jewish either – was a full-blooded Jew, which made Mitzi half Jewish, and, as Hermann had increasingly come to realize, despite his affection for her, a real liability.

He should have been a police captain by now; he had been with Hitler since the beginning. He had cracked heads at those early Nazi rallies and had marched in the failed Putsch in 1923. True, he had failed the detective exam several times. But finally, thanks to his mentor, Major Reineke, a Hitler enthusiast and a chief of detectives, he had passed the exam and become a detective.

Reineke had made it clear early on, though, that as long as Gruber was married to Mitzi, he would remain a sergeant. And being assigned to partner with Willi Geismeier had been another stroke of bad luck. Willi Geismeier . . . Whenever Hermann thought of the man, he felt bile rise in his throat. Willi had been nothing but trouble, always going his own way, violating every department regulation in the book. He was always investigating matters he wasn't supposed to investigate, making things difficult for everyone, especially Party members, like Reineke and those higher up too, and thereby making things difficult for Gruber. How much, he wondered, had Geismeier's bad behavior cost him in terms of advancement and success? No use crying over that spilled milk though. What could he do about it now?

Anyway, he had invested too many years in his career to let it all go now because of an incorrect marriage. That was something he *could* do something about. He looked around the Golden Pheasant at the SS in their sharp, black uniforms, true Aryans with their Aryan wives and girlfriends, and decided then and there that he had to divorce Mitzi. What choice did he have? She was a Jew. She hadn't even produced any children, which he momentarily regretted, until he realized they would have been Jewish too.

Of course, he would do the right thing by her. He wasn't a cad. He would provide for her, support her, protect her, when it came down to it. Once he was admitted into the SS and rose through the ranks, he would have influence and be better able to protect her and her whole family. That thought put his mind at ease.

It was as though Mitzi had read his mind. A few days later she started making preparations for what was coming. 'I'm going to move in with Mutti and Vati,' she said.

'What? Why, Mitzi?' he said, all innocent and surprised.

'Because,' she said. 'It's for the best.'

Hermann left it at that. He appreciated Mitzi all the more for her willingness to make this sacrifice.

A judge granted the divorce immediately. Most of Hermann's police colleagues didn't react when they heard, although a couple of them solemnly shook his hand, as though he had been freed from a great burden or awarded a prize. Major Reineke said, 'You did the right thing, Gruber. It's only too bad it took you so long.'

Hermann did not get promoted after the divorce. In fact, months and then years passed and he remained a sergeant in charge of a small squad of detectives. Major Reineke, the closest thing Hermann ever had to a mentor, was transferred to Berlin, and Hermann was left on his own.

Hermann's new commander, Captain Robert Wendt, who had once been a detective under Hermann's command – the insult was almost unbearable – sent down the latest case-closure statistics. Hermann found his squad near the bottom of the chart again, his numbers circled in red pencil. With Willi Geismeier's departure – Willi had closed more cases than the rest of the squad put together – the squad's numbers had plummeted to the bottom of the chart and for the last few years had stayed there.

Hermann suddenly had a thought – an inspiration really. Everyone knew Geismeier was responsible for the death of Otto Bruck, and Bruck had been one of the Führer's favorites. And yet Geismeier was still at large somewhere, still tempting fate, still waiting to be caught. Many believed Willi had fled the country for England or America, but there was no evidence that this was actually true. What if Geismeier was still here? And what if he, Detective Sergeant Hermann Gruber, could manage to find the son of a bitch and arrest him? Willi Geismeier was a big fish and that would change everything. No one would give a shit about the squad's closure rates or any of that crap after he arrested Willi. Willi Geismeier would be Hermann Gruber's path to redemption. Hermann knew as much about Willi as anybody did. After all, they had even once been partners. If anyone could find Willi Geismeier, it was Hermann Gruber.

Hermann stepped to his office door, full of new exuberance and hope. 'Bergemann!' he bellowed. 'Come in here.'

Bergemann jumped. 'What is it, Sergeant?'

'I'd like you to get me whatever we have on former Detective Geismeier.'

'Willi Geismeier? Boy, there's a name from the past,' said Bergemann. 'I doubt we have much in our files, but I can check in Central Records. What are you thinking, Sergeant?'

'How well did you know him, Hans?'

'Not that well, Sergeant. I heard he's in America.'

'I don't buy it,' said Gruber.

'What? You think he's still in Germany?'

'Not only that. I think he's still in Munich,' said Hermann triumphantly.

'Really? That's interesting,' said Bergemann. 'Do you have new information?'

'Gut instinct,' said Hermann, thumping his ample stomach.

'I see,' said Bergemann. 'OK.'

Gruber was a big believer in his own instincts, despite the fact that they were usually based on a combination of his misreading a situation and wishful thinking. He had always been a terrible detective. He had hardly ever investigated a case on his own, unless it had been in order to impede it. His rare interrogations of perpetrators gave away more information than he ever gleaned. He telegraphed his intentions so that the dimmest of suspects could tell what he was after. And yet once in a while even a terrible instinct could turn out to be correct, and even a terrible detective could catch a break.

The Steins

It was time for one of the Horvaths' Sunday evenings. Benno was polishing champagne glasses in the kitchen. Margarete sliced a cucumber, smeared some paté on each slice, and arranged them prettily on a china platter. They laid out French cheeses on another platter beside a porcelain bowl with small crisps and thin squares of pumpernickel bread. There was a crystal bowl of pickled herring in thick cream, and various other treats, both savory and sweet.

For as long they could remember, the Horvaths had been hosting occasional small Sunday evening buffets for a group of their friends where they talked about culture and politics and whatever else came up. Benno and Margarete both wanted to keep the Sunday evenings going, to keep something like normality alive. You really couldn't tell what was going to happen next. And even Benno Horvath – who was later arrested, tortured, tried, and executed for being part of a plot to assassinate Hitler – still managed to believe, or maybe he just hoped, that Germany could somehow come to its senses. A lot of people thought that way. *Somehow we'll get out of this mess.* The champagne was cold, the glasses shone in the candlelight, the hors d'oeuvres were spread on silver trays.

Recently, however, the gatherings had changed. Gerhardt Riegelmann, for instance, a longtime guest and an acquaintance of

Margarete's from her university days, had always been a true conservative, a royalist even. He brought with him interesting and strong opinions about world politics and the like. He had seemed to be a supporter, with reservations, of the Weimar Republic, but had recently let it be known that he had come to think of Hitler as 'the right man for the moment, the leader we need,' to defend the country against the rising tide of Bolshevism. 'He has the Bolshis on the run. And just look at the economy,' he said. 'You can't argue that we're not all better off under the Führer.'

Bad enough, thought Benno, but then one Sunday, Riegelmann was suddenly castigating 'world Jewry' for seeking to undermine Germany's rising well-being. 'I don't know why I tolerated his crap for so long,' said Benno. Riegelmann was no longer invited and soon broke off relations with the Horvaths altogether. Subversives, he called them both, even though Margarete deplored politics of every sort.

Then there was Gottfried Büchner, the theater and book critic. He had also fallen in line with the Nazis, publishing the most ridiculous movie reviews, criticizing the 'decadent Jewish tone' of one movie, or praising the 'Germanic grandeur' of another. He was no longer invited either. Presumably neither man had known that the Steins, who had sat beside them at the Horvaths' on more than one occasion, were Jews. Or maybe they *did* know and liked offending them. That sort of cowardice was common these days. In any case the Steins had sat there silently and let it pass, and Benno and Margarete had both apologized profusely afterwards for their uncouth guests.

In the old days Willi had sometimes come to the Horvaths' Sunday evenings. He had mostly kept his opinions to himself. But then, once in a while, he had a way of unexpectedly and yet artfully skewering an ignorant remark so that the culprit could tell he had been skewered but couldn't quite put his finger on how it had been done. Neither Riegelmann nor Büchner liked Willi and wondered to one another why a simple police detective was even invited to an intellectual evening. Of course, Willi could no longer be there anyway, now that he was a fugitive.

Edvin Lindstrom was back in Munich after a few years in Tokyo and then Stockholm, posted once again at the Swedish Consulate. He had Ella, his new wife, with him. Edvin was a friend of Willi's. They had first met at the Horvaths' and had stayed in touch after

that. Edvin and Ella were welcome back at the Sunday evenings, although Edvin was no longer as outspoken or as interesting about politics as he had been in earlier times. Now when the conversation turned in that direction, Edvin and Ella listened but did not join in. They talked about how beautiful the summer in Stockholm had been, or about starting a family, or the lovely apartment they had found overlooking Munich's English Garden. But even when someone asked directly about Hitler, or the new race laws, or the struggle against Bolshevism, Edvin demurred. 'It would not be appropriate for me as a diplomat to comment about your politics.' Ella just smiled when she was asked and didn't say anything.

This evening the guests – they were ten – were subdued. Someone brought up the new production of Schiller's *Wallenstein* at the Deutsches Theater. Then, of course, someone brought up the Olympics. Everyone was eager to see the great American Jesse Owens run. But inevitably every topic they touched – even a foot race – turned into a political discussion. The evening ended early.

The Lindstroms were the last to leave. 'I would like to see Willi Geismeier,' said Edvin. 'Do you think you could put us in touch?'

'You know he's no longer with the police?' said Benno.

'Yes, I do,' said Edvin. 'We wrote each other for a while. We had to break it off. But do you think you could arrange a meeting?'

'I can get a message to him,' said Benno.

'And we, Benno, you and I, we have to talk as well,' said Edvin.

'Yes,' said Benno. 'We do.' Benno knew enough about international diplomacy these days to understand that, while Edvin might be the Swedish cultural attaché, he probably had other, more sensitive duties as well. Back in the 1920s Edvin had already revealed an interest in matters beyond his diplomatic purview. He had warned and briefed his German friends – Benno and Willi among them – about Hitler, well before anyone believed he could ever come to power. Outsiders could sometimes see things Germans couldn't.

Now, as a senior diplomat, Edvin found himself in a particularly advantageous position for conducting extra-diplomatic activities. Since the Nürnberg race laws had come into being, many consulates and embassies had been helping people whose lives were in danger to leave Germany – mainly Jews, but others as well. The Swedes in general, and Edvin and Ella in particular, were part of that effort. They also had other, more clandestine duties.

Josef and Marta Stein, while still invited to the Horvaths'

evenings, had not been there for several months now. Then one day – not a Sunday – they called on the phone and made an appointment to stop by.

'We've come to say goodbye,' said Josef. Marta burst into tears.

The Steins said they were emigrating to the United States. Marta had cousins there who had agreed to sponsor them. Armed with the signed affidavits and all the other required papers, they had gone to the American consulate and gotten visas for themselves and their two children. They had had to wait in line.

That line, however, was nothing compared to what it would become. By late 1938, just two years from now, the deportation and murder of Jews had begun, and leaving legally became very difficult. Every consulate and embassy of every country had long lines of desperate people snaking around the block trying to get out of Germany. By then, just standing in such a line made you an easy target for harassment. At first it was the SS and storm troopers who harassed you, but eventually it was your former friends and neighbors.

For now, Hitler's government was happy to have Jews leave voluntarily. All they had to do was turn their worldly goods – their property, their wealth, including the proceeds from the sale of Josef's law firm, family jewelry, art – over to the Reich. They could get their passports – imprinted with a big red J for Jew – with relative ease. Of course, often enough the official issuing the passport demanded a bribe. Why not? He was a poor office drudge who was paid a pittance for doing tedious and distasteful work. Why shouldn't he get his little piece of a Jew's money? The Führer said it wasn't even theirs to begin with; they had stolen it from real Germans.

The official looked the Steins up and down, saw their nice clothes, their proper manners. No jewelry was showing, but that didn't mean anything; by now all Jews knew not to wear jewelry when they went to get their passports. But the official had been doing this long enough to be a pretty good judge of what a Jew could afford to pay. He just had to be careful not to get too greedy or he'd get in trouble with his boss. 'A hundred Reichsmarks,' said the official, and held out his hand. 'Each.'

Josef Stein had known this was coming. He reached into his pocket several times until he had pulled out four hundred. The official wiggled the fingers of his outstretched hand impatiently. He knew there was more money in there. But he didn't have the right to order Josef to show him. So he settled for the four hundred and regretted not asking for six.

When the Nürnberg Race Laws had been passed, Josef had been outlawed from owning the law firm he had founded – in fact, from practicing law at all. Marta had also been forced to dismiss their children's nursemaid, Frieda Schultze, who had been part of the family for many years. As a young woman she had been Marta's nursemaid. But it was now against the law for an Aryan woman to be working for a Jewish family. Frieda couldn't stop crying.

'The writing is on the wall,' said Josef. 'Thank you, Benno and Gretl, for your friendship, your kindness and hospitality. It means the world to us. But we can't stay in Germany any longer.'

'How can we?' said Marta. 'Our families have been here since the middle ages. But we're no longer thought of as Germans. How can we stay here? How can we raise our children here? There is no future for us or for them.'

Josef's parents were dead, but Marta's were still alive and, to her distress, they refused to leave. 'This is our home,' said her father. 'We are Germans. I am a war veteran.' He was more than a war veteran. He had retired as a colonel after the Great War ended, a renowned fighter pilot, an ace with thirty-six air victories to his name. He had ended the war with one eye, one hand shot away and a chest full of medals. He was sure that would protect them from Hitler's wrath.

It didn't.

Lili Marlene

'Here are the files you asked for, Sergeant.' Bergemann held a thin packet in Gruber's direction. Gruber looked puzzled. 'The Willi Geismeier files from Central Records,' said Bergemann.

'That's all there is?' said Gruber.

'Yeah,' said Bergemann. 'I thought there'd be more.'

'There has to be more,' said Gruber.

'This is all I could get.'

'Anything useful?'

'No. Mostly old official complaints, Sergeant. And a few papers about his suspension. But nothing about the arrest attempt back when he went missing. And nothing recent. Whatever there was is gone.'

'Gone? What do you mean, gone? Signed out maybe?'

'Could be. Nobody would say. They wouldn't even show me the logbooks.'

'Do we have any of his old case files here?'

'Everything should be in Central Records.'

'But it isn't.'

'Maybe somebody else is interested in him too,' said Bergemann.

'Somebody else . . .' Gruber thought for a moment. 'Who?'

'I don't know, Sergeant. Gestapo maybe?'

Gruber took the packet of documents into his office and sat down. Bergemann watched him frowning at each page before turning it over to study the next. He stopped once in a while to write something down. After a while he got up and closed his door. Bergemann could hear him talking on the phone but couldn't make out what he said. Gruber put on his hat and coat and came out of the office.

'I looked again, Sergeant,' said Bergemann. 'There aren't any records here. Did you learn anything useful?'

'No, not really,' said Gruber, and headed for the door.

'Where're you off to, Sergeant?'

Gruber stopped and studied Bergemann for a moment. 'Aren't you supposed to be working on something, Bergemann – that robbery case or something like that?'

The sun had just set when Bergemann met Willi to warn him about Gruber. The clouds turned crimson around the edges and then went black, and the temperature seemed to drop ten degrees at the same moment.

'That doesn't sound like Gruber,' said Willi. They sat on a park bench looking out at the Isar. The ice had mostly melted except along the banks. Some ducks were swimming around, diving under the water and bobbing back to the surface.

'No, this isn't the Gruber we know,' said Bergemann. Gruber was lazy and uncurious. Except now he was running off to Central Records to do research. 'Could I have missed anything?'

Willi shook his head, but he looked worried. 'What's he up to?'

'I don't know.'

'Do you think something has come his way?' He thought of Heinz Schleiffer and his earlier snooping around. Frau Schimmel was sure he had filed at least two complaints against Karl Juncker. And there were the two men, Weber and Meier, who had gone into his apartment and rummaged around. These things could have worked their way through the system and finally found their way to Gruber.

'If he's on to anything, he's not giving it away,' said Bergemann. 'And that's not like him either. I'll keep looking, though, and I'll let you know what I find out.'

'Be careful, Hans,' said Willi. 'You know, if you try to drag your feet or get in the way of whatever he's doing, he'll know it. If he's paying attention, you could be in a lot of danger. So do whatever he expects of you. Help him out if you have to.

'We shouldn't meet again for a while,' he said finally. The two men stood and shook hands. Willi turned away, swung his leg over his bicycle, and rode off into the night.

Gruber's determination, a quality that had mostly been missing from his character until now, continued unabated. He spent hours each day going through papers he dredged up from who knew where. 'SS files,' said Gruber.

'Can I help?' said Bergemann.

'No. It's on a need-to-know basis,' said Gruber.

Bergemann got busy on the robbery case. Someone had been holding up businessmen, three so far, all late at night, all claiming to be on their way home from work. Two admitted to having stopped for a drink. Well, maybe a couple of drinks. All three surmised they had been followed. Then a man grabbed them from behind and held a pistol against their cheek while they fished out their wallets. He instructed them to face the wall and count to ten slowly while he disappeared. None had seen the robber or could say anything useful about him.

The trouble was, Bergemann was pretty sure all three were lying about why they had been in the locations where they were robbed. There were plenty of decent bars and restaurants along the routes they would normally have taken home from work, while the bars where they had stopped and the sites of the robberies were far from any such route. Moreover, the bars they named were seedy establishments in a seedy neighborhood, not the sort of places a well-heeled businessman would be likely to stop. Unless he was trying to cover up something illicit or embarrassing. Since these were married men, a sexual adventure came to mind. And sure enough, Bergemann found a well-known whorehouse on Pfortzheimgaße, not far from where the men had been robbed.

Werner Deutlich was the eldest of the three victims. His wife answered the door when Bergemann knocked. When Werner recognized Bergemann, he quickly stepped past her and into the hall. 'It's business, sweetheart,' he said. 'I'll be right back.' He steered Bergemann down the hall and around a corner.

'You lied to me, Herr Deutlich,' said Bergemann.

Werner Deutlich pleaded with Bergemann not to disclose what he had discovered. Yes, he had visited the whorehouse. Yes, more than once. 'My wife is not well, Herr Detective.' He confessed he was a sometime client of a voluptuous blond who called herself Lili Marlene. 'Just like the song.' For some reason Werner sang the first lines:

Vor der Kaserne, vor dem großen Tor
Stand eine Laterne und steht sie noch davor . . .

A dim red light illuminated the door at number seven Pfortzheimgaße. Bergemann knocked and the door was opened by a man with slicked-back hair, a pencil mustache, and a complexion that looked sallow even in the red glow. He wore a suit that may have fit him once, but now made him look like a scarecrow.

Bergemann showed his police ID and asked to see Lili Marlene. She was with a client, said the man. Bergemann said he would wait. He was shown into a dimly lit room with pink wallpaper, a badly worn Persian rug, and plush chairs and a sofa in various states of decrepitude. Some awful perfume had been sprayed around the room. The skinny man disappeared. Bergemann took a seat and waited.

Women and girls in various stages of undress wandered through from time to time, mostly ignoring Bergemann. Thirty minutes passed before Lili Marlene – her real name was Ingeborg Lützmann – swept into the room. Her chubby face was framed by a cloud of platinum-blond hair. She wore a filmy, flowered shift that revealed more than it concealed. Despite her near nakedness, she had an air of authority about her. Bergemann wondered whether she was the proprietress of this establishment, and she assured him she was. She produced a folder with permits and health exams for all her girls. 'It's all in order and up to date,' she said.

Bergemann explained that none of that concerned him now. He wondered whether she herself still saw customers.

'Why wouldn't I?' she said, tossing her platinum locks and allowing her shift to open even wider. She received only men she favored. 'Only gentlemen,' she said, giving Bergemann an appraising look.

'And is Werner Deutlich one of those gentlemen?'

She said he was. Bergemann named the other two.

'Yes, them too,' said Lili Marlene. 'What's this all about?'

'And were they with you on these particular evenings?' He listed the dates and she checked them against her calendar. They had been there then, yes.

'All three of these men were robbed after they left you on those nights, Frau Lützmann.' Lili Marlene looked startled, then thoughtful. 'What can you tell me, Frau Lützmann, about the man who works your front door?'

'Jacky? Jacky Prinz. He belongs to one of the girls, Liesl. He's been on the door about two months now.'

'Do you know where he was before that, Frau Lützmann?'

'Liesl told me he was down on his luck, that he needed the work. He seemed all right, so I didn't ask too many questions. But I had my suspicions.'

'And what were those suspicions, if I may ask?'

'He looked to me like somebody just out of prison. Herr Detective, I don't . . .'

'Do you have any other men in your employ, or are there other men – I'm thinking tradesmen – who come by on a regular basis? Delivery men, cleaners, anyone like that?'

'There are occasional delivery men, but nobody regular.' Lili Marlene pulled her shift tighter around her again, like she suddenly wanted to hide her nakedness.

'Frau Lützmann, I'm going to insist you not talk to anyone about our conversation.'

She nodded her head adamantly.

'Certainly not to Jacky Prinz,' said Bergemann. 'Or to Liesl – I'll need her full name.'

Jacky Prinz had done two years for armed robbery and assault with a deadly weapon. He had come out of prison a few months back with a raging drug habit. Liesl had pleaded with Frau Lützmann to give him the doorman job, and had told Jacky which of Lili Marlene's clients were worth robbing. Jacky followed them a few blocks, held the pistol up to their faces, and took their money. Bergemann went with two uniformed policemen to arrest the two of them.

'Nicely done, Detective,' said Hermann Gruber after listening to Bergemann's summary of the case. Bergemann handed him the paperwork and Gruber leafed through it. 'What was the whore's name? And where's the house?'

'Number seven Pfortzheimgaße, Sergeant. Lili Marlene.'

'Don't know it,' said Gruber, a little too quickly.

The Logbooks

G ruber was momentarily distracted from his pursuit of Willi Geismeier. While he didn't know Lili Marlene well, he had met her, and he knew a number of her girls and had enjoyed their services – of course, only after his divorce from Mitzi. Still, if it was discovered that he had been diddling local whores, his closure rate would be the least of his worries. He saw the girls' faces go by in his mind's eye, one after the other. This imagined parade of faces suddenly made him think of someone else.

Hans Bergemann was putting together the final version of the robbery report – Gruber had read through the first draft and ordered some changes to it – when he sensed Gruber standing behind him looking over his shoulder. He continued working, waiting for Gruber to speak.

'Hans,' he said finally. 'Do you remember? It's been a long time now, two or three years at least, maybe more. This pretty redhead came in, said she was looking for Willi Geismeier?'

Bergemann paused and thought. 'When was that, Sergeant?'

'No, I'm sure you were here, Hans. Let's see: when would that have been? Do you remember when that was?'

'I don't think it was me, Sergeant.' Bergemann went back to assembling the robbery report, but his heart was pounding. Of course he remembered. He had followed Lola from the station that day. She had overheard talk of the SS raid that was meant to arrest Willi. He had warned her, and then had told Gruber that he hadn't found her. He had hoped that would be the end of it, and it had seemed to be. Except he hadn't remembered one thing: her name and probably her address would be in the desk sergeant's log. Damn it! He had forgotten about the logbook.

'Yeah, Hans, I'm pretty sure you were here then.'

'I'm sure you're right, Sergeant. I just don't remember it.'

Gruber nodded, stepped to the outer office door, and called out to the clerk. 'Would you bring me the logbooks from 1932 up to now?' The clerk soon brought a stack of thick green ledgers and dropped them on his desk with a thump. Gruber spent the rest of the day with his door closed, scanning the columns of dates, names and signatures, moving his index finger slowly down one page and then down the next. That evening he turned off the light in his office later than usual, and locked his office door. 'Goodnight, Hans,' he said.

'Goodnight, Sergeant.'

Normally, when Bergemann wanted to speak to Willi, he used circuitous means to make contact. But this was different. Bergemann had made a serious error, and Willi and Lola were in danger. He left the office and headed for the Mahogany Room. Lola saw Bergemann at the far end of the bar. She headed for the door that opened on to the alley where they met.

The following morning Gruber came to the office early. Bergemann was already there. 'Did you find what you were looking for, Sergeant?'

'Not yet,' said Gruber.

'You know, last night I was thinking about what you said. I think I *do* remember that woman, the redhead looking for Geismeier. As I recall, I even tried to follow her. By the time I got outside, she was gone. Do you remember that?'

Gruber grinned at Bergemann. 'Here, Hans.' He dropped the stack of ledgers on Bergemann's desk with a resounding thud. 'See what *you* can find.'

'Oh, c'mon, Sergeant. I've got two new cases . . .'

'Boo hoo,' said Gruber. 'Poor overworked Hansl.' He went back into his office and closed the door.

Bergemann found the ledger page with Lola's name and address. He briefly considered removing the page or rendering it illegible, but that was a foolish idea. Maybe he could somehow use Lola's logbook information – name, address – to get ahead of Gruber. If he could do the interview with Lola, even if Gruber were present, he might manage to control some of the damage. Maybe with luck he could turn this whole episode into a dead end.

He knocked on Gruber's door and handed him the ledger. 'Here she is, Sergeant.'

Gruber's eyes went straight to her signature; he had seen it already the day before.

'You want me to track her down?' said Bergemann.

'Never mind,' said Gruber with a grin. 'We're already on it.'

Corpus Delicti

Two schoolboys spotted a woman's body bobbing face down amidst sticks and other debris against a bridge piling. Once the police pulled her from the water it became obvious that she had been savagely murdered. She had countless stab wounds up and down the entire front of her body. She was young and had been dead for several days.

Gabriella Mancini, seventeen years old, had been reported missing by her parents two weeks earlier. When Bergemann showed them a photo of the dead girl's face, they both began to cry. After some difficult questioning, they admitted that Gabriella had left school at fifteen, had worked as a nanny for a short time, but more recently had been working as a prostitute. She still looked in on her parents every week and gave them part of her earnings. 'She was a good girl,' said her mother between sobs.

Gabriella had been found some distance from Pfortzheimgaße. But the spring rains had been heavy this year, and the Isar was running high and fast. She could easily have been washed that far down stream. Lili Marlene burst into tears as she confirmed that Gabriella had been one of her girls. 'She was just a child,' she said. 'Girls come and go; I just assumed she had moved on.' She paused and thought back to the earlier case of her robbed clients. 'My God, was it Jacky Prinz?'

'No. He's locked up,' said Bergemann. 'Anyway, it's much too early to know about suspects. We're in the very early stages of our investigation.'

Sergeant Gruber went pale when Bergemann told him that Gabriella was one of Ingeborg Lützmann's girls. This thing could screw up his life even more than it already was. *At least I didn't know her*, he thought. He went into his office, shut the door, and spoke to someone on the phone.

'I want you to take over this case, Hans,' he said a little later. 'And make it your number one priority. A dead girl in the water can really spook the public.'

From the coroner's report and the circumstances, Bergemann concluded right away that this was not what was normally called a crime of passion so much as a crime of rage. The savagery with which Gabriella had been killed – the coroner counted over fifty stab wounds, mainly in the breast and pelvic area – led Bergemann to wonder whether there might have been similar killings elsewhere in the city. Bergemann sent out a query to surrounding precincts. He heard nothing back for a long while, until one day a Detective Prager from the Nineteenth called. 'We had a case like this back in 'thirty-five, a young prostitute stabbed multiple times. Really butchered. Twenty years old. She was found in an alley, near our station, actually.'

Bergemann wondered why he had not heard about that case until now. Prager couldn't say. He had expected that his Sergeant would send out queries, but for some reason he never had.

'What's the status?' said Bergemann.

'Still an open case,' said Prager. 'But a cold one.'

'Did you turn up any suspects?'

'A bunch. Mostly customers of hers. They all had alibis.'

'Where was she found?'

Detective Prager named the street. 'An alley not far from the whorehouse she worked at.'

'Any evidence at the scene?'

'Nothing.'

'So, where are you now with the case?'

'Understaffed,' said Prager. 'We're down to five detectives total, so we have to deal with the cases where we can get some results. The sergeant's always worried about the closure rate.'

'Tell me about it,' said Bergemann.

'And you know the attitude: "She's just a whore."'

'Can I look at the file?' said Bergemann.

In both cases the medical examiners had determined that the

murderer had stabbed with both hands using one knife, stabbing with his left hand for a while and then switching to his right. In the Nineteenth's case, the body had been found near where she was murdered. She had staggered a few steps as she was being stabbed and died right there. The killer had paused when he was finished to wipe off his knife on the girl's dress. But aside from all the blood, there was no evidence. Bergemann sent out more queries, this time to all the precincts in the city.

Bergemann decided to walk the riverbank from the point where Gabriella had been fished from the water to the point nearest Pfortzheimgaße. Gruber was against it at first. 'Waste of time,' he said. After thinking about it, though, he said, 'Take a couple of uniforms with you.'

The sun was out. The sky was dotted with white fluffy clouds. There was a light breeze. Bergemann and his two young juniors were happy to be outside. 'What are we looking for, Detective?' said young Hans, a strapping blond boy with just the beginnings of a mustache.

'Anything that doesn't belong where you find it,' said Bergemann.

They walked the two kilometers slowly, keeping as close to the water as possible, their eyes to the ground. In any city there is usually trash on the riverbanks, but the south bank of the Isar seemed to be the exception. Young Hans explained that the Hitler Youth had been along the day before, picking up trash, doing their part for civic virtue. They were unlikely to find any clues. Young Hans beamed with pride.

Two days later, when Bergemann arrived at work, a detective from the Fifth was waiting. He took two file folders from his briefcase. Two young women had been stabbed to death in the same fashion about a year ago, one a clerk in a department store and the other an elementary school teacher. The store clerk's body had been found in a small park across from the building where she lived. The teacher was found in a different park. Both had been killed late at night, the clerk coming home from a night out with friends, the teacher returning home after an evening cultural program at the school where she worked.

'Come in, Sergeant Gruber,' said Captain Wendt. Gruber had called Wendt with the news that Munich had a serial killer on its hands. Wendt had immediately notified his superiors, both police and SS. The political authorities had also been notified.

Gruber and Wendt took a police car to police headquarters on Ettstraße. They sat side by side in silence on a hard wooden bench in a waiting room. A large colored photo of the Führer seemed to be looking at something just behind them.

After a while they were summoned, and Gruber followed Wendt into a large conference room. A dozen men sat around a massive table. Gruber was relieved to see Major Reineke among them. 'Heil Hitler!' said Gruber, standing at attention with his arm raised in the direction of yet another Hitler portrait. Gruber couldn't help thinking, *He's everywhere.*

'Now, Sergeant Gruber,' said Reineke, 'tell us what we know so far.'

Gruber had written out extensive notes and had even rehearsed the report he intended to deliver. He wanted to present a thorough and cogent summary of the case. *His* case! After all, his squad had discovered the connections between the four murders and were gathering evidence at that moment. He didn't want to leave anything out of his report (except his connection to the whores at Pfortzheimgaße). If he played this right, it could be a career-making moment for him.

No sooner had Gruber begun speaking, though, than he was interrupted by a small man in an SS uniform. 'Spare us the details, Sergeant,' said the man, drumming his fingers on the table. 'A broad overview will suffice.' After Gruber said a few more words, the man interrupted again. Gruber realized then that it was Heinrich Himmler interrupting him. Gruber managed to stammer out a few more words before falling silent. An animated discussion began between Himmler and others around the table.

'We have to keep this out of the papers.'

'It may be too late for that.'

'What kind of political fallout should we expect?'

'And what will the international press do if they get hold of this?'

'We can't let them get hold of it.'

'The killer is probably a Jew.'

'Probably? I'd say certainly. We will make certain he is.' They laughed at that.

'When do we tell the Führer?'

'And how do we tell him?'

'And what will he say?'

Himmler noticed Gruber still standing there. He gestured with

his chin and gave a dismissive wave with the back of his hand to
the policeman standing by, and Gruber was escorted from the room.

Erna Raczynski

By the time all the police precincts in and around Munich
had checked in, eight murderous attacks on women had
been reported over the last three years, all obviously
committed by the same killer. Only one woman – Erna Raczynski
– had survived, and only because the attack on her had been interrupted and the killer had been scared off.

Munich had a serial murderer who had been killing women
for three years without the police command even noticing. How
was this even possible? The Führer was furious. 'The utter incom-
petence!' he fumed. 'Heads will roll!' Himmler should take over the
case in person and should devote himself to it until the perpetrator
had been caught and brought to justice. And that had better be soon.
The entire resources of the SS and Gestapo and police departments
in all of Germany must be mobilized, and it would all fall under
Himmler's purview.

First of all, they were to go through case records to find every
similar unsolved case and to report all relevant information about
each case to Himmler's office and to the office of Gruppenführer
Heinrich Müller of the *Sicherheitspolizei*, the security police. The
matter was to be considered top priority and top secret. The news
that there was a serial killer at large was to be kept from the public
as long as possible.

Hans Bergemann stood at the bulletin board reading the police
directive signed by Gruppenführer Müller. 'What's going on,
Sergeant?'

'What do you mean, Bergemann?'

'You were there, weren't you, when the decision was made?'

'You read the directive, didn't you, Bergemann?'

'Yes, Sergeant, I did. But what are they thinking? When this gets
out, there'll be panic. That's not—'

'It's not going to get out, Bergemann. That's the point. As to
what they are thinking, that is none of your business. One thing

they're thinking is you should get your nose to the grindstone and find this killer.' Bergemann was becoming more and more like that goddamned Geismeier, asking questions when he shouldn't, meddling in matters that were way beyond his responsibility. Yes, all right, he had been the one to discover that there was a serial killer. But the search for this monster was just getting started – the real work was yet to be done. Everyone had to do his part to solve it and to see that the story remained a secret. Was that entirely clear?

'Yes, Sergeant,' said Bergemann. Even his obedience came out sounding like an insult. *Just like Geismeier*, thought Gruber.

Gruber's humiliation at Himmler's hands had stung. But at the same time, when he gave it a bit more thought, he was glad the serial-killer matter was out of his hands. No one was going to escape this case undamaged. His best bet was to get back to finding Geismeier. That was where his career would be made. And he had already turned up some good leads, not the least of which was Lola Zeff. He had her address, and if, as he suspected, she was somehow connected to Geismeier, Gruber was one giant step closer to bringing that son of a bitch to ground.

Bergemann decided to tell Willi about the serial killer. Willi was liable to have some useful ideas about the case. As it happened, Willi already knew something about the case. The story was out, and he had been thinking about it plenty. It had brought to mind the attack on Lola.

'That was at least four years ago,' said Bergemann.

'More,' Willi said.

'But they're nothing alike,' said Bergemann.

'That seems true,' Willi said. 'We'll see.'

'These were all stabbings. Lola wasn't attacked with a knife.'

'That's true,' Willi said.

The leads in the case were few and insubstantial. Muddy footprints at one of the scenes suggested the murderer was not very heavy. He was young and fit and dexterous. The soles of his shoes were lightly worn, suggesting he was not impoverished, but there was nothing beyond that. As far as the killing went, his stabbing motion was always the same, stabbing upward with his left hand and downward with his right. He had used the same large knife in all the known cases, switching it from hand to hand, and then, when he was finished, cleaning the blade on the victims' dresses, a chilling detail that revealed an odd cold bloodedness – odd in light of the fury that had gone beforehand. He went from collected to enraged and then to fastidious. He held the knife in his left hand while he cleaned it with his right. He did that in every case with ritualistic regularity. None of the women appeared to have been robbed. The victims had not been sexually violated. However, given how the stabbings were directed toward the victims' pelvis and breasts, these murders had to be seen, in part at least, as sexual assaults.

Bergemann studied the victims' photos. Though the women ranged in age from sixteen to forty, they all looked young and bore a superficial resemblance to one another. They all had light complexions and were slim-waisted and full-figured.

Bergemann travelled across town to meet with Erna Raczynski. It had been over a year since her attack, and the stab wounds she had suffered on her arms and shoulders had largely healed. She had been through multiple surgeries, but she still suffered muscle pain, and her doctors told her she probably always would.

The thirty-year-old housewife and mother of two small children had been walking from the streetcar to her home at five o'clock one morning after sitting all night with her ailing mother. The old lady was suffering from dementia, and Erna sometimes spent the night at her bedside. Just as she arrived at her own house, she was grabbed from behind, spun around, and stabbed. At that moment her husband, Horst, a streetcar conductor on his way to work an early shift, came out of the building. Erna screamed, fell backward against the iron fence, and was flailing against the slashing knife. Horst dived down the three stairs, knocking the murderer back and taking a serious cut to his arm. The murderer jumped up and ran off.

He had worn a dark shirt, a suit jacket and dark pants. He was in shadow and his face was mostly distorted with emotion. Erna described him as clean-shaven with a narrow face, a long nose, and thin lips. His hair was trimmed close on the sides and longer on top, what some called a Nazi haircut. When he grabbed her by the throat, his hands seemed soft, not hard or calloused. As she thought of it now, she started to cry.

'She already told police investigators all of this,' said Horst. 'Does she really have to go through it all over again?'

'I'm sorry, Frau Raczynski, but sometimes repeating a story jars something loose – a sound, a smell, words, gestures, something you've forgotten.'

'A smell?' she said.

'Anything,' said Bergemann.

'He smelled like soap,' she said. 'Like he had recently bathed.'

'It was soap, not cologne?'

'No, definitely soap. That hard, brown soap you can buy every-where. We use the same soap. Everybody does.'

'Did he say anything?'

'He was talking – muttering, more like it – but I couldn't understand anything he said.'

'Could you make out any words?'

'No. It was gibberish to me.'

'Could it have been a foreign language?'

'No. It was German, except it didn't make any sense.'

'Do you remember any phrases or even just words?'

She thought for a moment. 'No. Nothing. It made no sense. I wish I could. Oh, God!'

'That's fine, Frau Raczynski. I know this is hard. But we might just hit on something that makes a difference.' Bergemann paused. 'Can we go on?'

'Yes,' she said. 'I'm all right.'

'Did he ever say your name?'

'Really, Detective . . .' said Horst.

'Wait. He may have,' said Erna, surprised then frightened at the thought.

'You think so, but can't be sure?' said Bergemann.

'Yes . . . No.' She closed her eyes as though she were listening. 'I can hear his voice, a soft voice. He was kind of screaming and whispering at the same time, if you know what I mean?'

'I do,' said Bergemann. 'Was it a voice you recognized, a voice you had ever heard before, or heard since?'

'No, I don't think so. But if he spoke my name? How . . .?'

'Can you remember how he said your name? Was it a greeting, a threat?'

'I can't say what it was. I can't be sure. I may just have imagined I heard my name. I couldn't understand anything he was saying. He was angry, raging.'

'Is my wife in danger?' said Horst.

'I don't think so,' said Bergemann. 'It's been over a year. If he meant to attack her again, he would have already tried. I think he has more to fear from you, Frau Raczynski, than you do from him.'

Erna thought about that.

'The pitch of his voice,' said Bergemann, 'was it high or low?'

'It was high, quite high.'

'Did he curse, or call you bad names?'

'I don't know. Maybe.'

Horst's recollection of the killer was that he was youngish, he guessed late twenties, early thirties. He didn't seem to Horst to be strong, so much as furious. Horst was not very big, but he said he thought he could have overpowered the killer, given the opportunity.

'Did he actually try to stab you, or did you just get in the way of the knife?'

'I think I got in the way of the knife,' said Horst. 'He actually seemed shocked and frightened that he had stabbed me. That's when he ran off. He was a very fast runner. I knew I could never catch him.'

Bergemann spoke with the Raczynskis for nearly an hour. Which direction had the man fled, what was the night like, the weather, what had Erna been wearing, what was she carrying, what was Horst wearing? Everything he could think to ask, he asked.

Bergemann looked through his notes. 'One last thing, Frau Raczynski. You were an amateur actor, weren't you?'

'That was years ago. But yes, I was.'

'It's just an idea, but do you think you could . . . I understand if you don't want to do this . . . but do you think you could imitate his voice? Just to give me the sound of his voice as you heard it?'

'Oh, God!' she said.

'Really, Detective!' said Horst yet again. 'You're asking her to mimic the man that tried to kill her. Can you imagine what that—?'

Erna suddenly jumped up from her chair. Her eyes were wide with fury, her mouth was contorted with rage, the veins in her neck bulged, her fists were clenched in front of her. She made a slashing motion in Bergemann's direction as she screamed, 'You filthy bitch! You slut, you goddamned whore!' It was not Erna's voice, it was the killer's voice, a high growl, hoarse and venomous, and filled with hatred.

Both Bergemann and Horst stared at her in astonishment.

'It was like that,' she said, sitting back down.

Briennerstraße 20

The Berlin Olympics were a smashing success, many were saying the greatest Olympics ever. Hitler had overseen the construction of new facilities, including a stadium that seated more than 100,000 spectators along with other halls and arenas for a multitude of sports. The facilities were superb, and the German athletes were triumphant, winning more gold medals than any other country, including the United States. Tens of thousands of visitors had come from around the world to marvel at Germany's miraculous rebirth, to partake of its thriving culture and booming economy. One could imagine – and many did – that the world was entering a period of peace and prosperity.

Hitler basked in the Olympic glow for months. And yet now his great propaganda triumph was being tainted by the exploits of a lone, sick serial killer. It was no wonder that he was furious. The Führer ranted at anyone and everyone. How could one pathetic murderer outwit the entire Gestapo, the SS, all the police in Germany? His underlings scrambled to keep a lid on the story. Everyone was sworn to secrecy. Joseph Goebbels, the Propaganda Minister, forbade newspapers from printing a word about it.

Still, rumors sprang up and grew wilder with each retelling. Every effort to suppress the lurid details and damp down speculation inspired new rumors and intensified the fear. Before long the papers had to publish the facts of the case, as terrible as they might have been, in order to keep rumors and conspiracy theories that were even worse from taking over. The *Völkischer Beobachter* wrote:

'That such criminality should have been allowed to run rampant for more than three years is an unforgivable betrayal of the Führer's vision for our great German Reich. It is moreover a grave betrayal of the purity and sanctity of German womanhood. The perpetrator of these eight brutal murders must be brought to justice. Unspeakable crimes such as these sully our noble German blood, and blaspheme against the essence of our German existence. These crimes are so

grotesque, so counter to everything that is good and pure in the German spirit, that a Jewish cabal must be behind them. Only the Israelite sinks to such depravity. He must be caught and cast into the deepest pit of hell.'

People were afraid to leave their homes. They started reporting false sightings of the killer, even though no one had any idea what he looked like. And because denunciation had become popular in Germany, people began denouncing one another. The man next door was acting suspiciously, or the likely killer was lurking at the train station. The police were running in circles chasing down endless stories like these.

That the police, with all their resources and control, had been unable to solve the case and bring an end to this reign of terror was no mystery. The German police and security establishment, from the lowliest patrolman all the way up through Heinrich Himmler himself, was now completely politicized. Genuine communication among different (and often rival) departments about ongoing crime – about anything, in fact – had all but ceased. Prevailing politics made even the most basic communication dangerous to careers great and small. What passed for communication consisted entirely of administrative orders and political directives up and down the chain of command. And there was also the fear, widespread in official circles, that the killer might be one of their own.

Bergemann had repeatedly warned Willi that getting too interested in any police investigation, particularly this one, would be foolhardy for him. He reminded him that Sergeant Gruber was now obsessed with catching him, and this obsession was to be taken seriously. Willi was in serious danger even without taking into account Heinz Schleiffer's imaginings about Karl Juncker or the fact that his reports on Juncker had finally gotten the attention of the SS. Bergemann gestured around the bicycle workshop where he and Willi stood. 'You have the perfect cover, Willi. Karl Juncker is a certified bicycle repairman. Don't jeopardize it.'

The trouble was bicycle work was not in Willi's blood. Fixing a bicycle, while it had its satisfactions – tuning a machine to run smoothly depended on a delicate touch and meticulous sensitivity to the machine – it had none of the allure of detective work.

Bergemann tried again. 'You're still on the SS list of enemies of the Reich. If the police and the SS make common cause, if they somehow stop interfering with one another and getting in each other's way, you'll end up in Dachau.'

'I'm sorry, Hans. This case in particular is important to me,' said Willi.

'Important?' Bergemann was annoyed. He was trying to keep Willi safe, and Willi seemed to be going out of his way to make his task even more difficult and dangerous than it already was. 'Why? What makes it so important to you?'

Willi reminded Bergemann why he was in Munich in the first place: Lola had been savagely attacked.

'What?' said Bergemann. 'You're not saying that every violent attack on women is this one guy?'

'No, I'm not saying that.' Still, Lola worked at the Mahogany Room six days a week starting at three in the afternoon. And depending on how busy they were, she sometimes didn't get out of there until two in the morning. At that hour most buses and streetcars had stopped running, and she had to walk more than half an hour through dimly lit and sparsely peopled streets to get home. And now there was a killer prowling those same streets. Lola was frightened and so was he.

'Tell her to get another job,' said Bergemann. He knew, even as he said it, that it was a ridiculous thing to say.

Willi just gave him a look. 'Let me show you something,' he said, and pulled a city map from the drawer beneath his workbench and spread it out between them. There was a lamp above them on a pulley, and he drew it down so that it illuminated the map.

Bergemann shook his head in exasperation. 'I shouldn't have told you about it,' he said, as though he might have been able to keep Willi from finding out. 'I knew you wouldn't be able to let it alone.'

Willi ignored Bergemann's frustration. 'Look here, Hans. I was trying to find a way home for Lola so she wouldn't have to walk. Only a few buses and streetcars run all night. These here.' He slid his finger across the map in various directions.

'So this has nothing to do with the killer?' said Bergemann.

'None of the streetcars go in her direction,' said Willi. 'Then I noticed this.' He pointed out small circles he had drawn here and there.

'What are these?' said Bergemann.

'They mark where the women were attacked or where their bodies were found.'

Bergemann sighed, but Willi went on. 'Here's Gabriella Mancini,' he said, 'and over here, Erna Raczynski.'

Bergemann cast one last angry look in Willi's direction, then turned back to the map. It took him a minute before he saw what Willi had seen. 'They're all near streetcar stops,' said Bergemann. 'Erna Raczynski was coming home from seeing her mother. She had just gotten off the streetcar. So, do you think *all* the women got off a streetcar right before they were killed?'

'We can't know that for sure. But it's possible, maybe even likely,' said Willi. 'They might also have been going to or waiting for a streetcar. But, if you think about it, it seems more likely they'd gotten off, that the killer was on the streetcar with them and followed them off.'

'Why more likely?' said Bergemann.

'Because the killer staking out different streetcar stops around the city, picking out a woman and then killing her there makes no sense. Unless these women all fit together somehow, unless they were all connected to the killer in some way. But this feels way more random than that.'

'Did he know them?' said Bergemann. 'Erna Raczynski thought he might have said her name.'

'But you said neither she nor her husband knew the man. I think she might be mistaken about hearing her name. Erna sounds like many other sounds.'

'I had the same thought,' said Bergemann.

'I think these women had nothing to do with the killer, and he has nothing to do with them. He rides the streetcar, alone, late at night, and looks for women. He picks one out and gets off the streetcar with her. I think that's their entire connection.'

'So, you think these are the lines he rode . . .'

'Because they run late at night. It's just a theory, Hans. But look here.' Willi drew another circle on the map.

'What's that?' said Bergemann.

'It's where Lola was attacked.'

'Jesus,' said Bergemann.

'She was riding that line,' said Willi. Bergemann just stared at the map. 'She wasn't stabbed,' Willi said. 'But the guy's hand came through the umbrella and got caught. Think about it. I'm pretty sure even a strong man couldn't just punch his hand through the fabric of an umbrella.'

'So you think there was a knife,' said Bergemann.

'I do. I'm an idiot for not having thought of it earlier.'

'Jesus,' said Bergemann again.

Both men were silent for a long time.

'OK,' Bergemann said finally. 'So what's his connection to the streetcar?'

'One obvious possibility is he works for the Munich Transportation Authority,' said Willi.

'But you don't think so,' said Bergemann.

'Well, a streetcar man would fear that the tram routes might lead back to him. I think a streetcar man would avoid streetcars when committing his crimes. There's a good chance he'd be recognized by a conductor or a driver. Killing where he works would be stupid.'

'But he knows the system in detail. That could be useful.'

'Maybe. We'll keep an open mind on this . . .'

'But?' said Bergemann.

'Well, regardless of who he is, there is another tantalizing . . . possibility.'

'Which is?'

'If we're right about the victims and the killer getting *off* the streetcars where the women were then killed, we may also know where the killer gets *on*.'

'Really?' said Bergemann. 'How?'

'Well, look at the map. There are six streetcar lines that run through the night.' Willi pointed them out again. 'And of those six he only used three. Why *those* three?'

'Go on,' said Bergemann.

'Well, I think we can safely assume he's an orderly killer. The murders not only *look* similar. He kills exactly the same way each time; he is savage in the same way, he cleans the knife the same way each time – it's almost ritualistic. In any case, being involved in a very risky scheme, a man like this – compulsive, systematic – wouldn't deviate from his familiar ways any more than he has to. He wants to avoid surprises. He wants things to play out the same way each time. So he probably sets off from the same place each time.'

'Near home?'

'Maybe, but not necessarily. But somewhere secure, some place where he's familiar with the setting and feels safe. He might be anonymous there, or there might be crowds. But one place, the same place each time. Where the ritual begins.'

'And that would be?'

'That would be where the three lines cross.' Willi pointed to the map. 'Right here: Karolinenplatz. This is where he starts his hunt. It's central, near the train station.'

'Karolinenplatz?' said Bergemann. 'A safe place? I don't think so.'

'Why?' said Willi. 'What makes you say that?'

Bergemann slid his finger east from Karolinenplatz on Briennerstraße. 'Briennerstraße twenty,' he said.

'What's there?' said Willi.

'Gestapo headquarters.'

The Green Dress

It was ten in the evening. Big, wet snowflakes swirled around the street lights and were sticking to the ground. This had the makings of a substantial snowfall. Willi turned up his collar and pulled his hat down to his ears.

Heinz Schleiffer was out front clearing the walk with a broom. '*Guten Abend*, Herr Juncker,' he said, trying to sound friendly. He had decided to treat Karl Juncker respectfully, even though he took him for a suspicious character. That way, Schleiffer figured, he wouldn't arouse Juncker's suspicions in return.

Schleiffer had lately reported to Ortsgruppenleiter Mecklinger (or rather to Irmgard Kinski, since the Ortsgruppenleiter would no longer see him) that he suspected that Karl Juncker might be Munich's serial killer. Frau Kinski had written down Schleiffer's 'information' and given it to the Ortsgruppenleiter. Mecklinger had read her note, snorted, and thrown it in the trash.

Heinz Schleiffer watched Karl Juncker walk down the street until he disappeared into the blowing snow. He made a mental note to check the newspaper in the morning to see whether another woman had been killed. Willi turned the corner and got on the streetcar that was waiting there at the end of the line. He walked to the back of the second car. The conductor punched his ticket. After a few more minutes the streetcar rumbled off down the street.

Willi understood that there might be dozens of security people – SS, Sicherheitspolizei, certainly Gestapo – working on finding the serial killer. Himmler would probably have seen to that by now. And if he, Willi, had figured out the streetcar line connection, then they would soon figure it out too, if they hadn't already. In any case, he understood it was dangerous for him to be prowling around this way.

The streetcar's iron wheels squealed as they rounded corners. More people got on at the next station, and more at the station after that. They were mostly men on their way to or from work. They dozed or gazed absently through the windows at the falling snow. After several more stops Willi got off and transferred to the line along which Erna Raczynski had been attacked. There were twenty-five or so passengers in the two cars. They were heading toward the center of Munich. There was a uniformed policeman in the second car. Willi took a seat toward the front of the first car.

There was a pair of uniformed policemen at one stop. The policemen surveyed the streetcar as it rolled to a stop. The passengers tried to look as though they didn't notice. One started to read a newspaper, another checked his watch, meaningless gestures that, if anything, made them look guilty. Maybe not of murder, but of something.

The streetcar stopped at Karolinenplatz. Several men got on, including a man wearing a leather overcoat and carrying a briefcase. He sat two rows behind Willi. The man had the Nazi haircut. He fit the description they had from Erna Raczynski – mid-thirties, regular features, the right height, etcetera. *If only it were that easy*, thought Willi.

At the next station, two uniformed policemen got on. They walked down the aisle checking everyone's identification card. '*Guten Abend*,' they said. 'Your ID, please.' They looked at Karl Juncker's card, looked at Willi's face, said thank you, and moved on. At the next stop they got off and moved to the second car.

By the time the streetcar reached the end of the line, Willi and the man in the leather coat were the only two passengers left. Both got off the train. The man gave Willi a nervous look before walking off briskly toward home.

Willi waited for the next tram to go back into town. This time he got off at Karolinenplatz and transferred to a different line – three women had been murdered along this line. By now it was after midnight and both cars were sparsely populated. Two women sat together in the front seat of the first car opposite the driver, and three men were scattered about. Willi sat alone in the last car. After four stops, one woman got off. She was young, dark haired and not pretty, not the killer's type, he thought. A man followed her off the train. The woman walked off, presumably going home, and the man watched her go, then he turned around and walked in the opposite direction. Willi took the train several more stops and was about to get off, when two policemen got on. 'Your ID, please,' said one. Once again, Willi gave the policeman his card.

'Where are you going . . . Herr Juncker?' said the policeman. He studied the ID.

'Visiting someone,' Willi answered.

'Visiting someone?' said the policeman. 'At this hour?'

'You know,' said Willi, and smiled. 'A *certain* someone.'

'Ah,' said the policeman. He smiled back at Willi and gave the ID back. 'Well, have a good night.'

'And you too,' said Willi. 'Stay warm.' He got off the streetcar and waved at the policemen as the streetcar pulled away.

It was after two when Lola finished tallying the books for the night. She checked with her assistant to be sure everything had been taken care of. She pulled on her boots, buttoned her coat, and wrapped the mohair shawl around her neck. The snow had stopped falling. The night was clear and cold. The ground was covered with a glistening white blanket. Lola took a deep breath of the clean night air, pulled her collar tight around her neck, and set off for home.

The city was even quieter than it usually was this late. Every footstep, the noise of every passing car or bus was muffled by the snow. The stores that weren't shuttered cast light onto the white sidewalks. Lola stopped at a shop window to admire a dress she hadn't seen before. The shop changed its display once a week and today, Thursday, was the day. The dress was emerald green, a color that went well with her red hair.

Willi got to Lola's at about two thirty. She wasn't home yet, so he made a pot of tea and sat down to wait for her. When she wasn't back by three, he decided to walk out and meet her. He was sure she was fine. She was often late on Thursdays. Thursdays were always busy. There was no reason to worry. Lola's route didn't take her anywhere near the streetcar lines in question.

And yet, what difference did any of that make? What good was a theory? When a murderer is at large, all your most convincing theories about how a murder happens, why it happens, who is doing it, about the orderliness and predictability of the crime, seem like nothing so much as wishful thinking. Willi had quickened his steps and was nearly running when he finally saw her coming toward him.

'What a nice surprise,' she said when they met. He kissed her a little more vehemently than usual. 'I saw a dress on the way home,' she said. 'I love it. I'm going to stop tomorrow afternoon and try it on.'

'I can't wait to see it,' said Willi.

Degenerate Art

In the House of German Art, Joseph Goebbels and his Propaganda Ministry mounted *Die Große Deutsche Kunstaustellung*, the Great German Art Exhibition, a spectacular show of the pompous and heroic painting and sculpture favored by Hitler. There were grandiose bucolic landscapes and portraits of blond mothers clutching children lovingly to their ample bosoms. There were statues of gigantic men with strong jaws and bulging muscles straining forward on their way to save the world. The Führer swept through the exhibition with his entourage following behind, stopping by his favorites and holding forth to his bedazzled acolytes on the works' aesthetic superiority.

Goebbels had also mounted a second show, this one called *Entartete Kunst* – Degenerate Art – meant to demonstrate to Germans yet again the utter depravity and sickness of modern culture and art, and thereby the moral bankruptcy of the recently departed Weimar Republic. This exhibition had six hundred and fifty paintings and sculptures, which had been removed from Germany's great museums, jammed together in small, badly lit galleries. The works had disparaging labels attached decrying the 'sick Hebraic view that distorts and devalues life' or 'the failure of the so-called artist to manage even the most rudimentary representational skills.' Hitler went through this exhibition too, but as quickly as he could, scowling and snarling and denouncing its appalling horrors.

The crowds that followed, once Hitler had left, were enormous, attracted by the chance to see, one last time perhaps, masterpieces by Picasso, Matisse, Chagall, Van Gogh, Cezanne, Renoir, Duchamp. The great German Expressionists were there too – Ludwig Kirchner, Max Ernst, Georg Grosz, Otto Dix, Emil Nolde, Oskar Kokoschka, Ernst Barlach. The crowds remained enormous until November 30, the day the exhibition closed.

Once the show closed, Goering helped himself to several works for his collection of plundered art. So did other officials. The remainder of the work from the show was sold at auction in Switzerland. 'We might as well make some money from this trash,' said Goebbels.

Willi could not risk going to see the exhibition. Benno and Margarete went the first day and they described it for him. 'It's so crowded you can hardly move. Strangely enough, once inside, people are mostly silent, out of respect, maybe. Or maybe it's a sense of grief.'

Lola went to see it with her friend Sofia. She couldn't stop talking about it. 'I'm sorry you can't go,' she said to Willi. 'I think everyone should see it.'

Heinz Schleiffer did not think everyone should see it. He found the work just as disturbing as the labels said it was. He stood in front of a Picasso painting of 'Two Harlequins,' shaking his head from side to side. 'He can't even paint,' he said. 'It's dreary and smeared. They don't look like real people. It's depressing.'

Tomas Schleiffer stood beside his father. He had come to Munich just to see the show, then had decided – now he wondered what he could have been thinking – to invite his father to go with him. *Why not make peace with the old Nazi?* he thought. *Whatever else he is, he is still my father.* Heinz hadn't even recognized Tomas when he had knocked on the door. It had been that long. 'Hallo, Papa,' said Tomas and held out his hand.

'Ja, Tomas!' said Heinz. 'What are *you* doing here?'

Tomas explained that he had come to Munich to see the big art show, and his mother had suggested he look up his father while he was here, and, well, here he was. 'Why don't you come with me?'

'I can't, Tomas,' said Heinz. 'I've got stuff to do. I'm busy.'

'You're still in your pajamas, Papa. Please come. We'll get lunch together. My treat.'

What's this? thought Heinz. *The little pissant has grown up and learned some manners. Maybe I should go; I'm his father, after all.*

What have I got to lose? 'Give me ten minutes,' he said. It was a beautiful day. Tomas waited on the bench outside on Tullemannstraße.

Heinz got out his brown uniform, laid it across the bed and stared at it for a while before putting it back and taking out his suit and tie instead. He dressed and looked at himself in the mirror. He wet his hair and brushed it across his head, then he went outside. Tomas was standing talking to Frau Schimmel who was sitting on the bench. 'Herr Schleiffer,' she said, 'I've just met your charming son. He tells me you're going to the modern art show.'

'Yes,' said Schleiffer. 'He's studying art history, you know.'

'Yes,' said Frau Schimmel. 'So you've told me.'

'Oh,' said Heinz. 'Well,' he said after what seemed to him an interminable silence, 'we better be going.'

'Would you like to come with us, Frau Schimmel?' said Tomas.

'Oh, that's very kind of you,' said Frau Schimmel. 'But I'm a little tired after my walk. I think I'll just sit here for a while and watch the birds. But thank you, Tomas.'

'You do that, Frau Schimmel,' said Heinz, relieved – he wasn't sure why – that she wouldn't be with them. 'You sit there and take it easy.' They shook hands and parted. 'I help her out with her groceries sometimes,' said Heinz. 'She's really quite sick. Cancer.'

'Is she?' said Tomas, studying his father as though he were seeing him for the first time.

Heinz wanted paintings to be beautiful. He wanted them to look real. He wanted them to make him happy, not depressed. 'I understand, Papa,' said Tomas, trying his best to understand. Then he talked to Heinz about Picasso's 'Two Harlequins,' pointing at details as he spoke. He explained that the 'ugliness' that Heinz saw in the colors, in the brushwork, in the skinny, awkward, bent figures was intentional. Picasso meant for the two figures to be unsettling. He wasn't painting two people so much as he was painting their inner lives: their anguish, the pain of their poverty and loneliness and hunger. Here were two 'clowns,' whose job it was to entertain us, sharing a meager meal. They had been beaten down. Their lives were hard. They were hungry, maybe starving. The paint was thick, it was applied roughly and quickly, but with great skill to reveal their suffering and to give you a feeling for their world.

Not everything Tomas said made sense to Heinz, but some of it did. It didn't make him actually like any of the works either. But he did like hearing Tomas talk about them. He watched Tomas while he was talking, gesturing toward the painting. Heinz felt something that resembled pride. This was *his* son: a *man*. And he was smart and educated. And he, Heinz Schleiffer, could take at least some credit for what Tomas had become. Couldn't he?

At lunch at the Three Crowns, Heinz and Tomas talked about Germany and world politics. That was when things got tense. Tomas said he wasn't political, but in the next sentence he said something about how he didn't think it was right to censor art and literature. Free expression was important for a people. The right to express themselves freely and without fear in their art and writing was sacred. It was wrong to burn books or paintings; literature and art shouldn't be disrespected.

'Listen, Tomas,' said Heinz, 'you're young. You have a lot to learn. Germany has to speak with one voice. We are under assault from all sides. The Jews are undermining our culture. The French and the British have been bleeding us dry with their unjust reparations. We have to be one people under the Führer in order to be a great country again.'

'We can be one people, Papa, without having only one thought. We can be different and yet united as a people.'

'Tomas,' said Heinz, lowering his voice, suddenly aware that they were in a busy restaurant where their conversation could be overheard. 'Keep your voice down. Remember where you are. People might misunderstand what you're saying.'

Tomas looked around, and sure enough, the couple at the next table were looking at them. He smiled at them; they didn't smile back. Both Tomas and Heinz agreed they should talk about other things while they ate. 'They have a very good roast chicken here,' said Heinz, so they both ordered chicken and dumplings and beer.

'You know, Tomas, I've been with the Führer for a long time,' said Heinz, as they walked home. 'I believe in his vision for Germany.'

'I know, Papa.'

'And what about you, Tomas?'

'I don't believe in that vision.'

'You don't believe in one German people?'

'Does that include Jewish people?'

'No, of course not,' said Heinz.

'Why not?' said Tomas.

'They are an alien culture with different and alien ways,' said

Heinz. 'You know that. They have polluted our culture with their ways, and our blood with their blood.'

'You're just parroting Hitler, Papa. What about . . .?'

'I'm not parroting anyone,' said Heinz, growing angry. 'Damn it, show some respect. These are my own beliefs.'

'Show respect? OK. What about old Tante Jolesch?' said Tomas. 'Did she pollute our blood, our culture?'

Heinz hadn't thought about Jolesch for a long time. The old Jew from Prague everyone called Tante Jolesch had lived upstairs when Heinz and Renate had still been married and Tomas was a small boy. Jolesch had been a wonderful neighbor, taking care of little Tomas so Heinz and Renate could enjoy a night out once in a while. She had also cooked delicious meals for them. She would just show up at the door with casseroles, soups, desserts whenever the spirit moved her. When both Heinz and Renate had been sick with the flu during the big epidemic, Jolesch had moved in and taken care of them until they were better. Heinz had wept when Jolesch had died.

'What about the old Jew Jolesch?' Tomas said again.

'What about her?' said Heinz, truly angry now.

They walked the rest of the way home in silence. When they got there, Heinz went into his apartment and slammed the door.

'Goodbye, Papa,' said Tomas, speaking to the closed door.

The Ninth Victim

A young woman's body, mutilated in the usual way, was found not far from one of the late-night streetcar lines. She had been returning home from an assignation with her boss. The snow was crimson all around where she lay. How could one person have so much blood?

It turned out, however, that the blood was not all hers. When the police moved her body onto the stretcher, they found a small knife. She had apparently carried it to defend herself and, before she perished, she had wounded the killer, maybe seriously. He had not cleaned his knife in the usual manner. Instead, a large piece of fabric had been torn from her dress, possibly as an improvised bandage. The killer had run off, leaving a trail of blood in the snow along with his footprints. He had been running, not staggering, so the wound was likely not mortal. Not immediately anyway.

A streetcar conductor remembered a wounded man getting into his car at exactly three o'clock in the morning. He knew it was three because the nearby church bell was sounding the hour just as the man got on the streetcar. 'I always listen for the three o'clock bells. That way I know we're on schedule.' The wounded man's right sleeves had been slashed open. He had a bandage of some sort tied around the wound, but it was still bleeding. It had dripped on the floor. A freak accident, the man had said. A lot of blood, he said, but no serious damage.

'Can I help?' said the conductor. 'Don't worry,' said the man. 'I'll be fine.' He had smiled, but you could tell he was in pain. 'Thanks for your concern,' he had said when he got off the streetcar.

'Where did he get off?' said Detlev Lettauer, the detective interviewing him.

'Why are you asking me all these questions again?' said the conductor.

'What do you mean again?' said Lettauer.

'Well, another detective interviewed me yesterday, and he asked the same questions. And then some. I told him everything I know.'

'Another detective? What was this detective's name?'

'I didn't get it,' said the conductor.

'Did he show you his credentials?'

'Well, he said he was a detective. Who else would be asking that kind of questions?'

Detective Lettauer asked for a description.

'About your height,' said the driver. 'Glasses, a mustache. Is this connected with those murders?'

'What more can you tell me about the other detective?' said Lettauer. 'Where did he interview you?'

'I was just starting my shift,' said the driver. 'Yesterday afternoon, the day after they found her. Five o'clock.'

'You mean he met you here, at the streetcar yard?'

'No. He just got on the streetcar.'

'Where?'

'Julius-Hemdstraße. First stop out of the yard.'

'How far did he go?'

'I think he got off at Dreiheiligenplatz.'

'Did you see which direction he went?'

'He may have gone toward the river, but I'm not sure.'

Willi was risking his life. The police now knew somebody was impersonating a detective, and that meant the SS and Gestapo knew. He didn't need to be told about the danger he was in. Bergemann told him anyway. Lola didn't know what Willi was up to. But there was no mistaking that he was keyed up and on edge about something. He got out of bed in the middle of the night and sat in the dark. You could almost hear him thinking. She tried to warn him too, but she didn't even know what to warn him about.

There were five clinics and hospitals along the streetcar line between the scene of the latest murder and Karolinenplatz. After talking with the driver, Willi had retrieved his bicycle and ridden from one clinic to the next. At the very last clinic – a small private one – he struck gold.

Late on the night in question, someone had rung the emergency bell. A man had a badly wounded right arm and hand. He had lost a lot of blood. The night nurse rousted Doctor Rosenberg, the doctor on duty, and he had given the man an injection, cleaned the wound, and sewed it up. It went from between his thumb and fingers, up his hand and around his wrist. It had taken more than fifty stitches. 'It was a very serious wound,' said the nurse.

She showed Willi the log entry. The name – Friedrich Grosz – and the address the man had given were undoubtedly false.

'Why do you think they were false?'

'The way he looked at me when he gave his name? The sound of his voice? I don't know exactly, but I'm pretty sure he was lying.'

'Is Dr Rosenberg here tonight?' said Willi.

'No,' said the nurse. 'He won't be in until tomorrow.'

'Would you give me the doctor's address?' The nurse hesitated. 'This is an urgent matter,' said Willi.

The nurse, Irmgard Grosz, gave a good description of the patient.

'Well, of course I was watching him for signs of shock, that sort of thing, so I got a good look. Thirty or so years old. Boyish, in any case. Light brown hair, cut short on the sides, clean shaven. His ears stuck out. Blue eyes, a bit too far apart. He had a long thin nose, and almost no lips. When he smiled his lips disappeared altogether.'

'He smiled?'

'Sort of. He had perfect teeth. Not a friendly smile though. He even laughed once, at the coincidence of our same last names.'

'What do you remember, if anything, about how he spoke?'

'He had a soft voice, a high voice, almost like a boy's voice.'

'Anything else you noticed about him?'

'He bit his nails. They were bitten to the quick.'

'How was he dressed?' said Willi.

'A suit and tie and an overcoat.'

'A tie? Was he disheveled?'

'No, and that surprised me. And he didn't want to take anything off.'

'But he did?'

'He had no choice. We had to help him, of course. Overcoat, suit coat, and shirt all had blood on them. He kept trying to cross his arms over his chest, like he was ashamed of his body.'

Willi continued in this direction, asking about body hair, scars, tattoos, jewelry. 'Was he wearing any military insignia? What about his undershirt, his belt, his shoes?'

'Nothing seemed to be military.'

'He came in with some sort of bandage around his arm?'

'He did. More of a rag than a bandage.'

'What was it like?'

'Odd,' said Irmgard. 'It was yellow, with a small red and green pattern, tiny flowers, I think. I remember wondering where he had got that. I mean, when you have an accident like that . . . the bandage looked like it came from a curtain or a dress or something. So, how did that become his bandage? I mean, he had obviously been outside, probably when it happened – his pant legs were wet from the snow – so where do you find a piece of fabric like that lying around outside?'

'I understand,' said Willi. 'What happened to that rag, Frau Grosz? Do you think it might still be in your trash?'

'No. That's odd too,' she said. 'I started to throw it away – it was soaked with blood – but he grabbed it out of my hand. Really grabbed it. He wadded it up and stuffed it in his pants pocket. I wondered why. Now I know.'

'Frau Grosz, have you ever thought of going into police work?' said Willi.

'No. Why?'

'It's just, I think you might be very good at it.'

It was late in the evening when Willi rang the Rosenbergs' bell. Samuel Rosenberg answered the door himself. Willi identified himself as a detective. He could hear there was a party going on. Dr Rosenberg was not happy to have his evening interrupted. But once Willi explained that it was about the wounded man he had treated, and that this man was a person of interest in a criminal investigation, Dr Rosenberg showed Willi into a small office just off the entry hall. The office was comfortably furnished with leather chairs, a desk, and what looked to be a Tiffany lamp. The walls were covered with paintings and drawings.

'Paul Klee?' said Willi, nodding toward one small painting.

'He was a patient,' said Doctor Rosenberg. 'This person of interest, are you talking about the young woman who was killed the other night?'

Willi said that he was.

The doctor remembered the wounded man very clearly. He confirmed Irmgard Grosz's description of the patient and of his treatment of the wound as well. 'It was a deep and violent injury.'

'Did he need more medical attention?'

'He did. I told him I thought he might have suffered some nerve damage and that vascular surgery might be necessary as well. In any case, someone should check the wound to see that it is healing properly. And he'll need the stitches removed.'

'How did he react to your advice, Doctor?'

'He didn't react. And given what I now know, I doubt that he'll follow my recommendations.'

'Did he say anything about how he was injured?'

'I asked,' said the doctor, 'but he didn't answer.'

'You mean he didn't say anything?'

'I told him I was required to keep a record of all injuries in the treatment log, to which he said, "Put down: accident." I remember thinking that was odd. Not "It was an accident," but "Put down: accident."'

'Was he in pain?' said Willi.

'A good bit of pain, I think, yes. I knew he'd be in a lot more pain soon, and I told him so.'

'How did he react?'

'He seemed frightened and asked me to give him something. I had given him an injection earlier, and I wrote him a prescription for later. But he wanted something right away.'

'What did you give him, and what was your prescription for?'

'Eukodol in both cases. It's an oxycodone-based pain killer.'

'Do you have a list of all-night pharmacies, Doctor?'

'There are four in Munich.' The doctor paused and thought for a moment. 'You know,' he said, 'even without knowing about the murder, I still suspected Grosz wasn't his real name.'

'What made you think that, Doctor?'

'He had a way about him. I thought he was Gestapo.'

'And what made you think that?' said Willi.

'I'm Jewish, Detective. I've seen the Gestapo. Why would I *not* think that?'

One of Munich's all-night pharmacies was across from the train station and one stop from Karolinenplatz. Willi rode his bicycle the three kilometers on back streets. Except for the drunks and vagrants around the station, the streets were mostly empty now.

Sure enough, the pharmacist had filled the Eukodol prescription within hours of Friedrich Grosz's visit to the doctor. Grosz had said he was in pain and immediately took one of the tablets even though Doctor Rosenberg had given him one a short time ago. The pharmacist had not paid much attention to what the man had looked like, although he recalled that his hand was heavily bandaged and his arm was in a sling.

He found the prescription and showed it to Willi. He then looked it up in the logbook where all controlled substances were registered. The false name was there along with the same bogus address he had given the doctor. 'What additional information is required for controlled substances?' Willi said.

'The prescribing doctor's name, address, the reason for the prescription, and exemptions and exceptions.'

'Exemptions and exceptions?' said Willi. 'What's that?'

'Well,' said the pharmacist, 'that's for special uses, for instance, scientists or doctors working with controlled substances, certain military and government officials who have . . . a privileged . . . dispensation . . .'

'I don't understand,' said Willi. 'Are you talking about addicts?'

The pharmacist was silent for a long time. Finally he said, 'In recent years, Herr Detective, the uses of some of these substances, and the laws controlling them have . . . evolved, shall we say, so that more people now have access to them than was once the case.'

'And Herr Grosz had such an exemption or exception?'

'He did, Herr Detective. A police and military exemption.'

'Is he an addict?'

'There's no way for me to know.'

'So this number here?' Willi pointed to the number the pharmacist had written beside Grosz's address.

'That is his exemption number,' said the pharmacist.

'And you have this number how?'

'It was on his ID card.'

'And he showed you his ID?'

'Certainly. That's required by law.'

'And it had his picture and the name Friedrich Grosz?'

'It did.'

'And you looked at the picture to make sure it was him?'

'I did.'

Willi turned the logbook toward him and read the number aloud: 'SS47840. An SS number.'

'Yes,' said the pharmacist, and for some reason only he could have known, he clasped his hands over his mouth, as if to indicate there was nothing more he could say.

The Mind of a Killer

Reinhard Pabst was just thirty years old. He had only been in the Gestapo for a few years, and in a very short time had achieved the rank of Obersturmbannführer, lieutenant colonel. He had been extraordinarily successful in exposing and arresting various enemies of the German people, including a small group of army officers who had been planning a *coup d'état*, which he had prevented from even getting off the ground. Thanks to Reinhard, three army colonels had been liquidated and two brigadier generals now found themselves crushing stones in Dachau.

This had been a triumph for Reinhard, a man who only a few years earlier had been a confused young man, riven with self-doubt, and trying and failing at one thing after another. And now he had just been put in charge of the Gestapo's largest ongoing investigation, the pursuit of the serial killer bedeviling Munich and unsettling the entire country.

Since Reinhard was himself the killer, he had thought it urgent that he take over the case so that he could direct the investigation away from himself. And he had been brilliant yet again in accomplishing this objective. Reinhard's unique combination of gifts – an innocent face, a modicum of intelligence, and an effortless and lethal duplicity – had allowed him to maneuver other more senior Gestapo officers aside to get the assignment.

Reinhard, taking the Führer as his model, had looked into his rivals and then spread the word about their insufficiencies – real or imagined, it didn't matter. The rumors he started inevitably found their way to Himmler and then to Hitler. When these candidates were interviewed, they suddenly found themselves on the defensive. 'No, Herr Reichsführer, I did not fail to accomplish the assignment. There was no failure on my part. It was an administrative failure.' An administrative failure? That was almost like blaming the Führer himself! One by one Reinhard's rivals were eliminated from consideration.

Reinhard was the last candidate to be interviewed. 'Thank you, my Führer, and you, Herr Reichsführer, for this opportunity to serve you and the German people.' Reinhard summed up his accomplishments since joining the Gestapo, being careful to repeatedly give the Führer credit as his inspiration and model.

Reinhard laid out in detail several interesting things he knew about the serial-killer case that Hitler and Himmler were both unaware of. For instance, Reinhard had discovered that someone had been posing as a detective and interviewing people about the case. Reinhard believed that this person might himself be the killer. Reinhard also said he had evidence that the killings were part of a Jewish plot to destabilize the Führer's regime as a step on the way to Jewish world domination.

Hitler looked at Himmler. Himmler nodded.

'So, Pabst,' said Hitler. He clapped his hands together, and smiled. 'I think we've found the man for the job. What will it take to bring this pig to slaughter?'

'I have a very sharp knife, my Führer,' said Reinhard. The Führer laughed at the joke. 'I will formulate a plan of action, my Führer.'

'This must be accomplished quickly, Pabst. Do you understand me?' said Himmler.

'I understand you perfectly, Herr Reichsführer.'

'Do you think he will kill again?' said Hitler.

'I am certain he will, my Führer.'

Since that first time long ago with the prostitute when he was still a Jesuit, Reinhard had had many catastrophic attempts at what he thought of as sexual union. But a lusty woman trying to reach into his pants, another one cooing in his ear, or one holding her own breasts toward him and moaning with desire, all had the same terrifying effect. The sexuality of woman, whatever shape it took, threatened him. It represented what he perceived to be mortal danger.

Reinhard stayed late in his office in Briennerstraße. When the pressure had built up and he felt compelled to act, he went down to the basement gym where the showers were. He stripped off his clothes and scrubbed every centimeter of his body under nearly scalding water with a stiff bristled brush and hard, brown soap. It was like a ceremonial cleansing before a sacred ritual.

At Karolinenplatz he got on a streetcar going in one direction or another, it didn't matter which. He sat toward the back of the front car. Like the streetcar, the woman was random too. She had to be a particular sort, though: alone, of course, youngish, slim, large breasts. He recognized her immediately as soon as he saw her. His mother had been like that, so it was almost like he already knew her.

Most nights he rode the train to the end of the line and back again without seeing her. He felt both relieved and disappointed when she wasn't there. Then one night there she would be. There was that look, that mocking confidence as she got on the streetcar. Her eyes would scan the car, would sweep right past him, without seeming to notice, although he could tell she had seen him and was prepared to destroy him.

She took her seat, her back to him. She crossed her stockinged legs. He could hear the whisper of the silk on silk that made him shudder. Or she casually brushed the hair from her neck. Except it was not casual at all. He felt the hair on his own neck stand up. 'Look at me,' she said without speaking, without looking in his direction, without even moving.

Once Reinhard was off the streetcar and behind her, the rest went very quickly. He had to be quick or she might overpower him. He struck like Abraham sacrificing the ram caught in the bush. Then it was over – she was vanquished, the sacrifice was accomplished. Reinhard took the streetcar back to the office. Sometimes, if it was a nice night, he walked.

Suzanna Merkl had almost killed him. A woman using her lethal, demonic skills. He had gotten careless, had forgotten how dangerous

the enemy could be, and it had almost cost him his life. He could
not afford to make a mistake like that again.

The Third Report

Heinz Schleiffer had observed Karl Juncker leaving home
late the night before, and now there it was in the paper a
few hours later. Another poor woman, Suzanna Merkl, had
been butchered in the same way as the other eight victims, and her
killer had gotten away. The paper had photos of all nine women
across the top of the front page.

Heinz had suspected Karl Juncker all along, and now he finally
had the proof. The timeline – Juncker leaves home at night, Merkl
is dead the next morning – was irrefutable evidence. They would
have to pay attention to him now. He took out a pad of paper, a
pen and ink, and wrote a letter. He used a dictionary to be certain
everything was spelled correctly. He wrote in what he thought of
as official language.

To: Ortsgruppenleiter Gerhard Mecklinger
From: SA Mann Heinz Schleiffer
Subject: Serial Killer Herr Karl Juncker
Herr Karl Juncker, residing at Tullemannstraße 54, Apartment
21 has been engaged in suspicious activity for long durations
of time. He regularly leaves the above referenced address at
extremely odd hours. His professional activities are unknown.
On the evening of December 19 at approximately 22:15 he
departed from his residence under peculiar circumstances
for parts unknown. On the following morning of December
20 the body of Suzanna Merkl was found dead in the snow.
I am convinced that Karl Juncker's suspicious activity means
that it is extremely likely in all probability that he is the
killer who is terrorizing the city and warrants a further
investigation.
With utmost respect,
Heil Hitler.
Heinz Schleiffer

SA Mann Heinz Schleiffer was not one to violate protocol lightly, to skip over the chain of command, to go behind the back of his commanding officer, even an incompetent like Mecklinger. After all, the Reich was founded on order, and order had to be maintained. But, Schleiffer reasoned, these were not ordinary circumstances. Women were dying, and the killer was known to him. He had a responsibility.

Heinz put on his uniform and marched off to deliver this latest evidence to Ortsgruppenleiter Mecklinger – or rather, to Frau Kinski. He knew Mecklinger had been ignoring his warnings and might well ignore this memo too. But Heinz would give Mecklinger one week, and if he didn't hear anything back by then, he would find someone who *could* see how dire the circumstances were and who would take him seriously. Heinz was no fool; Mecklinger was the fool. Mecklinger would eventually be shown to be the impediment to solving this crime.

Heinz had made a copy of the memo which he carried in his jacket pocket. When the occasion presented itself, he would show it to someone who could get this important information to the Führer. Well, maybe not the Führer himself. But the Führer had people who could take action on such matters. If Heinz could get his memo into the proper hands, the crime would be solved, and he would be a hero.

Imagine Heinz's shock when the SS knocked on his door a few mornings later. Two men in black uniforms inquired whether he was the author of the complaint that had been filed a while back – it had been so long ago that Heinz had all but forgotten – about a neighbor who had been receiving mail from England. Heinz said he had indeed filed that report, and he set about summarizing all his complaints as best he could remember since that first one about Karl Juncker. He saved the best for last. He excused himself and went to his jacket to get the memo.

'This is urgent,' he said. 'I gave this memo to Ortsgruppenleiter Mecklinger three days ago. But since you are here, I don't see any harm in giving it to you too.'

One SS Mann read through the memo and passed it to the other. They exchanged meaningful glances.

'When did you last see this Juncker?'

'The night of the murder. That would be last week, Thursday night.'

'What do you know about Karl Juncker, beside your suspicions?'

'Not very much. He's very secretive and not very friendly.'

'Can you describe him?'

'He's a bit taller than you, wears glasses, has a mustache. He's arrogant. Thinks he's better than everybody else.

'Do you know if he is employed?'

'I wrote in the memo . . .'

'We know what you wrote, Herr Schleiffer. We would like to hear it in your words.'

'I don't know if he is employed or not.'

'Do you know whether he has ever been employed as a policeman?'

'A policeman?' said Heinz, astonished.

'Or a detective?'

'Are you serious?' Heinz remembered the rosette in Juncker's lapel.

'Please answer the question, Herr Schleiffer.'

'No, I can't imagine that he ever was. No, impossible,' said Schleiffer. 'Was he?'

'Herr Schleiffer, we'd like you to come to headquarters with us to look at some photos.'

They allowed Heinz time to change into his uniform. He had never been to Gestapo headquarters in Briennerstraße. There he sat at a wooden table and leafed through a book with pages and pages of photos of men, six photos to a page.

'This could be him,' said Heinz.

'Are you sure?' said the man standing over him.

'Pretty sure. It looks like him.'

Heinz was driven home in an official car. He hoped everyone saw him. Frau Schimmel certainly did. That afternoon as he was washing the front windows, she came back from shopping, pulling her grocery cart. 'Herr Schleiffer, could you help me up the stairs with my cart?' Heinz was glad to do so. He used the opportunity to warn her about their dangerous neighbor.

'Herr Juncker? Dangerous?' said Frau Schimmel. 'I hardly think so.'

'*Extremely* dangerous,' said Heinz.

'Come in, Herr Schleiffer. Please. I'll make us some tea, and we can have some of the strudel I made yesterday. Pear this time. The apples didn't look especially good.'

'No, thank you, Frau Schimmel. Really . . .' He always refused her invitation and Frau Schimmel never accepted his refusal.

She took him by the arm and walked him into the kitchen. 'Come in, sit down.' She cut off a slice of strudel and put it on a plate on the table in front of him. She got a bowl of whipped cream from the ice box. She poured them both tea.

'I'm serious, Frau Schimmel, Juncker is not what you think.'

'Oh, he seems like a very nice man.'

'Frau Schimmel, take it from me, he is a suspect in . . . a very serious matter.'

'You must be mistaken, Herr . . .'

'No, Frau Schimmel, really. Believe me. I know what I'm talking about.'

'Would you like another slice of strudel?'

He did not refuse.

'Frau Schimmel, I'm not supposed to say anything. But I expect him to be arrested very soon. I was briefed on it this morning.' Before ten more minutes had passed, and with very little prompting on her part, Heinz had told her all about his trip to Gestapo head-quarters, how Karl Juncker – not his real name – had once been a police detective, and how he was now the lead suspect in the serial killer case.

The Lion and the Hyenas

Lola had bought that green dress, but Willi would not see it for a very long time. He was now being hunted from several directions at once by Reinhard Pabst and the Gestapo and SS task force he had assembled, as well as by the police in the person of Detective Sergeant Hermann Gruber. Gruber was the only one so far that knew Lola was connected to Willi. The address for Lola Zeff in the logbook led him right to her door.

Both Lola and Willi had been warned by both Bergemann and Frau Schimmel that something was afoot and that Willi should disappear. They didn't think Lola was in immediate danger, since no matter where his suspicions might have led him, Gruber didn't know anything for sure of her life with Willi, and neither did the

Gestapo or the SS. She might get a visit, but it shouldn't amount to more than that.

There was some art on the walls of Karl Juncker's apartment these days, along with a few vases of artificial flowers. But there was no sign that anyone had lived there recently. There was no food in the kitchen closet or in the ice box. There was no clothing in the wardrobe or the entry closet. The SS came to search the place on several occasions. Each time Heinz Schleiffer went with them and unlocked the door. But Karl Juncker had disappeared.

Bergemann knew how to send Willi messages – they had a system of signals and drops around the city – but he kept his messages to a bare minimum. Frau Schimmel could warn Willi too using a code they had agreed upon. Different objects in her window had different meanings. The blue vase on the left side of the window signaling imminent danger now remained in place.

When Lola said she had no idea of Willi Geismeier's where-abouts, it was not a lie. Detective Sergeant Gruber pressed the issue. 'Isn't it true that you and he are close? When did you last see him?' he asked.

'Of course we're not close,' she said. 'How could we be? I haven't seen him since we were children.' Bergemann had warned her that Gruber would be coming to question her. Though she was nervous about the interview at first, she was prepared now and quite calm. 'You probably don't remember, Sergeant, but I actually came to your precinct once trying to find him.'

'Oh, Frau Zeff, of course I remember that. That is how I was able to find you now.' Gruber seemed quite pleased with himself.

'Well, I never found him,' said Lola. 'You must know that as well.'

Gruber tried to trick her. 'You were seen together, Frau Zeff.'

'Whoever told you that, Sergeant, is mistaken.'

'And remind me, please, Frau Zeff, why were you looking for him?'

'I told you: we were childhood friends. I was fond of him; I would like to see him again. That's all.'

'And yet you gave up looking for him?'

'Sergeant, if you, with all your detective skills, haven't been able to find him, how should I be expected to?'

Gruber was pleased to have his detective skills mentioned, but he would not be distracted. 'Are you political, Frau Zeff?'

'Political? No. I can't afford to be political in my work, Sergeant.'

Gruber had been his usual careless self. He knew nothing about what sort of work she did.

'I work at the Hotel zur Kaiserkrone, Sergeant. In fact, if I don't leave shortly, I will be late for my shift.'

'Well, Frau Zeff, why don't we go there together, and we can continue our conversation on the way?'

Lola and Gruber walked side by side, and he imagined for a moment that they might be lovers, which made his head swim a little. He had forgotten how wonderful it felt having a pretty woman walking beside you. They got to the hotel and went in the service entrance, then through a narrow, dimly lit service corridor past the kitchen. 'Here we are,' said Lola. She opened a swinging door and they stepped through. Gruber found himself behind the bar in the very grand Mahogany Room with its high ceilings, its enormous chandeliers and mirrors, and colorful tapestries and paintings in gilt frames. He and Lola faced a long row of SS officers arrayed along the bar. They were young and fit. They were among their own, laughing, or deep in earnest discussion, completely at ease.

'Who's this then, Lolly, a new boyfriend?' said a grinning lieutenant.

'You know, Jürgen, you're my one and only,' said Lola with a laugh.

Gruber was knocked off balance. He was somewhere he hadn't expected to be and definitely didn't belong. The SS were an elite aristocracy and they regarded his sort of official, with his big belly and his ill-fitting brown uniform, as the fascist underclass. The storm troopers were thugs. Yes, they were useful for some tasks. But they were not serious political warriors, like the SS, highly trained and prepared to both kill and die for the Führer. The SA was the old guard, thick around the middle, out of shape, the remnants of an earlier, pre-Third Reich world. Gruber tried to laugh along with Lola's joke, but the SS men just looked at him with their killer eyes.

Gruber would have liked to say he had stood with the Führer since the early days, when he had been an enforcer and they had been schoolboys. He had knocked heads in the Bürgerbräukeller. He had been part of the putsch. He thought of himself as one of the old lions, and these SS types as hyenas. They were after Willi Geismeier too – Gruber knew that from his various inquiries. He also knew that if he got to Geismeier first, they would soon be there too, circling, trying to steal his prey. And determined hyenas could kill a lion.

Still, Gruber thought he had several advantages over the SS and the Gestapo. First of all, he had worked with Willi Geismeier for years, and knew how he operated. Second, he doubted they knew anything about his own investigation. For instance, he was sure they knew nothing about the precinct logbook or Lola's connection to Willi. And he didn't for a minute buy her claim that she knew nothing about Willi's whereabouts. It was a bit worrisome that she was friendly with some in the SS. He would have to be more careful now when it came to Lola Zeff.

He started following Lola. He followed her to and from work a few times, although he never went inside the Mahogany Room again. He questioned the hotel manager, Alex Kusinski, who could say only good things about Lola. Kusinski said he was certain she didn't have a partner or boyfriend. 'I would know,' he said.

'Nobody in the SS?' said Gruber.

Kusinski just raised his eyebrows.

Gruber followed Lola to her parents' house. She went there – usually on Tuesdays, her day off – for an early supper. He stood and watched in the small park across from their building. It was rainy and cold, and by the time she came out an hour and a half later, he was soaked and shivering.

One Sunday he followed her to Tullemannstraße. After a half hour, she left in the company of a little old lady. Willi had taught Lola how to tell if someone was following her. But this was the first time Lola had noticed Gruber. 'Don't be alarmed, Frau Schimmel,' she said, 'but I think we're being followed. It's the policeman I told you about.'

'So that's who he is,' said Frau Schimmel. She had noticed him when they left her building. She knew all about being followed from her old Berlin days. The two women walked arm in arm to a cafe where they drank coffee and shared a slice of Linzertorte.

Gruber had the feeling that whenever he was following Lola, Willi was lurking somewhere behind him. And the feeling grew stronger all the time. Gruber would turn suddenly, hoping to catch him, but of course Willi was never anywhere to be seen.

It occurred to Gruber that if he were to arrest Lola, Willi would have to come to her defense. He would have to arrest Lola somewhere public, at night maybe, just to make sure Willi was there.

But under what pretense could he arrest her? And if he were to arrest her, and Willi *wasn't* nearby, it would alert her to his suspicions. And it would drive Willi so deep underground that there would be no finding him, ever.

'What the devil are you up to, Sergeant Gruber?' It was unusual for one of his detective sergeants to be gallivanting around the city the way Gruber had been, and Captain Robert Wendt wanted to know the reason for it. The latest case-closure figures were out, and once again Gruber's squad was at the bottom of the standings.

'I'm working on a priority case, Captain,' said Gruber.

Wendt pulled furiously on his mustache, a sign Gruber understood all too well. 'Damn it, man, it's not for you to decide whether a case is a priority or not,' he said. 'If you're not up to the task of running a squad, I can put Bergemann or somebody else in charge . . .'

'It's Geismeier, sir,' said Gruber.

'Geismeier? What about Geismeier?'

'He's been spotted,' said Gruber. This was a lie.

'What? When?' said Wendt.

'A short while ago,' said Gruber.

Wendt looked at his hapless sergeant for a long minute. He looked at the case board. There were six open cases on it, some dating back to the beginning of the year and even earlier. Wendt rapped the board hard with his knuckles. 'Take care of these cases, Sergeant. I don't want to hear another word about Geismeier. Leave Geismeier to the Gestapo.'

The easiest case on the board, a robbery, had all the earmarks of a gang of well-known villains. They often hung out at a pool hall on the outskirts of the city, a place where, unfortunately, Willi Geismeier had never been seen or been known to have any business. It was a cool April evening; a warm breeze was blowing from the south. Gruber, along with another detective and two uniforms, drove out to roust the robbers.

The pool hall was on the second floor of what had once been a newspaper printing plant. They parked a block from the building. Gruber and the detective walked toward the building's front entrance while the two uniforms went through an alley to get to the back entrance. As Gruber and the detective were about to enter the building, a bicycle approached from a side street. Willi and Gruber recognized one another at the same moment. Willi tried to swerve out of the way, but Gruber leapt and grabbed the handlebars, pulling the bike down on top of himself. Gruber hit Willi hard, then hit him again and again until he lay still. The other detective put the cuffs on Willi, and that was that. Dumb luck, thought Gruber. But that's just how it works sometimes.

PART TWO

PART TWO

Dachau

The clouds were low and leaden. It was raining. Puddles formed here and there, turning the *Appelplatz*, the Roll Call Square, to mud. The weather, the cold rain, which outside Dachau was merely a nuisance, inside was a lethal menace. You had no protection from it. Your inadequate clothes soaked through and chilled your body and made you sick. Your broken-down shoes, which had already been worn out by someone else, collapsed into mush in the mud and rain, and scraped your heels raw so you walked in agony.

When you were not in Dachau you couldn't imagine what life in there was like. Willi certainly hadn't. And once you were in Dachau you could no longer remember what life was like out in the real world. These were two worlds apart. Eating, sleeping, walking, defecating, conversing, remaining silent, these were the banal and forgettable aspects of daily life out there. In Dachau nothing was banal or forgettable, and every aspect of daily life could mean the end.

The men had been awakened at four and had gotten their breakfast of thin gruel with a chunk of stale bread and coffee. They had straightened their beds, such as they were: a sack of straw, a threadbare sheet or light blanket, if you were lucky, laid out on wooden platforms stacked three high. There were about fifty men to a room, five rooms to a barracks, thirteen barracks altogether. More were being built by the current prisoners for all the new prisoners who would soon be arriving.

The men had cleaned their rooms, and now they marched in the rain down the alley between the barracks on the camp road that led to the *Appelplatz*. They were led by their kapo, a prisoner selected by the SS to oversee them. The kapos usually came from the criminal population who were all too eager to have advantages over the other prisoners. Their collaboration with the SS was rewarded with alcohol, drugs, even visits to the Dachau camp brothel, but, most of all, with being allowed to go on living.

The prisoners were required to sing while marching – folk songs, or Nazi songs, or anything else you could march to. You would be punished for not singing. Even music was a means of abuse and humiliation in Dachau. The kapo in charge decided what you sang. Today it was the Horst Wessel Song.

> Raise high the flag! Our ranks are tightly closed!
> The SA marches with a calm and steady step.
> Our comrades, killed by red reactionaries,
> March on in spirit with us in our ranks.
>
> Make way the streets for all our brown battalions,
> Make way the streets for all our SA men!
> Millions look to the swastika with hope,
> The day of liberty and bread is dawning now!

When they reached the *Appelplatz*, they stood at attention. Suddenly there was shouting and screaming behind them. Someone had fallen out of formation or looked around when he wasn't supposed to. He was being battered and kicked to the ground. If you turned to look, the same thing might happen to you. You marched with your eyes on the neck of the man in front of you. You stared straight ahead while the roll was called. It could take hours, and you stood as long as you had to. You saw nothing, you heard nothing, except when a command was issued or your name was called.

Sergeant Gruber and his men had bundled Willi into the car and driven him back to the station. His head was bloodied, one eye was swollen shut. Just breathing hurt. He thought some ribs might be broken.

They put him in a holding cell, and handed him over to the Gestapo the next morning. The Gestapo sentenced him immediately to what was known as 'protective custody,' an arbitrary and indefinite sentence for the protection of German society from its ruinous elements. There was no trial. There never would be.

In Dachau, Willi's personal information was taken down. His photograph was taken. He was stripped naked and given a perfunctory physical examination. Despite the huge purple and black bruises covering his body, his eye swollen shut, the cuts across his face, he was pronounced healthy and fit for work. His clothes were taken away. He was assigned a number, and given new striped prison clothes. The striped pants were too short. The striped jacket, also too small, had the red triangle badge and his number – 27944 – sewn on. The red triangle indicated he was a political prisoner, which meant that he, along with the Jews, was subject to the least consideration and the worst treatment.

Dachau the camp, in the village of the same name, had been opened in 1933 in a refurbished munitions factory. At first it was a 'labor camp' for career criminals, political criminals, the so-called 'work shy,' Jehovah's Witnesses, and other general misfits. There were few Jews at first. And in the beginning some inmates were released once their sentences were done. Some prison guards had even showed sympathy toward the prisoners, but those days were over.

In addition to the new barracks, the prisoners were building roads and other facilities, including a swimming pool for the resident SS officers. They were preparing the fields around the camp for cultivation. It was all being done at a punishing pace. SS Reichsführer Heinrich Himmler had taken over the running of Germany's prisons and prison camps and he had come up with a brilliant plan. Himmler realized you could house prisoners in inadequate quarters, feed them starvation rations, work them without mercy, and as they died, you could replace them with new 'workers.' The prisoners would be building the camp while at the same time ridding German society of its worst elements. There was an almost unlimited supply of disposable labor, especially once foreigners and Jews started showing up.

Of course, the success of Himmler's plan depended in large part on a new generation of guards, the SS Death's Head units, who could be trained to be merciless and brutal. They were not necessarily hardened sadists to begin with. But having been recruited as impressionable and insecure young men, boys even, they were malleable and, with the proper training, could be turned into killers.

Hans Loritz had recently taken over as Dachau's Oberführer, its commandant. He liked to assemble the young guards and officers from time to time for a motivational speech. They stood at attention in their grey uniforms, jodhpurs tucked into their heavy boots, the death's head on the collars of their smart tunics, their fresh faces eager, their eyes shining.

Loritz stood facing them, feet wide apart, hands on his hips, his senior staff lined up behind him. 'Comrades of the SS!' he said.

'You are here because you are the Reich's future, its promise, its best hope. And your mission is to assure the Führer's vision for Germany.

'Always remember, your assignment here will place you among the dregs of human society, the worst of the worst: criminals, Jews, traitors, pig dogs all. Do not be fooled by what looks like a gentle face. Behind it lurks the heart of a pig. Stand fast, hold firm. Do not allow your decent German spirit to be misled.

'There is no room here for sympathy or kindness or patience toward these pig dogs. Always remember that there are no human beings here, only swine. If any of you does not wish to see blood, you should go home immediately. And most of all remember this: no one who does harm to a prisoner need fear reprimand. After all, the more you shoot, the fewer we have to feed. Also, I am opposed to torture for the Jews. Bugs are not exterminated by tearing out their legs, but are stamped upon.'

The young SS guards lived in close quarters in special barracks. They trained together, had their meals together, socialized only with one another, and, at the same time, competed with one another for the favor of their officers. To win favor you had to be the hardest, the most brutal, the most relentless. You had to drive every sense of mercy and kindness from your mind. There was only room here for the merciless, the unforgiving.

If a prisoner fell, he was to be beaten until he stood. And if he couldn't stand, you could beat him to death. Those SS men who weren't hard enough, who showed even the faintest traces of sympathy, the slightest hesitation at committing meaningless and horrifying violence, would be ridiculed, held in contempt, and driven from the ranks in disgrace.

Outside

Hans Bergemann had arrived at the office early. He was busying himself with the contents of his briefcase, looking for his latest notes on the serial-killer case, when Sergeant Gruber came marching in.

'Well, Bergemann,' crowed Gruber. 'Guess what.'

'What, Sergeant?'

'I caught Geismeier.'

Bergemann had known all along that this might happen, and if it did, it would happen suddenly, when he least expected it. Willi was shrewd and clever, but his pursuit of the serial killer had been reckless. He had been obsessed. He wouldn't let go of the thing until he caught the killer or was caught himself. Bergemann had been bracing himself for a long time against just this moment.

Still, there was no way he could have been ready. He had seen Willi only the day before. He certainly hadn't thought it could be Gruber who caught him. He continued rummaging through his papers and dropped his head even lower while he gathered himself. He managed to say, 'What do you mean, Sergeant?'

'I caught that bastard, Bergemann. He's finished, done for! Gone!'

Hans was finally able to look up. Gruber was almost dancing in triumph.

'How'd you do it, Sergeant?'

Gruber didn't want to admit to Bergemann he had gotten lucky. 'I just nailed that asshole,' he said with a grin. 'Last night.'

'Geismeier?' Bergemann said again, just because he couldn't come up with anything else to say.

Other than Gruber, Bergemann was the only detective in the office who had known Willi. But the younger detectives had all heard of him and his reckless exploits. They listened in astonishment as Gruber told how he had wrestled Geismeier off his stupid bike, cracked his head against the pavement, not once but twice, punched the bastard hard in the ribs again and again to quiet him down, once and for all.

Geismeier was pretty groggy when they loaded him into the car for the drive to the station. Every time he seemed about to get a little frisky, Gruber let him have it again. 'He's not such a tough guy,' said Gruber, holding up his massive fists. They were bruised and raw. 'He didn't get in one good punch. Not one.'

Gruber could hardly wait to report to Captain Wendt. Detective Sergeant Hermann Gruber, and nobody else, had singlehandedly brought Willi Geismeier's reign of insurrection and mischief to an end. There would be a medal for sure. If there wasn't a promotion in it for him, he didn't know what it would take.

Bergemann didn't say anything more. Willi was in Dachau now. Bergemann had to go about his business with extreme caution as though nothing were different. Gruber had always been a little suspicious of him. If anyone was ever able to make the connection between him and Willi, it would mean the end. The slightest misstep could mean Dachau for him too. And that wouldn't do Willi or Lola or anyone else any good.

Over the next few days, Bergemann set about notifying people of Willi's arrest and imprisonment. Some of them already knew. The police grapevine was buzzing, so Benno Horvath, who still had police contacts, had already heard. Benno notified Edvin Lindstrom, the Swede, but Edvin had also heard already. Bergemann let Frau Schimmel know, but even she had already worked it out somehow. Willi was right about her: she had connections only she knew about and an uncanny understanding of what was going on almost before it happened. And Lola was already in hiding somewhere. Bergemann didn't know where, and it was best that way.

Sofia Bergemann could see that Hans was troubled. But she didn't ask him why. He got upset if she asked too many questions about what he was up to, what he called his 'work,' by which he didn't only mean his job as a policeman. Willi Geismeier had been outside the law for some time, and she knew Hans still had some sort of relationship with him. But she didn't know anything about it – for her own good, is what Hans said.

The first few times Sofia had met Willi – that had been years ago now – she had found him arrogant and aloof. He seemed to almost make a point of avoiding her. She eventually came to realize his aloofness was a necessary precaution, for him and for her. Then once, after she thought she understood him, he had showed up right before Christmas with a big box for the boys. It was a wooden train set that had been his as a boy. Willi had sat down on the floor and helped them set it up. It had bridges and tunnels, a station with a stationmaster and semaphore signal. It took more than an hour and Willi had lost himself in the task.

From little things Hans said, she knew Willi lived dangerously. And Hans himself did things that, if discovered, could place her and the boys in danger. So she had learned never to ask. That's how it was now. If you didn't accept the fact that someone close to you – a husband, a colleague, a friend – might end up in prison, you were living in a fools' paradise.

Keeping your head down, walking the straight and narrow, was no longer enough to keep you safe. And Bergemann was in the difficult position of investigating a very high-profile case whose clues – those gathered by Willi and a few additional clues Bergemann had uncovered on his own – led straight to the door of the Gestapo.

Bergemann's earliest, tentative inquiries in that regard had been met with stony resistance. But eventually Captain Wendt had authorized an interview with the Gestapo official responsible for police relations. Bergemann sat waiting in a sparsely furnished office in Briennerstraße. It was his first time in the building, and he was struck by the empty silence of the place. His footsteps had echoed down the empty hallway. The venetian blinds had been lowered in the office where he waited, but were open just enough so that he could see the iron bars over the windows and the traffic beyond them moving by in all innocence.

The door opened and a short, chubby, middle-aged man came into the room. He wore a gray suit and tie. His round head was bald with a well-trimmed fringe of mouse-colored hair. His prominent nose held his small, rimless eyeglasses away from his face, so that when he looked at you over his glasses, which he often did, you saw his eyes both on his face and refracted in his glasses. *It looks like he's got four eyes*, thought Bergemann, *like he's seeing twice as much.* His handshake was firmer than Bergemann had expected.

'Herr Braun,' he said by way of introduction, and gestured for Bergemann to take a seat. 'I understand you are investigating the serial killer,' he said. 'A terrible case. Terrible.'

'That's right,' said Bergemann. 'I assume the Gestapo is looking into it too.'

Herr Braun ignored Bergemann's implied question. 'How can I help you, Detective?' he said.

'Well, I'm not sure you can,' said Bergemann. 'But I wanted to alert you to something that could concern you.' He waited for a response, but Herr Braun just peered at him with his four eyes. 'We don't have that much to go on, of course,' Bergemann continued. 'The killer has been careful and has left very few clues. But one thing does point to the possibility that he is somehow connected to the SS.'

'Really?' said Herr Braun. 'I'm surprised.' He did not sound surprised. 'And what is that one thing?'

Bergemann told Herr Braun about the drug exemption and the SS number and the killer's likely addiction. He did not mention the

intersecting streetcar lines or Doctor Rosenberg or nurse Grosz or
the killer's Gestapo alias Friedrich Grosz.

'I see,' said Herr Braun. He did not ask Bergemann how he had
come by that number or whether he knew whose number it was.
Bergemann concluded from this that it was likely that Braun and
the Gestapo were already aware of these facts. 'Thank you, Detective,
for bringing this to our attention. We will certainly look into it,'
said Herr Braun.

Bergemann had come intending to push Herr Braun for information if it seemed opportune to do so. But Braun's lack of
curiosity about Bergemann's information suggested that, if the
Gestapo knew more than Bergemann had told him, they weren't
going to give anything away. Herr Braun had also convinced him,
without saying so, that the Gestapo did not want the police to
pursue the case. If there was an SS connection, as seemed likely,
the Gestapo would likely want the investigation closed down and
covered up. They might shut down the case and yet still go after
the perpetrator, find and punish him. It was not in their interest
to have a serial killer on the loose. But whatever they did,
Bergemann thought it certain that none of it would ever be known
to the public or to the police.

In fact, when Bergemann got back to his office, Gruber was
waiting with the news. 'You're off the case, Bergemann.'

'All right, Sergeant,' said Bergemann.

'And no arguments, Bergemann. You hear me? It's not my
decision.'

'Yes, Sergeant,' said Bergemann. 'I understand.'

No arguments? thought Gruber. *What the hell is he up to now?*

Bergemann was not up to anything. He was just making necessary adjustments, taking prudent precautions. Being taken off the
case was a relief. It was a dangerous case, after all. His visit to
Briennerstraße would have brought that home if he hadn't already
known it. In fact, being taken off the case was a sort of warning.
It meant the Gestapo was now aware of him, if they hadn't been
before. And even though he was no longer officially investigating,
they knew he knew something, and they would be watching him.

Since the *Anschluß,* since Austria had 'rejoined' the German
Reich in March, the Gestapo was more active than ever. This had
to do with the Führer's decision to prepare for war, and the opposition coming from his generals. They were either scheming traitors

or short-sighted weaklings. The Führer saw betrayal and defeatism around every corner, so of course the Gestapo was busy.

This included them interfering in what until now had been strictly police business. Two Gestapo had shown up one hot July day to talk to Gruber. *Why do they always come in twos?* Bergemann wondered. *Are they always checking on one another?*

He could tell from the look on Gruber's face that this visit was unexpected and unwelcome. They were in his office for a good hour. No voices were raised, but there were no smiles either. Once they had gone, Gruber came out mopping his brow.

'What did they want?' said Bergemann.

'I'll be damned if I know,' said Gruber, and Bergemann believed him. 'Damn it, Hans, someone has poked a stick in the hornets' nest.'

Schleiffer in Trouble

The Gestapo also came one day to question Heinz Schleiffer. Over the years Heinz had dutifully done his part, been watchful and responsible, trying to help the Führer keep order, doing, he thought, his patriotic duty. And yet there they were early one Sunday morning. Heinz answered the door still in his pajamas with a piece of buttered toast in his hand. It was Sunday morning after all.

This was not too long after Willi's arrest, and the two men, one short, one tall, both wearing ill-fitting suits, were interested in understanding Schleiffer's interest – what seemed to them *undue* interest – in Willi Geismeier, aka Karl Juncker.

'We're just trying to get the whole story,' said the tall one as they stepped past Heinz and into his apartment.

'But I didn't even know his real name,' said Heinz.

'No? So you say.'

'All I did was identify him . . . for your colleagues from photos they showed me. I thought they . . .'

'Yes, you identified him. But you denied that he was a policeman.'

'I didn't deny it. I just didn't know it,' said Schleiffer.

'He wore a police rosette in his lapel,' said the first man, the tall one. He kept his hat on. 'Why the devil do you think he did that?'

'You seem to know almost nothing about this man,' said the short man. He kept cracking his knuckles. 'And yet you filed numerous reports about him.'

'Yes. I didn't know. I thought he acted suspicious, that's all,' said Heinz.

'So, how could you file so many complaints and know so little?' said the first man. 'You filed your complaints based on what?'

'My suspicions,' said Heinz.

'I see. Your suspicions,' said the tall man. He began walking around the room, looking at the furnishings, lifting a magazine from the table as though he expected to find something illicit under it, opening a cupboard. Of course Heinz had nothing to hide, but when someone started opening cupboards, you didn't know what they might find that could arouse their suspicions, even if you were perfectly innocent. Then you started acting nervous, giving wrong answers, *seeming* guilty. That was how they worked.

'All right,' said the short man, leaving his knuckles alone and opening his notebook, touching his pencil to his tongue, as though he were about to get to the heart of the matter. 'So, tell us what you know about his associates.'

'His associates? I don't know anything about his associates.'

The man lowered his pencil and looked at Heinz in astonishment. 'Did he have visitors?'

'I suppose he did, but I didn't see them.'

'You're the building supervisor,' said the man. 'How is it possible that you never saw his visitors? Didn't you notice *anyone*?'

'No, I didn't. I never saw anyone,' said Heinz.

The man spoke as he wrote: 'Says . . . he . . . never . . . saw . . . anyone. What about friends? Did you ever see him with friends?'

'I don't remember ever seeing him with friends,' said Heinz.

'Herr Schleiffer, you *are* a loyal Party member, aren't you?' said the tall man while the second man continued making notes. He stepped up to Heinz and loomed over him.

Heinz regretted being in his pajamas and not in uniform. Still, how could they doubt he was a loyal Party member after everything he had done for the Party? 'Yes, of course I am,' he said indignantly. He wondered whether he should salute and say 'Heil Hitler!' to prove it.

'I'd watch my tone, if I were you, Herr Schleiffer,' said the short man, as though he had read his thoughts. 'You're on thin ice here.'

'I still wonder, Herr Schleiffer,' said the tall man, 'why you filed so many frivolous denunciations. I haven't heard a reasonable explanation yet for that.'

'Frivolous?'

'You know it's a crime to denounce someone falsely. Our dockets are virtually filled with false denunciations, which makes it all the more difficult for us to catch the real malefactors. Making a false denunciation is a serious misdemeanor, Herr Schleiffer.'

'Very serious,' said the short man. 'A false denunciation is tantamount to obstruction of justice.'

'Well, you caught Herr Juncker, didn't you?' said Heinz. He assumed still that Juncker had been arrested for his crimes.

'Caught him?' said the tall man. 'Who said anything about having caught anyone?'

'You mean he wasn't arrested?' said Schleiffer.

'That is none of your business, Herr Schleiffer.'

'The point is, you led us down many false trails with all your denunciations,' said the short man.

At that moment, as Heinz was wondering how he should respond to their accusations, he remembered Karl Juncker's girlfriend, the redhead. What was her name? Lola! He *had* met Lola. Here was a name he could give them! And he was about to do so when he had the thought: how would it look now, right after they had accused him of making frivolous denunciations, if he mentioned Lola at what was obviously a convenient moment for him? And Lola who? He didn't even know her last name. And not only that. What if she turned out to be a completely innocent bystander to whatever they were investigating? That would be *another* frivolous denunciation on his record. For the first time ever, but not the last, Heinz Schleiffer felt like the Gestapo was not his friend, and, instead of mentioning Lola, he remained silent.

Three weeks later, when the papers reported that yet another woman had been attacked and murdered by the serial killer, Heinz, who by this time knew from Frau Schimmel that Karl Juncker was in custody, wondered whether his accusations of Juncker had not been wrong after all. 'Still,' he said, 'at least Juncker or Geismeier or whatever his name is must be guilty of something.'

'What makes you think so?' said Frau Schimmel.

'Well, he was using a false name.'

'He was a policeman, Herr Schleiffer. Maybe he was undercover.

They use false names all the time. Maybe he was actually investigating the murders of all those women.'

'Well, they arrested him, didn't they?' said Heinz. 'He must have done something wrong, or they wouldn't have arrested him.'

'But they wouldn't tell you what he had done wrong, would they?' said Frau Schimmel. 'And you know as well as I do, Herr Schleiffer, they arrest people all the time these days for very flimsy reasons.'

Even Heinz had heard those stories, and now he had come within a hair of being arrested himself, for what, he didn't even know. And when he thought about it, he really had denounced Herr Juncker for what Frau Schimmel would have called flimsy reasons. 'They must have their reasons, though, for asking me all those questions,' said Heinz.

'What reasons, Herr Schleiffer? They weren't just asking you questions, were they?' said Frau Schimmel. 'They were interrogating you.'

'Oh, I don't think so,' said Heinz, trying, without success, to rehabilitate the Gestapo in his own mind and to make himself feel better at the same time.

Frau Schimmel knocked on his door more often these days. She needed help getting up the stairs; the grocery cart had gotten too heavy for her to manage. The doctor had recently told her she didn't have much longer to live. You could see that just by looking at her. She had gotten thinner and thinner until she looked like a twig. She could hardly walk, even with her cane.

Heinz was always glad to help. He went to the grocery store for her now when she couldn't go because of the pain. He looked in on her, to make sure she was all right. He always learned something useful when he did. Besides, he found that he actually enjoyed her company.

'I haven't done anything wrong, Frau Schimmel,' he said. 'I've been with the Führer since the very beginning.' The Gestapo visit was weeks in the past, but it still stuck in his craw.

'Well, we've all been with him since the beginning, Herr Schleiffer, haven't we? Still, they *did* interrogate you . . . I worry about Herr Juncker,' she added.

Heinz said nothing.

She slid another slice of strudel onto his plate. Pear again. His favorite. 'I'm sure you had only the best intentions when you filed your reports,' she said. 'But I wonder what Herr Juncker was really up to. To me it's hard to imagine it was anything criminal. You know I always think of him as a good man.'

'I like to think he was up to no good,' said Heinz, trying to convince himself all over again. But his certainty about both Karl Juncker's guilt and his own virtue had abandoned him, and so he said, for the fifteenth time, 'They wouldn't have hauled him off if he hadn't done something bad.'

'Did they even admit they hauled him off?' said Frau Schimmel.

'Not exactly,' said Heinz.

'You said he was a policeman, didn't you?' said Frau Schimmel.

'That's what they told me when they showed me the photos, Frau Schimmel. Frankly, right now I don't know what to believe.'

'That's understandable, Herr Schleiffer.' She thought for a moment. 'You know, your SA commandant Mecklinger's office could help you there, Herr Schleiffer. Why don't you ask them?'

'Ortsgruppenleiter Mecklinger won't give me the time of day . . .'

'Which is why you befriended his Frau Kinski, isn't it, Herr Schleiffer?'

This was true. Thanks to Frau Schimmel's reading of the situation, Heinz had found a way around Ortsgruppenleiter Gerhard Mecklinger and a reliable source of information. Frau Kinski knew everything that went on even better than Mecklinger himself, and was, it turned out, friendlier than she had at first appeared. Heinz had learned from her all about Mecklinger's dalliance with the voluptuous Lorelei, who was now happily ensconced in police headquarters, and his very tenuous connection through his wife to Heinrich Himmler, which apparently had both its advantages and dangers. He learned a few other things too about meetings and planned actions and such. And Frau Schimmel always generously helped Heinz make sense of everything.

The German army, supposedly limited to 100,000 men by the Versailles Treaty, had now swollen to over three million men. You didn't need Frau Kinski to know that. It was no secret; it was in all the papers as cause for celebration. Soldiers in uniform were every-where. The British and the French had let it happen, but short of going to war, there wasn't much they could have done about it.

Tomas stopped by one day to tell Heinz that he had been drafted. Tomas and his father were friends again. Tomas had shown up a month after their falling out to patch things up. Tomas said art and politics weren't worth fighting over, and Heinz agreed. And now Heinz's only son, whom he had only recently gotten to know, was probably going to war.

'Mama told me I should desert, should leave the country,' said Tomas. 'Go to America or Canada or Australia.'

'That's just like her!' said Heinz.

'I just couldn't do it,' said Tomas.

Heinz didn't know what to say. Tomas stood before him, handsome in his gray uniform, a faint mustache on his lip, but now seeming still very much a boy, at least to Heinz. Heinz felt proud one minute and frightened the next.

Tomas had orders to join a tank division near Dresden, hard by the Czech border. He would almost certainly be part of the invasion of Czechoslovakia, when it came. The thought of Tomas being wounded or, God forbid, dying, filled Heinz with fear, but the thought of him deserting filled him with shame.

'Let's go up and see Frau Schimmel,' said Heinz. 'I know she'd like to see you. She's very sick, you know.'

Heinz told Frau Schimmel what his ex-wife had said. 'Well, that's how mothers are,' said Frau Schimmel, and from the sound of her voice, Heinz wondered whether she might be speaking from experience. She had never said anything about having children, or, for that matter, about being married. But with her you never knew. The anguish in her voice sounded real.

The Sudetenland

The Gestapo had followed Edvin Lindstrom almost every day since he had been back in Germany. They did so in plain sight. If he went to a cafe to meet someone, they chose a table nearby and drank coffee or pretended to read the paper. Edvin had diplomatic immunity and couldn't be arrested. But the Gestapo's purpose was only to harass him and scare those he met, so it was better that he saw them and knew they were there.

Most of the people Edvin met and spoke with had no immunity. And these days if they met with a foreign spy – and like every foreigner, Edvin was presumed to be a spy – they could expect to

be arrested, or at least pulled in for questioning: How do you know him? Why did you meet? What did he want to know? What did you tell him? What did he tell you? When do you expect to meet again?

It wasn't that hard for Edvin to give the Gestapo the slip as long as he didn't make a habit of it. He did so during off hours or on weekends. Then he met Benno Horvath to share some of what he had learned about political developments within the German government that might be news. And through Benno, Edvin connected with Willi.

Edvin and Willi had met in the Westfriedhof not far from the Olympic stadium. Willi was carrying a bouquet of flowers. 'Why else visit a cemetery?' he said. They shook hands. 'Everything you predicted has come to pass,' said Willi.

'I'm sorry to say it has,' said Edvin. 'Nonetheless, I'm happy to see you after all these years.'

'Me too,' said Willi. 'I hoped it would be different. What can I help you with?' Willi always got straight to the point.

'It's getting harder and harder for Jews to leave,' said Edvin. 'Where possible, my government wants to help them get out. We're able to arrange for transportation and visas. But certain documents – passports, identity cards – are another matter.' By now the Swedes and everyone else trying to help refugees were using illegal means. It was a matter of saving lives.

Willi connected Edvin with Gerd Fegelein. The print shop in the basement of Lerchenau Bicycles was up and running.

'On another matter,' said Edvin, 'what do you know about any organized resistance? Is there any?'

'No,' said Willi. 'None. There isn't any organized resistance that I know of. That's not to say there's no resistance at all. Only it's mostly lone wolves, people operating on their own, slowing down production in factories, sabotage, that sort of thing. And there's been some opposition among a few politicians. You probably know who they are. But one by one they're being found out, arrested and hanged.'

'What about among the police? Anything there?'

'Nothing organized that I know of,' said Willi. 'Again, a few lone wolves is all. But what do you know? What about the army? Anything stirring there?'

'Ah, the army,' said Edvin, shaking his head. 'That's a pitiful case. They're the one group that could overthrow him. Ella has some contacts there, and she's heard rumblings. So have I. But it never comes to anything.

'Officers tell me they're horrified by Hitler; they find him reprehensible. But they can't imagine rising up against him. They're afraid, yes. But it's more that they're completely paralyzed by their idiotic Prussian code of honor, their nobility, the duties and loyalties of rank. He's reprehensible, abominable, evil, they say, but he's their Führer, their commander-in-chief, no matter what. Attacking him in any way would amount to treason, which is out of the question.

'Besides that, and this is interesting, they are reluctant to turn against him because he's been successful. Marching into the Rhineland, for instance. The generals warned him that was doomed. It wasn't. Austria, last March, the same thing. He succeeds where he is bound to fail. And they embrace his successes.

'He's gotten rid of whatever opposition there might have been in the general staff, you know. Von Blomberg, von Fritsch, both damaged, yes, but they offered some opposition. And now even they're gone.'

There was a funny story making the rounds about General von Blomberg, the field marshal and minister of war. Blomberg was a widower and wanted to marry again. He proposed to his young secretary, Erna Gruhn, and she accepted his proposition. This, of course, scandalized the Prussian officer corps because Erna Gruhn was of the lower classes and not suited to be the wife of a general and a Prussian aristocrat. But the Führer gave the marriage his blessing – maybe he liked the fact that the Prussians objected – and he and Goering served as witnesses at the wedding.

A short time later, rumors started flying, and then the story broke that General Field Marshal von Blomberg's new wife was not just a commoner. She had once been arrested for prostitution and pornography. There were photos. 'Doesn't that make the Führer a pimp?' someone said. It was a good joke, but too dangerous to repeat.

Edvin and Willi met repeatedly. Edvin offered Willi help. Was there anything he could do? Willi said he was working on a case, which caused Edvin to raise his eyebrows. 'A case?' he said.

Willi explained that he had been pursuing the serial killer who, he was all but certain, had attacked Lola years earlier. Willi was also fairly certain the killer was in the Gestapo. Certain other evidence indicated that he was also a senior SS officer. Willi thought he was getting close, but thought also that the Gestapo was getting close to him. He thought he would probably be warned by a contact in the SS when his arrest was imminent and it was time for him and Lola to leave the country. Edvin promised he would arrange their departure. Willi had never imagined he would be caught by Gruber. How could he have imagined that?

A light rain began falling. Willi left his flowers by a stranger's grave, and the two men went their separate ways. They arranged for another meeting two weeks later. The persecution of Jews was being stepped up; Edvin was trying to establish a network of safe houses and could use Willi's help. The day of the meeting Edvin waited in vain for Willi to show up. Edvin had two Swedish visas in hand, but Willi was already in Dachau.

Benno and Margarete Horvath listened every night to the BBC. You could hear the world unraveling and stumbling toward war. Chamberlain, the British prime minister, had made repeated trips to Germany to meet with Hitler to prevent an invasion of Czechoslovakia. Chamberlain gave up the Sudetenland, a corner of Czechoslovakia with a German population, for vague promises by a known liar. Were the English that blind, Benno wondered, or desperate, or both? Chamberlain tricked himself into believing he was preventing a larger invasion of the entire country of Czechoslovakia and the war that would necessarily follow, when in fact he was enabling both.

The Czech border with Germany had strong defenses, but thanks to Chamberlain's Sudetenland concession, the German army got past them without firing a shot. The rest of Czechoslovakia lay there for the taking, defenseless and without allies. The French and the British had made it clear their promises weren't worth the paper they were written on. Within five months Czechoslovakia ceased to exist.

Hard Labor

The Dachau kapos treated prisoners badly. The kapos' survival depended in part on their brutality. A kapo who wasn't sufficiently brutal could find himself back in the general prison population where he would be treated with particular contempt by SS and prisoners alike. Willi's barracks kapo was a man named Franz

Neudeck, a gang member whom Willi had arrested more than once. As a result of his many arrests Neudeck had been classified a habitual criminal. Even though it was not Willi who had landed him in Dachau, when Neudeck saw Willi for the first time, he turned his rage about being in Dachau in Willi's direction.

He came up behind Willi in the barracks early one morning. 'Geismeier,' he said, and when Willi turned, Neudeck hit him hard in the ribs with a short metal pipe he was carrying. Willi crumpled to the floor. 'Welcome to my world, Geismeier,' said Neudeck. He spat and walked away.

It was time for roll call. Two men helped Willi to his feet and out to formation. They marched beside him in the middle of the company, helping keep him upright. They sang a folk song as they marched.

> I love to go a-wandering
> Along the mountain track
> And as I go, I love to sing
> My knapsack on my back
> Val-deri, val-dera
> Val-deri, val-dera

The two men were also in Willi's work group of twenty men, so they helped him march to the work site. They were part of a crew building a road between the new barracks. Half the men carried rocks from a nearby pile while the other half used sledgehammers to pound the rocks into gravel.

Despite his beating that morning, Willi was not in the worst condition of the men in his crew. One man could barely lift the sledgehammer overhead. He let it fall on the stone at his feet without having any effect on the stone at all. The kapo in charge came running, spitting and fuming at the man who stopped his efforts and stood at attention. The kapo punched the man in the arms and chest, shouting at him the whole time.

The crew worked nonstop twelve hours a day with a ten-minute break for lunch which consisted of 'soup' with a few scraps of potato. In the evening they marched back to the *Appelplatz* for another roll call, then eventually back to the barracks for supper and sleep.

One evening, Juergen Diehn, the man who been punched for not working hard enough, wouldn't eat his supper. He lay on his thin mattress with his arms folded across his chest and refused to eat. Juergen had once been a professional soccer player and then a conservative member of the last democratically elected Reichstag. He had been imprisoned in Dachau right after Operation Hummingbird. He had been brimming with health and resolve, expecting to outlast this ridiculous Führer. But more than four years had passed and he had been turned into a tattered and ruined skeleton. His cheeks were caved in, his hair had fallen out, his neck was too thin to hold up his head. You could count his vertebrae and his ribs. His hips stuck out and his knees were swollen knobs.

'Eat,' said Dietrich Dominick. He cradled Juergen's head in the crook of his arm, holding a spoonful of that wretched soup in front of Juergen's mouth. But Juergen kept his mouth pressed shut. Dietrich had been a Lutheran pastor. He was in Dachau because he had written, signed, and then circulated among his fellow pastors an open letter to the Führer criticizing his racial policies. Like Martin Niemöller, who would eventually land in Dachau himself, Dietrich Dominick had been an anti-Semite and ardent nationalist to begin with, but had, as he said in his letter, renounced nationalism and anti-Semitism as antithetical to his Christian faith. 'Please eat,' said Dietrich. 'For the love of God.'

Juergen just stared past Dietrich and said nothing. What did the love of God mean to him? Juergen was taken to the infirmary the next day and was never seen again.

Everyone in Dachau found himself forced into a sort of existential solitude, and if you allowed yourself to become truly alone, you would go mad or die. Willi had been a solitary person most of his life, but while solitary, he had also always believed that the only way forward for humanity was humanity itself. And so now he struggled not to allow his instinct for solitude to keep him away from his fellow prisoners. For better or worse, they were a community. They shared everything now. He could even sympathize with Neudeck's rage. In Neudeck's mind, Willi had sent him to hell.

In addition to the physical work each man was forced to do, which seemed beyond endurance, there was also the mental and emotional work. In Dachau you were quickly reduced to your essence. You consisted entirely of what your body and mind could do, and were held fast by what they could not do. You were alone with your fears, and they were abundant. You were alone in your own particular anguish, which was profound. And you were alone with your hope. 'The miserable,' Shakespeare reminded him, 'have no other medicine, but only hope.'

All of the prisoners hoped to survive somehow, to come out of this on the other side, whether in this life or another. But each man's hope had its own shape and dimensions which were molded and formed by his life experience, by the choices he had made, by his beliefs, dreams, and aspirations, by the happiness and unhappiness he had known, by what he saw as possible. Some had grandiose hopes. Some just wanted to be returned to their families. Some found hope in the idea of freedom, in just the thought of not being locked up. Neudeck was like that. He dreamed of being on the street again, up to no good, finding a woman.

For Willi, hope was not about anything he wanted. Hope was just something he had. Hope was like fuel. It was propulsive, it was in his muscles and bones and not in his mind. He was not conscious of hope. He did not hope to see Lola again: he *expected* to see Lola again.

Hope entered his body with every breath and never left. He did not know where it came from; he might not even have known it was there. Once when he was asked if he was ever hopeful, he answered, 'What do you mean?' When he was carrying rocks, or breaking rocks, or even suffering torture, even there, his hope was just something that was present, like his heartbeat, a small kernel, a flame that would not be extinguished. When he finally realized that about himself, he was amazed.

The First Interrogation

After two weeks of breaking rocks, Willi's crew was harnessed to heavy rollers which they pulled non-stop back and forth over the crushed rock to create the road bed. The rocks tore through their shoes and bloodied their feet. The ropes and timbers of the roller tore at their arms and shoulders and necks. However, this work, as terrible as it was, had the advantage, if you could call it that, of tying a group of men to one load so that the stronger could help the weak.

Dachau, the prison camp, was surrounded by a no man's land overseen by machine gunners in towers with orders to shoot anyone in or even near this 'death zone.' Beyond the death zone was a high fence of reinforced concrete posts and multiple strands of electrified barbed wire.

Once Willi's team had finished the road bed to the engineer's satisfaction, they were marched out the gate and into the marshland beyond the fence where they were to clear boulders from the muck and prepare the ground to be cultivated. They were guarded by SS men. All you had to do was look like you were thinking of running, and the SS guards would shoot you down.

One morning Willi was called out at roll call. He was marched by Franz Neudeck to another part of the camp where the old armaments factory had been, to a square stone building that had been reconfigured for interrogations and punishment. Once inside, Neudeck pushed Willi ahead of him down a long concrete corridor lined with heavy wooden doors crisscrossed by iron straps. These might have been prison-cell doors, except they dated from the building's early days as an armory. They stopped by one such door, and Neudeck knocked and then entered, again pushing Willi ahead of him.

They were in a small room, no more than four by four meters. An SS Hauptsturmführer, a captain, sat at a table. Carefully arrayed on the table in front of him, as if on display, were his hat, an open portfolio, and an oxtail whip, made up of multiple strands of wire. A second SS man stood beside the captain. He looked to Willi to be a boy barely out of school. Two kapos stood against the wall behind them, just under a small window, the source of the only light in the room. Attached to the wall to Willi's left were some heavy canvas straps.

The captain signaled Neudeck that he should leave. Willi stood at attention while the captain leafed through the papers in the portfolio, turning back and forth until he settled on one. 'Shall I call you Herr Geismeier or Herr Juncker?' said the captain.

Willi didn't answer.

'Geismeier, then,' said the captain. 'According to your file, Geismeier, there was a time when you were a good policeman. You closed a lot of cases. You were highly decorated, weren't you?' He looked up expectantly, but Willi remained silent.

'Fine,' said the captain, as though he considered Willi's silence a response. 'You didn't like the rules or regulations, though, did you?'

Again, Willi said nothing.

'I see,' said the captain. 'You thought you were of a higher order, didn't you? You could operate outside the rules, beyond the laws. You disobeyed your superiors because you thought you were smarter than they were?'

Silence.

'Is that really the way you want to play this, Geismeier? Let's try once more, shall we?'

Willi knew how this worked. The captain played a patient man. He even said 'I am a patient man' at one point. Willi understood the captain would then choose a moment to lose his patience, and his rage would come suddenly and violently. Then Willi would be strapped to the wall and beaten.

'When did you last see your Fräulein Zeff? We have her in custody, you know.'

Willi had been expecting the captain would say this or something like it. There was no way to know for certain whether it was true or not, but Willi doubted it. He and Lola had made contingency plans to get her away from Munich. But even if it was true, nothing he could say now would save her.

'We know about Schleiffer, your neighbor, too,' said the captain.

This gave Willi comfort. There was nothing to know about Willi and Schleiffer. The captain was either fishing or laying a trap. Either way, it meant they had only general knowledge about Willi's more recent misbehavior, but no specifics, no names, no places, no actions. In fact, the more questions the captain posed, the more he gave Willi the rough outlines of what they knew about him and what they didn't know. They didn't know much.

The captain wanted to know who, for instance, among Willi's higher-ups during his time as a detective, had been directing him in his treasonous behavior. Who were his confederates among the police and detectives he knew? Bergemann? Gruber? Wendt? Who had wanted Otto Bruck killed? What were Willi's connections to the Communist Party? Why had he recently been impersonating a detective?

The captain surprised Willi in one regard: he did not lose patience. When, after a considerable amount of time, he had gotten no response of any kind from Willi, and the only thing left to do was punish him, the captain still leafed through the file folder one more time, looking for more questions to ask, looking for some way he could continue the interview and forestall the punishment. Whatever allure inflicting pain had once held for him, it was long gone by now.

The captain rose from his chair, picked up his hat and put it on his head. He fussed with it a bit, getting it just right, delaying again, Willi thought, what they both knew to be inevitable. 'You leave me no choice, Geismeier.' They always said something like that. He picked up the file folder and left the room.

The two kapos who had stood silent and motionless against the wall the entire time now stepped forward, seized Willi, pulled off his jacket and shirt, and wrapped the leather straps tightly around his biceps with him facing the wall. The larger of the two picked up the whip and without hesitation began lashing at Willi's back.

As the first blow struck, Willi was already elsewhere in his mind. It was a stormy spring day. The wind was whistling and driving hail down on them. He and Lola had been hiking around the Murnauer Moos. He wore shorts, a jacket, and a cap. It had been sunny earlier. He had finally broken in his boots and they no longer hurt, so they were running, seeking shelter, their steps pounding along the path. There was a chunk of black bread, Emmental cheese, and a bottle of water in his backpack. It bounced and crashed against his back with each step. There was a sweater too, he remembered. Suddenly they were swimming in the icy Riegsee until their skin could stand it no longer. Lola laughed as they ran from the water, shaking the water droplets from her body like a dog might, shaking and laughing. The sun danced in the droplets. The lake shimmered. The sun scooted from behind a cloud. It began to shower lightning all around them, then snow began falling in great gouts. The last thing Willi remembered was Lola rolling in a snowdrift and pulling him down on top of her.

Hearing shouts and screams, the captain came running back into the room and found the young SS man beating Willi's torn and bloody back, kicking at his legs, and screaming like a wild animal caught in a trap. Willi hung on the floor from the straps, obviously unconscious, while the boy slashed at his body again and again and again, shrieking with each blow.

This boy, a seventeen-year-old who had finished his training just weeks earlier, had seen an opportunity. He had cursed the kapo and declared the beating he was administering weak, inadequate. He had torn the whip from the kapo's hand, pushed the man aside, and flailed away in blind desperation. This would show his worth, this would teach the others in the barracks not to mock him. This would put an end to all the teasing about his thin, hairless chest, his baby face.

The captain yelled 'Stop!' three times and finally seized the boy's arm before he stopped. The boy's shirt was soaked with sweat and flecked with Willi's blood. His face was red, his eyes were wild, and his body was heaving with his panting. 'We don't want him dead yet,' said the captain.

The Riegsee

I n one of those peculiar and meaningless coincidences that are sprinkled throughout life and usually go unnoticed, Lola found herself beside the Riegsee at the very moment Willi was being whipped, the very lake Willi had dreamed of as he was being beaten senseless. Thunder clouds were building over the lake and she was taking in laundry, pulling sheets and towels off the line and stuffing the clothes pins in her apron pocket. She almost tripped over Mephi, the big black poodle. He barked happily. He had fallen in love with Lola on the day she had come up the walk for the first time, and now he followed her constantly.

'You're not helping, Mephi,' she said, laughing.

Mephi belonged to Fedor Blaskowitz. Fedor had named him for Mephisto, who first appears as a poodle in Goethe's *Faust*. Fedor, Mephi and Lola lived in the steep-roofed, green cottage beside the lake. It was Fedor who, alerted by Bergemann, had gone to the Mahogany Room the day after Willi's arrest to warn Lola, and to escort her to the first stop on her flight from Munich.

By the time Detective Sergeant Gruber showed up at the hotel to question and, if need be, arrest her, Lola was gone.

'Where did she go?' Gruber demanded.

Alex Kuzinski, the hotel manager said, 'She got sick. She was vomiting.' This was not a lie. The news from Blaskowitz had made her ill. 'I ordered her to the hospital,' said Alex. This *was* a lie. Alex was taking a big risk by lying about something Gruber could easily check. But Alex cared about Lola and could tell she was in trouble. What other choice did he have? And Gruber, true to form, didn't check.

Bergemann had given Blaskowitz exact instructions. Lola and Blaskowitz had taken a taxi to an intersection not far from the Lerchenau Bicycles shop. They watched the taxi drive off and then walked the last few blocks to the shop.

On hearing the password, Gerd Fegelein, the one-time burglar, sprang into action. Many years retired from the only occupation he had ever truly enjoyed, Fegelein was pleased to be employed once again in illicit activity. He escorted Lola and Fedor a few blocks further to a safe house, a basement storeroom in an apartment building. The room was full of tools and equipment, but also had a bed and a few sticks of furniture.

Seeing how distraught Lola was in these early hours of her flight, Fegelein offered to visit her apartment and bring her whatever she might need to make her life a bit more comfortable and mitigate her distress. Blaskowitz was horrified. 'Are you crazy? Her apartment will be watched,' he said.

'Of course it will,' said Fegelein. He seemed to relish the thought. He described some of his professional successes for Blaskowitz, like the time he got away with some Fabergé knickknacks from the bedroom of a certain prince, while a party was going on in the very next room. 'The apartment was on the top floor, by the way.'

'But you were younger then, weren't you?' said Blaskowitz. 'And you were eventually caught.'

'But that was by Willi,' Fegelein said, as though that didn't count. Fegelein would not be dissuaded. He even asked Lola whether there was anything in particular that she wanted. He was happy for the adventure.

Lola lay down on the bed and almost immediately fell asleep. When she woke up many hours later, she was alone. A small lamp on the wobbly little table by the bed was burning dimly. And someone had brought a plate with some grapes, some cheese, a hunk of dark bread, and a kitchen knife. Bedside the bed stood a small cardboard suitcase, *her* suitcase, which, when she opened it, contained some toiletries, some clothes, including, for whatever reason, the green dress.

Now that Detective Sergeant Gruber had arrested Willi, he seemed determined to find Lola as well. He ordered his detectives to stake out her apartment. Bergemann was assigned to be part of the stakeout, but even though he was there the night Fegelein visited, he didn't see anything. Fegelein went in over the roof and down the airshaft.

After two days Bergemann decided it would be safer if Lola left Munich altogether, and Fegelein had to agree. Blaskowitz offered to take her to the green house on the Riegsee, and that seemed the perfect solution.

Years earlier Fedor Blaskowitz had been a teacher of Greek and Latin at the Herder Gymnasium in Munich. While there, he had been blackmailed because of his homosexuality and forced by the notorious Otto Bruck, the school headmaster at the time, to give false evidence in a murder investigation. Fedor could have been charged with obstruction of justice and sent to prison, and Willi had helped him extricate himself from that situation. Fedor soon left Munich for Murnau, where he had found another teaching position.

Fedor's brush with criminality and his friendship with Willi had changed everything for him. He didn't think of himself as a brave man by any measure, but he was no longer the fearful man he had once been either. And because Fedor had experienced injustice followed by justice, he became devoted to the cause of justice, and to Willi, whom he saw as an instrument of justice. He knew that by bringing Lola to Murnau he was placing himself in danger, but that didn't matter to him.

They could not very well take the train to Murnau; the SS would be watching the trains. And Fedor did not drive or own a car. Bergemann asked Frau Schimmel whether she had anyone who could help, and of course she did. At the appointed hour on Saturday morning a young man named Pierre drove up and stopped outside the safe house. Frau Schimmel had sent him, he said. He knew the password which he pronounced with a French accent.

He was a fast and sure driver. He drove in silence. A little over an hour later they all got out at the green house by the lake. Mephi was excited to see them and danced around Lola's legs barking as they walked to the door. Pierre insisted on carrying Lola's suitcase.

It was lunchtime and Fedor opened a bottle of wine. He brought out a loaf of black bread, some ham, cheese, apples, and some pickles he had made the summer before. Because it was a sunny, unseasonably warm day with only the slightest breeze coming off the lake, he flung a red and white checked tablecloth across the rustic picnic table outside the back door. They sat down on the benches by the table, and the three of them had a relaxed picnic lunch as though they hadn't a care in the world. Mephi dozed at their feet.

Frau Schimmel Again

B ertha Schimmel's doctor told her that the sharp pain she had been experiencing in her legs indicated that her cancer had spread further throughout her body. The tests he performed confirmed that she probably had less than a year to live. He was surprised and bit horrified when she laughed at the news.

'Come now, Doctor,' she said. 'Why are you surprised? You know me. You know all about me.'

This was true. The doctor was only a few years younger than Bertha, and had been her doctor since before she became Bertha Schimmel. In addition to knowing her real name, he knew she was Jewish, knew she was a former revolutionary, and thought that she was probably somehow involved at this very moment in something subversive. As a socialist and a Jew himself, he knew what fate might await her if she fell into the hands of the regime.

'Well then, Doctor' – she still called him doctor after all this time, as though that were his name and not Albert – 'why wouldn't I be happy to learn that, despite the dire political circumstances and the imminent threat to us Jews, despite the fact that our country is almost certainly headed into another terrible war, why wouldn't I be thrilled to learn that I have a fair chance of dying a natural and peaceful death, maybe even in my own bed? I can hardly imagine better news. Can you?'

'I take your point,' said Albert.

'Can you give me something for the pain?' she said.

'I can,' said Albert.

Bertha Schimmel felt liberated by the news of her impending death. She even felt rejuvenated in a sense. Her communist comrades were all either dead or scattered to the wind. Resistance to Hitler was pretty much non-existent. She yearned to take up the battle herself, or at least do whatever she could. Oh, to man the barricades again! Of course, there were no barricades to be manned. And given her illness, she could barely make her way up and down the stairs.

'Good morning, Herr Schleiffer,' she said one morning.

Heinz had been mopping the floor and hadn't heard her come down the stairs. 'Good heavens, be careful, Frau Schimmel. It's slippery.' He took her shopping cart from her – how had she even managed? He took her by the arm, and walked her gently to the door. 'Do you need me to come with you, Frau Schimmel?'

'Don't be silly, Herr Schleiffer.'

'Well, I'll watch for you when you come back.'

She was about to get on her way, when she had a thought. 'By the way, Herr Schleiffer,' her voice was now more of a whisper, 'have they done a search of Herr Juncker's apartment?'

'They?' said Schleiffer.

'You know,' she said. '*They.*'

There was nobody else in the lobby, but Schleiffer looked in every direction anyway before he spoke. 'Of course they have,' he whispered.

'Well, what did they find?'

Schleiffer was a bit taken aback; she was not usually this direct. 'I can't say, Frau Schimmel.'

'Can't say because you don't know, or because you're not allowed?'

'Of course I *know*, Frau Schimmel, but it's official business.'

'I was just wondering whether they found anything that indicated to you what crimes he is supposed to have committed. Whether anything they found put your own doubts to rest.'

Schleiffer hadn't thought of it that way. 'They took some papers, that's all. Police records, I think.'

'Well, Herr Schleiffer, if you have cause to be in his apartment again, could you do me a favor? There's a little green vase in there he borrowed from me. Would you please get it for me?'

As guardian of the building, Heinz had a key for every apartment. And he had been tempted more than once to explore Karl Juncker's apartment. But he hadn't had any 'legitimate' reason to do so until now. A few days later he brought her the vase.

'No, no, Herr Schleiffer, that's not mine. That's the wrong vase. Let me show you.' Two minutes later they were both inside the apartment. 'Where is that darn thing?' she said. Before he could stop her, she was opening and closing drawers and cupboards. 'Ah, here it is,' she said finally, holding up a small vase triumphantly. 'It's more blue than green, isn't it? It just shows how mistaken you can be, even about something you think you know. My mother gave this to me. What have you found there, Herr Schleiffer?'

Heinz had been looking around too and had just pulled an intriguing small brass box from the top desk drawer. He opened it. It was full of medals in all colors and sizes, including an iron cross. Heinz leafed through the folder of citations that was in the same drawer: citations for valor in the war, for excellent police work, for outstanding service, citation after citation after citation.

'My goodness,' said Frau Schimmel. 'That's a surprise, isn't it? Who could have known?'

Heinz found he was unable to answer.

The Second and Third Interrogations

The striped clothes that had been too small when he had first arrived in Dachau were tattered and threadbare now, and much too large. After being beaten, Willi had been allowed one day in the infirmary to recover enough to be returned to his barracks and put back to work. He didn't know how long he had been in Dachau. Trying to keep track of time was a fool's errand. He thought it was probably now late February, early March of 1938. Some kept track, but he didn't.

Quite a few faces were gone from his room and new faces had arrived to take their place. The new prisoners brought news. Mobilization for war was in full swing. Hitler planned to invade to the east – Czechoslovakia, Poland, Russia. Hitler said Germans needed *Lebensraum*, living space, room to expand. That's what people were saying anyway.

One morning Willi was marched, again by Neudeck, to an interrogation room more or less identical to the one where he had been beaten senseless. This time Neudeck was told to stay. He stood against the wall next to another kapo. A different SS interrogator, also a Hauptsturmführer, was seated at the table. He had his hat on, cocked at a rakish angle. Not a good sign, Willi thought. A file folder lay open in front of him. He looked at Willi for a long time.

'You don't recognize me, do you, Geismeier?' He paused. Willi thought the voice sounded familiar. 'From the precinct,' said the Hauptsturmführer. Another pause. 'Ah, well,' he said, sounding a little disappointed.

The interrogation did not go well. The Hauptsturmführer asked Willi again about various conspiracies within the police department against the government. Who besides Willi had wanted to overthrow the Third Reich? Who besides Willi had sabotaged Otto Bruck and brought about his death? He asked about Frau Schimmel. He asked about Lola, about various other people of Willi's acquaintance. Willi knew nothing about most of what the captain asked, but in every case, whether he knew anything or not, he remained silent.

Once the Hauptsturmführer stood up, Willi saw that he was a gigantic man, two meters in height easily and a muscular hundred kilos. He took off his hat. His head was shaved. Now Willi recognized him. He came around the table and stood in front of Willi. He put on his gloves, as though hitting Willi might damage his enormous hands. He slapped Willi's face hard. 'Why, Geismeier?' he shouted. 'Why make things harder for yourself? And for me?' Willi tasted blood. The man slapped him again, then turned away in disgust.

This time Willi was not whipped. Instead he was taken to a cell in the so-called Bunker where he was to be held in total darkness with only a tin of water and almost no food for an indeterminate length of time. The cell was small and filthy and pitch dark. Despite a small ventilator in the door, the air was thick and foul. There was no bed and no bedding. A slop bucket in the corner was the only furniture.

After sitting against the wall or standing for the better part of his first day, Willi started walking around the periphery of the cell, his right hand on the wall to guide him. He had to be careful not to stumble over the slop bucket. The wall was mostly smooth stone; the floor was uneven, damp and slippery. There was a sharp metal burr on one edge of the door he had to be careful of. He had to walk slowly so he didn't get dizzy. He counted his steps. One circuit took ten steps, so he counted each time he passed the door. Ten times was a hundred steps, a hundred times was a thousand. Every thousand steps he reversed direction.

Deprived of liberty, food, and now even light, Shakespeare came to mind. 'I must become a borrower of the night for an hour or twain,' he said to himself. Willi began to recite as he marched around the cell. Of course, even having read the plays many times, Willi didn't know them by heart. But he knew some bits – openings, soliloquies – and was familiar enough with the rest to assemble the characters and arrange the scenes into a facsimile of the original.

So he set about writing the plays in his mind, reimagining them. He constructed dialogue, using the language he remembered, and improvising the rest out of the darkness in which he found himself, constructing a sort of amalgam of punishment and poetry. His steps around and around became the meter of his verse. Sometimes he spoke the words and sometimes he thought them. He wasn't sure when he was doing one thing or the other. It seemed natural, to him at least, that he should begin with *A Midsummer Night's Dream*.

'Now, fair Hippolyta,' he whispered, 'our nuptial hour draws on apace; four happy days bring in another moon. But I think how slow the old moon wanes. She draws out my desires.

'Four days will soon become four nights and dream away the time. Why not seven indeed, since we are seven nights here? And the moon, unseen but yet there somewhere, shall see the nights of our solemnities.

'Go Philostrate, stir up the Athenian youth to merriments, wake up the nimble spirit of mirth, send melancholy, dark melancholy, this my melancholy, send it to funerals. It is not fit for our inner light. Hippolyta, I woo'd thee with my pacing, remember? And I won thy love marching in circles, but I will wed thee differently, elsewhere and at a later time with triumphant reveling.'

And so it went on.

There were periods where he could not remember what came next, and he paused in his reciting to sort it out. But it mattered less and less, because as the play unfolded, it got further and further from Shakespeare's version and closer and closer to his own. It took him many hours to finish his *Midsummer Night's Dream*. He collapsed on the floor, not knowing whether it was night or day. He wept as he fell into a terrible sleep.

He took on *Macbeth* next, then *Hamlet*, then *The Tempest*, each one seeming more appropriate to the moment than the last. Once – he didn't know whether it was night or day, or how long he had been there – his madness was interrupted by the small trapdoor at the bottom of the entry door opening and spilling light into the cell. 'Geismeier!' someone whispered. 'Geismeier!'

'Yes,' Willi said. It was more a croak than a voice.

'Here,' said the voice at the door, and two hands reached in with a tin of hot soup – real soup with vegetables and even bits of meat, and a large hunk of bread.

'Thank you,' said Willi, taking the food.

'We're not dogs, Geismeier!' said the other voice. It was Neudeck, the kapo. 'You and me, Geismeier. We're not animals!'

One day – it could have been a week or a month as far as Willi knew – the door opened. Willi was blinded by the light. He was taken by the arms – despite all the pacing, he was unsteady on his feet. He was taken to a shower room and told to wash himself, but the water was cold and there was no soap. He rinsed the feces and urine from his legs and feet, the filth from his hands and face as best he could. He was given no other clothes, so he put his filthy clothes back on.

Willi was marched to the interrogation room and the gigantic Hauptsturmführer was there again, his hat cocked at the same rakish angle, as though he had been waiting the entire time. Muddled Shakespeare tumbled through Willi's mind. 'The hour's now come; the very minute bids thee ope thine ear; obey and be attentive.' He almost spoke the words, but recognized his own madness and kept silent.

'Let's try again, Geismeier, shall we?' said the captain. He spoke almost gently, reacting to Willi's physical state. Willi looked a wreck. His eyes were wild, his beard had grown, his hair had started falling out. And despite the shower, he stank. The two kapos moved to the corners of the room to be as far from Willi as they could get. The captain held a white handkerchief in front of his nose and mouth, a gesture that was both dainty and ridiculous. Nevertheless, now that he considered Geismeier's state, he was satisfied with the results of the punishment and obviously with himself.

'So, Geismeier, are you finally ready to talk?'

To the captain's surprise, Willi said, 'Yes, I am.'

'Well, Geismeier, now you're behaving in a reasonable manner.' He moved the handkerchief from his face, as though Willi's reasonableness might make him stink less. But it didn't, so he covered his nose and mouth again.

'So, Geismeier, do you remember that you impersonated a detective?'

'I do,' said Willi.

'You do what?' said the captain, just to make sure he was talking to a rational man.

'I remember impersonating a detective.'

The captain was astonished and relieved that the admission had come so easily. He hated doing interrogations at Dachau. 'And do you remember why you decided to impersonate a police detective, which I'm sure you know is a grave offense?'

'I remember that as well,' said Willi. 'I was trying to do what the police had evidently been unable or unwilling to do, and that is to find the serial killer, the man who was killing all those women. He had already killed . . .' Willi had momentarily forgotten how many women had been murdered. 'Is it nine?'

'No, it's even more,' said the Hauptsturmführer. 'It's thirteen.' He knew because he had been paying close attention to this story. The Hauptsturmführer had been raised the only male in a house full of doting sisters and aunts. They had fussed over him like a collective of very attentive nursemaids, granting his every wish, ignoring his follies, and treating him like a prince. And now he lived a similar pampered life in a comfortable villa with his wife and their four daughters who saw to his every need, bringing him his cocoa in the morning and his cigar and brandy at night.

His interrogation of Willi had originally been meant to discover Willi's supposed political activities and criminal connections while he was a policeman. But Willi's interest in the murder of these women now completely diverted his attention. He was by no means sympathetic toward the treacherous former policeman, but he was *very* sympathetic toward Geismeier's professed desire to put this killer out of commission. The Hauptsturmführer was a man who loved women. *All* women.

'But damn it, man, you're no longer a cop,' said the Hauptsturmführer. 'If you had been a proper policeman you might have solved the case by now. But, damn it, Geismeier, you disgraced yourself. You threw away the right to investigate anything. So, tell me: on whose authority were you impersonating a police detective and investigating this crime? That's what I want to know.'

It was a rhetorical question, so the Hauptsturmführer was surprised when he got an answer. 'Grosz,' said Willi. 'Friedrich Grosz.'

'Friedrich Grosz?! Friedrich Grosz is the authority?' said the Hauptsturmführer, sounding confused and indignant at the same time. 'Who the hell is Friedrich Grosz?'

'Friedrich Grosz is the killer, Hauptsturmführer Altdorfer.' Willi had finally remembered the captain's name.

Altdorfer realized that all he knew about the murders of the thirteen women was what he had read in the paper. And Geismeier seemed to know more. And Willi was correct: the police were still no closer to solving the case than they had been when he had been arrested. And the Hauptsturmführer found himself wondering for the first time why they hadn't caught the killer. Was this beast really that cunning that he could evade the Reich's entire security apparatus? He had been murdering women for years; they certainly ought to have caught him by now.

In fact, they probably would have solved the case if they had just followed the evidence. But they were completely distracted by other things – departmental politics for one – and Willi's impersonation of a detective for another. That was politically safer to investigate than a murder that might involve one of their own, or worse, someone above them. And so, their investigation had veered off in the relatively harmless direction of Willi's criminality. Some of the departmental higher-ups – superiors Willi had bedeviled when he was still a detective – believed, or pretended to believe, that his playing detective might be part of a plot against their departmental regime. Or maybe he had played detective just to show them up. Altdorfer had heard that argument and had thought it might be true.

'Who is this Friedrich Grosz, Geismeier?' he asked.

'He is the murderer of those women, Hauptsturmführer, and an officer in the Gestapo.'

Altdorfer jumped to his feet and left the room without another word. That allegation crossed the line. It just couldn't be. The Gestapo would have rooted out and punished such a heinous malefactor long ago. The Führer wouldn't stand for such a monster in his regime. And yet, the thought stayed in Hauptsturmführer Altdorfer's mind and wouldn't let go.

Kristallnacht

The clouds were low; it felt like snow. Heinz had a letter from Tomas. He took it up to show Frau Schimmel. He made a pot of tea and brought it to her along with the letter. He helped her sit up in bed and plumped the pillow behind her head. 'Drink this, Bertha,' he said. 'It'll warm you up.' They had finally, after years of knowing each other, begun using first names.

'Nothing warms me up any more,' she said. 'Other than your company.'

'Drink it anyway,' he said.

She did as she was told, taking small careful sips. Her hand trembled and the cup rattled on the saucer as she set it down. 'This was my mother's china,' she said. 'Limoges. I never cared much for it, you know. But I always kept it. And now I'm glad I did. It seems important somehow.'

He gave her the letter. The paper fluttered in her hand as she read it. 'Tomas sounds well,' she said.

They sat silently for a while. The only sound was the radiator banging and the ticking of the clock on the dresser. 'I need to bleed the radiators some day soon,' said Heinz.

'There's no rush, Heinz.'

'Still,' said Heinz, but had nothing to add. The clock ticked.

'You said you had something to tell me, Heinz.'

'Yes. Maybe. I don't know, Bertha. I don't want to alarm you.'

'What is it?'

'Well. It's probably nothing really, probably routine. And nothing for you to worry about. But two SS men stopped at my apartment yesterday. They asked for a list of residents, which I gave them. I heard they did the same thing in other buildings on the street.'

'Don't the police already have the names on our residency permits?'

'Yes. That's why it's odd.'

'Well, did they ask for anything else?' said Frau Schimmel.

'Yes, Bertha, they did. They asked about several residents in particular. Gruenhaus on the third floor, Penemann on four, and you. They asked about you.'

'Did they? And what did they want to know?'

'They wanted to know if you were a Jew.'

'Did they? And what did you tell them?'

'I told them no! I said, of course not.'

'But I *am*, Heinz. I *am* a Jew.'

'What?'

'I'm a Jew, Heinz.'

Heinz felt dizzy, he swayed on his feet. He went pale. He couldn't speak. He could hardly breathe. He sat down heavily on the chair by her bed. Betrayal, confusion, and anger flitted across his face and back again. 'But . . .' he said. 'Why . . .?'

Because he was a storm trooper, Heinz had learned that morning about a planned 'action' in two nights. A seventeen-year-old Jew named Herschel Grynszpan had shot and killed the third secretary in the German embassy in Paris. The Nazis had deported Herschel's father to Poland, and Herschel, mad with grief, had gone to the embassy to kill the ambassador. Ernst Von Rath, the third secretary, came out to see what he wanted, and Grynszpan shot him.

For Hitler, the assassination of a German official by a Jew offered an opportunity to solidify German hatred of the Jews and to advance his Final Solution. It didn't matter that Von Rath was under suspicion and surveillance by the Gestapo. Any martyred Aryan would serve the Führer's purpose.

Storm troopers were instructed to 'spontaneously' attack Jewish-owned shops, synagogues, and homes in the early morning hours. And as many Jews as possible were to be rounded up and sent to concentration camps. This hadn't mattered to Heinz when he thought he didn't know or care about any Jews. But everything had changed with Bertha's announcement. 'Damn her! he said as he stormed around his apartment. 'Let her rot in hell!'

Heinz, who normally slept well, couldn't sleep at all that night. He thought of how Frau Schimmel had lied to him, betrayed him. It was just like a Jew to do such a thing, wasn't it? To lie and cheat and manipulate. She had taken advantage of him, used him for her own purposes.

Except, when he tried to think of ways she had taken advantage of him, all he could come up with was that he had hauled her groceries up the stairs in exchange for her wonderful strudel and her sound advice. When he tried to remember what her selfish and devious purposes might have been, the only ones he could come up with were friendship and survival. To make matters worse, when he tried to conjure sinister images in his mind of Bertha Schimmel as a devious old Jew, instead he saw her kindly face next to that of Tante Jolesch, his beloved neighbor from long ago.

At around two o'clock on the morning of November 10, 1938, a half dozen storm troopers banged on the front door of Tullemannstraße 54. When they saw Heinz come out of his apartment wearing his uniform, they yelled, 'Open up, *Kamerad*!' and '*Juden heraus!*' Out with the Jews!

Heinz unlocked the door. He recognized a couple of them, including Jürgen from the Three Crowns. They smelled of alcohol. Heinz had stopped going to the Three Crowns, so he rarely saw Jürgen any more.

They swarmed up the stairs to Frau Schimmel's door and started pounding and yelling. Heinz ran to unlock the door before they broke it down. They rushed shouting into the apartment. But Frau Schimmel was gone.

'Where is she, Schleiffer?' said Jürgen.

'Damn! I don't know,' said Heinz. 'The old Jew bitch was here yesterday.'

They ran around in the apartment, bumping into each other and cursing. Some of them pocketed knickknacks or whatever else took their fancy. There was no money or jewelry. One of them, finding nothing he wanted, turned over the dresser and broke some pictures instead.

Hearing the sound of other men yelling out on the street, Jürgen said, 'Let's go, men. We've got more work to do.' They rushed down the stairs and out the door to rejoin the mob sweeping from building to building.

Heinz followed them downstairs. He locked the front door. He watched through the front window. But all he could see in the darkness was the flickering light from flames somewhere down the street. Heinz set the brass umbrella stand upright again.

He went back up to Frau Schimmel's apartment. It was a mess. He lifted the dresser up, replaced the drawers, and maneuvered it back into place. He put the clock back on the dresser. Its face was broken but it was still ticking. A lamp had been knocked over and broken, so he stood that back up and swept up the glass shards.

He swept up the glass from the broken picture frames too, and hung the pictures back up as best he could. The light from a fire in the street danced on the ceiling. He closed the curtains so he wouldn't have to look at it.

When he was finished, he went back down to his apartment. The curtains were closed and only a small night light was burning, so he couldn't tell whether Bertha was awake or not. He tiptoed to his bed where she lay. 'How was it, Heinz?' she said.

'They made a mess, Bertha. I'm sorry. They broke some things and they stole some things.'

'And you?' she said. 'Are you all right?'

'Yes,' said Heinz, 'I'm all right.' But he wasn't. He didn't think he would ever be all right again.

Bertha Schimmel – this was not her real name – stayed with Heinz Schleiffer for a week to be sure the pogrom was over. Then he moved her back upstairs. She lived for another month, growing weaker all the time, but also somehow more radiant. Her skin was pale and paper like, her eyes were huge and dark. And her hair was thin. He brushed it for her, which frightened him the first time he did it.

When he found her the morning after she died, her eyes were closed. She looked just like she was sleeping. She had gotten her wish, to die a natural death in her own bed. Heinz knew who her doctor was and tried to contact him. But the doctor was gone, arrested along with thousands of others all over Germany and Austria.

Heinz reported to the authorities that Bertha Schimmel, age 84, had died. She had no next of kin that he knew of. Of course, he didn't even know her real name. So it was up to him to deal with her remains. She had wanted to be cremated and had given him money to pay for it when the time came.

Heinz took the little urn of ashes and went with Tomas, who was home on leave, to the banks of the Isar. They stood and watched as the little cloud of ashes, changing patterns and slowly sinking, drifted downstream. A pair of mallards came in for a landing just behind the dispersing ashes and drifted along with them. 'The funeral cortege,' said Tomas. He looked over at his father. He was weeping.

Heinz settled Frau Schimmel's affairs as best he could. He cleaned out the apartment and donated the furniture to a national charity.

He kept the Limoges in accordance with her wishes, although he wasn't sure what to do with a set of fine china.

In the top drawer of her dresser he had found letters carefully tied with string in small packets. Some from long ago were addressed to a Clara Dubinski. There was a small bundle of letters from Lola Zeff too. They were postmarked Murnau and would probably have made it easy to find her. In the end he burned all the letters without reading them.

Even though Heinz had come to love the woman he knew as Bertha Schimmel, he had also at the same time managed to remain a devout anti-Semite. He accomplished this by means of an ungainly but effective mental somersault. To his way of thinking, the Jews were absolutely responsible for Germany's woes. But Bertha Schimmel (and Tante Jolesch before her) were the exception. They were decent and loving people.

Such acrobatic exceptions were performed all over Germany, so often in fact that there came to be a word for these exceptional Jews – *Hausjude*. The house Jew was the one that lived in your building, or the Jew of your acquaintance who was different from all the other Jews. He was generous, or their children were well behaved, or she was kind and gave you strudel. In fact, given all these positive attributes, they probably weren't even Jews at all.

By doing another similar mental somersault, Heinz also absolved himself of the crime he had committed by deceiving his fellow storm troopers and protecting the old Jew Bertha Schimmel from deportation or worse. If she was a good person (and therefore probably not even a Jew), then it would have been a grave mistake to allow her to be harmed.

Heinz's mental acrobatics came in handy yet again a few years later, in 1943, when Tomas, having left his leg behind near Stalingrad, came home only to be implicated as a member of the White Rose resistance group. He had been caught distributing leaflets denouncing the persecution and murder of Jews. Tomas had to be innocent, said Heinz (to himself), because he had fought, and been wounded and then been decorated at Stalingrad. It had to be a case of mistaken identity or betrayal by some defeatist or malevolent person, maybe even a Jew. Tomas was a war hero after all. Sending him to the guillotine would be a terrible mistake. He went to the guillotine nonetheless.

Friedrich Grosz

Despite the dismal weather – ice storms and bitter winds from the east – the clearing of the wetlands beyond the camp of trees and stones continued at a frenzied pace. The Dachau directorate had decided that large numbers of prisoners should be used to prepare this area for farming before spring. The prisoners who cleared the fields would then do the farm labor, if they survived. Now teams of prisoners were cutting down trees, hauling them away, digging up their roots, and pulling stones out of the frozen swampy ground.

One morning two SS guards pulled Willi from a crew as they were being marched out to the work site. He was taken to a small windowless stone building adjoining the *Juhrhaus*, the squat building through which new prisoners arrived. An official car stood by the door. Willi watched his crew disappear though the gate carrying saws and shovels, preceded by kapos, and surrounded by SS guards armed with clubs and machine guns.

Inside the building, which had once been an ammunition storage room, Obersturmbannführer Reinhard Pabst was waiting. He wore the black SS uniform and a heavy black overcoat. It was as cold inside the building as it was outside, and his breath turned to steam as it came from his nose and mouth. He had a pistol strapped on his hip.

The Obersturmbannführer was pacing back and forth. As Willi came in, he stopped pacing and peered at Willi, trying to affect a relaxed stance, his hands clasped behind his back. Willi could see that this man was ill at ease. His body was tense and his breath came in short bursts of steam. Willi had never seen Reinhard Pabst or Friedrich Grosz before, so he wasn't sure who this man was, although he had his suspicions. Willi stood at attention, waiting for whatever was next.

Since his first Gestapo posting only four years earlier at Humboldt University in Berlin, Reinhard had uncovered one plot after another with skill and cunning. He had brought dozens of traitors to ruin. Dominating these wretched human beings and destroying their lives had become his passion. He believed he had made it into a science. He could not be defeated. Reinhard had taught classes on interrogation and entrapment techniques in Berlin, and had eventually been sent to Munich to teach the Gestapo there as well. Just over thirty years old and already a lieutenant colonel, he was, by all accounts, headed for stardom.

Reinhard had convinced himself, and so explained to his students, that every interrogation should be seen as a life and death struggle between himself and the subject, ignoring, of course, the fact that his victim was essentially helpless and at his mercy. 'The person you are interrogating is your enemy,' Reinhard would say. 'If he is strong, he will try to resist you. For he understands implicitly that resistance is his only hope. And so your objective is to destroy his resistance, and thus to destroy his hope.

'Without hope, he is nothing. And by hope I do not mean merely his hope for survival. I mean his entire hopeful system of beliefs, the foundation of his existence – Christianity, communism, humanism, whatever it might be. If he is a Christian, you must destroy his belief in Jesus Christ; if he is a communist, you must destroy his belief in communism; if he is a humanist, you must destroy his belief in humanity. Whatever his belief system might be, it must be systematically dismembered and undermined until he sees it lying in ruin at his feet. Once you do that, you have thoroughly destroyed all hope. And once you have thoroughly destroyed hope, he will have nothing left and will be yours.

'"And how do I do this?" you might ask. Here our Führer is instructive; learn from the Führer. Fear. Fear is your most useful tool.' When Reinhard said this, he usually got a nervous laugh from his audience. At that moment they recognized the part fear played in their own lives, and how the solution, the means to ending that fear, came about when they began inflicting fear in others. 'Fear is one lever by which you can make someone doubt his own perceptions and beliefs, deny and turn against what he has taken to be true up until now.

'As human beings, we are all driven by self-interest. I learned in the course of my theological studies – yes, I was once a theologian – that even Jesus was driven by self-interest. He had a compelling need to appear virtuous. Not to *be* virtuous, but to *exhibit* virtue, to appear virtuous to others. His grandiosity – proclaiming himself the son of God – sprang from his own weakness, his need to feel superior, and that need is nothing more than a need to gain power. Humanity, charity, generosity, these are various forms of the same weakness, and they run contrary to who we actually are.

'We men are power-seeking creatures. Rob a man of his power, make what was once his power yours, and he will tell you whatever you want to know, and do whatever you want him to do.'

Reinhard Pabst believed that the Gestapo and the SS had finally given him his manhood, after humanism and Christianity had sought to emasculate him, to turn him into a eunuch, or worse yet, a woman. Humanism and Christianity were feminine ways of being: insidious, seductive, devious. And if they were not vanquished, they were then mortally dangerous.

The Gestapo gave him the power to invoke fear in others and thus gave him absolute power over them and the liberty to do with them whatever he pleased. He believed that, thanks to the Führer, he had freed himself from all the destructive – that is, feminine – strictures society and religion had imposed upon him.

Reinhard could tell as soon as he saw Willi that this former police detective was resolute, despite his weakened physical state. He meant to find out just how resolute he was, and, by means of his own superior interrogatory skills, to dismember the prisoner's last remaining resolution, expose his hope as illusory, and then exterminate him. First though, he needed to find out how much the prisoner actually knew about Friedrich Grosz.

Reinhard saw that Willi was alert and watchful. In fact, he seemed almost relaxed, seemingly indifferent to his own fate. *We shall see about that*, thought Reinhard. He knew that every man nursed hope somewhere inside himself, and Willi would be no different in that regard. And every man also had fear as a constant companion.

Reinhard was right about that. Willi had hope. And he had plenty of fear too. He had faced his own fear again and again over the many months he had been in Dachau. He was fearful even now as Reinhard Pabst sized him up, afraid of the pain that might come, afraid he might be killed. But Willi had also learned that fear was about the future, about what lay ahead. And the here and now demanded his full attention. So he had learned over these months to lay his fear aside, as one might take off a hat and lay it aside.

Willi reminded himself that he had actually wanted this meeting to come about. This was where Willi's personal madness – his obsession with seeing justice done – had come into play. Here he was, a prisoner in Dachau, and yet he had imagined that he could somehow manipulate circumstances and make a serial murderer come to him. And now he had actually done it. After naming Friedrich Grosz as the murderer of many women during his earlier interrogation, he had guessed that word would get back to Grosz himself, and that Grosz might be strongly tempted to show himself.

Why not? The Gestapo was a relatively small and tight-knit organization. Willi's accusation would make Grosz nervous and fearful. After all, this prisoner Geismeier's allegation was a serious threat to his existence. Reinhard had to confront and deal with this threat once and for all. And now, if Willi's hunch was right, Reinhard was here to kill him.

Reinhard sensed something dangerous about this man Geismeier despite his ragged and emaciated being. He looked Willi up and down, walked around him, keeping his distance, as though Willi were a wild animal. Once he was satisfied that he had taken Willi's measure, he stopped in front of him and smiled. It was not a smile so much as an imitation of a smile, a facial grimace meant to convey confidence but conveying instead uncertainty.

When Reinhard anticipated a formidable foe – and he believed from what he knew about Willi that he would be formidable – he chose to interrogate them alone, one on one, with no one else present. He liked to imagine the two men would engage in a contest of wills. He wore his pistol, knowing it would be a distraction, that his opponent would focus on it, both as a threat and a temptation. And he was right – Willi was thinking about the pistol.

'Geismeier,' said Reinhard. It was more a statement of fact than a greeting.

Willi did not reply.

'You were once a student of Shakespeare, I understand,' said Reinhard.

Willi did not answer, but raised his eyebrows slightly.

Reinhard was pleased. 'Don't be surprised,' he said. 'I probably know as much about you as you know about yourself.' He offered Willi some biographical facts to prove his point – he knew about Willi's parents, about the Geismeier ceramic pipe business, about Willi's university studies, his year in England, even titles from the small library Willi had kept at Tullemannstraße when he had lived there as Karl Juncker. 'All your books had protective dust jackets. They're even in alphabetical order,' said Reinhard. 'You are an orderly man. I like that.'

Reinhard mentioned Lola. He knew about her job at the Mahogany Room. 'Pretty woman,' he said. 'Cute little apartment too.' Threats did not need to be explicit. He kept the tone light, conversational. Reinhard always told his students that congeniality could break some men who were impervious to torture.

Reinhard Pabst had succumbed to the myth of his office. He was convinced of his mastery of all people and all things. His destruction of his opponents over and over again had convinced him of that. He took the black uniform and his high rank to be irrefutable proof. That he had every advantage and his opponents had none did nothing to dissuade him. His advantages sprang, he believed, from his innate superiority.

'You see, Geismeier,' he said, 'like you, I am a student of human nature. I have read Shakespeare too, although, I confess, not as thoroughly as you. As a matter of fact, I saw through his little act quite quickly. You apparently haven't. I assure you: he is essentially boring. Good maybe at the poetry end of things, but wanting when it comes to understanding what really drives humankind, what truly motivates us. The comedies are silly, the tragedies contrived. Have you read any of the great modern thinkers?'

Willi did not answer.

Reinhard named a few of his favorites.

Willi did not answer.

'I thought not. It's no wonder then that you are on the wrong side of things, the wrong side of history. It's because you are an intellectual coward. You haven't thought things through, because you are afraid of where that might take you. You are afraid of the truth.'

Willi did not answer.

'Understand this, Geismeier. I am not here merely to abuse and humiliate you. I am, like you, an investigator. I am always interested in getting at the truth.'

Willi did not answer.

'Of course, I have ways of getting at the truth that are not available to you.' He plucked at a splintered fingernail, distracted for a moment. 'I have ways that were never available to you really. Do you know why? Because you were, how shall I say?' He steepled his fingers in front of him. 'You were an insincere investigator. Do you understand what I mean by that?'

Willi did not answer.

'I will explain it to you. When you were in pursuit of something or someone, you chose not to avail yourself of all the available investigative tools.' Reinhard raised his right hand to stroke his chin in what he took to be a thoughtful gesture. The cuff of his coat slid away and revealed the still raw scar on his hand and around his wrist. Reinhard was surprised and pleased when Willi spoke.

'What truth?' said Willi. His voice came out as a hoarse whisper.

'Would you like some water?' said Reinhard. 'Help yourself, Geismeier. There, on the table.' There was a crystal pitcher with two glasses. It was as though they were having a colloquy in the university faculty club. 'Go ahead, Geismeier.'

Willi did not move.

'Suit yourself, then,' said Reinhard. 'It is there if you want it.' Reinhard took a drink of water himself. 'I'm interested in the truth that lies above the smaller truths,' he said, 'the truth that guides nature and all being.'

'You mean the truth of chaos and power, force and violence,' said Willi.

'Bravo!' said Reinhard, and clapped his hands in delight.

Willi said nothing.

'Sit down, Geismeier,' said Reinhard, and pushed a wooden chair in Willi's direction with his boot. Willi recognized in Reinhard something he had seen in other criminals: a pathological absence of character, a hollowness. And he could see that Reinhard was only marginally aware of this absence. He was pretending to be human, looking for the part of himself that he understood to be missing. There was narcissism and sadism, to be sure, but they appeared to Willi to be masking a deep fear that Reinhard was only, again marginally, aware of. A fear of what? Of some troublesome moment at the core of his experience? Of being found out, perhaps?

Reinhard was a psychopath. And Willi was sure now that Reinhard was Friedrich Grosz, the particular psychopath he was looking for. Willi sat down and poured himself a glass of water. Reinhard watched him drink.

'So, explain the virtues of violence and force,' said Willi.

Reinhard was pleased. 'Violence and force are the true currency of power,' he said. He was giving Willi his favorite lecture.

'Everything else – Christian love, charity, generosity, justice, dignity, democracy, humanity, these things are all nonsense. They are counterfeit. They have no purchasing power; they buy you nothing.'

'Maybe they seemed counterfeit when you tried them out,' said Willi. 'You did try them out, didn't you? Others have had a different experience from yours. Others have found redemption in love.'

Reinhard was a bit taken aback, but then he recovered and snorted. 'Redemption! Hah!'

'And the end of fear,' said Willi.

'That is utter nonsense, Geismeier, and you know it. Here you sit, pathetic, filthy, destroyed, virtually destroyed, buoyed perhaps by some vague irrational hope. But there is no hope for you, Geismeier. That is what you need to understand.'

'And I suppose you're going to explain it to me,' said Willi.

Reinhard's face darkened. He stood up and walked around the table to where Willi sat. 'Are you being insolent, Geismeier, you pathetic worm?'

'I wonder, Herr Obersturmbannführer, how you can think of yourself as being all powerful, and yet be so threatened by a pathetic worm's insolence.'

Reinhard hit Willi hard enough to knock him off the chair and onto the floor. He took the pistol from his holster and pressed it into Willi's face. 'You're playing a dangerous game, Geismeier. Get up.'

Willi got up.

'Pick up that chair.' Willi did as he was told. 'I could kill you now, Geismeier, and the kapos would come in and throw your miserable body in a ditch, and no one would ever know what had become of you.'

Willi did not speak. The left side of his face throbbed. He could feel it swelling. He tasted blood. But he was convinced that Reinhard Pabst would not kill him, *could* not kill him, at least not until he felt he had won their argument, whatever that argument turned out to be. Willi also thought, as foolish, even mad, as it might seem, that he, Willi, was from this moment forward in control of their argument, and that only he knew where it was going.

'Sit down, Geismeier. I'm not finished with you yet.'

Willi sat down.

'The last time you were interrogated, Geismeier' – Reinhard's voice was calm; it was as though the violent moment had not happened – 'you spoke of someone named Friedrich Grosz as a murderer of women. Do you persist in that accusation?'

'I know it to be true,' said Willi.

'And how do you know it to be true?'

'Because,' said Willi, 'I interviewed his one surviving victim. I visited the scenes of his crimes, I interviewed the doctor and the nurse who stitched up his wound and the pharmacy where he got the drugs to dampen his fear and uncertainty.'

Reinhard tried to smile again, but his mouth couldn't quite manage it. 'Why are you so interested in these whores who were killed, Geismeier? What are they to you?'

'They were not . . .'

Reinhard was becoming agitated. 'Did you know them, *any* of them? Was one of them your sister or your lover or your mother?' He laughed at his joke.

'They interest me because they were human beings, and were the victims of a criminal assault by a psychopath, a human being devoid of humanity.'

'A psychopath?' said Reinhard. 'And you know about his psycho-pathy how, Geismeier, pray tell?'

'Because you can see his suffering in the crime itself, the slashing with the knife over and over and over, first one hand and then the other. He picks women because they are weak. And yet he is afraid of them. He is weaker than they are. He thinks they have some power over him. He is the one who is weak.'

'Not so,' said Reinhard. 'He picks the women . . . I believe he picks the women because they are whores. All women are whores, Geismeier. Don't you know that yet? Your girlfriend Lola in her green dress' – Reinhard made an hourglass movement with both hands down the length of his own body – 'isn't that what got you into the situation in which you find yourself? If you weren't mixed up with her, you might have paid better attention and not gotten caught. The world was made by men for men, and it has been corrupted and eroded by women. If someone eliminates a few of these whore-demons, then what is that to you?'

'I was once a detective,' said Willi. 'I investigated crimes. It is a hard habit to break.'

Reinhard laughed. 'It is a habit you have had no choice but to break, Geismeier. Look around you. Look at where you are.'

'These women were human beings. To me their killer is evil.

Even in my current circumstances it remains my business to pursue evil.'

'What colossal grandiosity! Look at yourself! What makes a worm like you the arbiter of good and evil? How do you know this murderer, as you call him, isn't someone simply doing the world a service?'

Willi looked at Reinhard, at the water pitcher, at the room, before he spoke again. He reached for the water pitcher and poured himself another glass of water.

'Have you ever dared to kill a man, Herr Grosz? Or do you only kill women? You are a coward, a psychopath, Friedrich Grosz. Peel off that uniform and you are a scared little boy. You are pathetic and ridiculous and inadequate. I think at some level you know that to be true.' Willi had spoken in a calm, almost indifferent tone, like he was saying, 'The sun is setting,' or 'Look at that dog.'

Reinhard sat motionless, his mouth half open in astonishment. He began breathing heavily through his mouth, sending rapid puffs of steam into the frigid air. He pressed his hand to his chest, revealing the scar again.

'You are unmasked, Herr Grosz,' said Willi. 'A killer and a fraud. You have no power. None. I'm not the only one who knows of your crime, either. There are police officers who know. The Gestapo knows. And I think you understand that even this evil regime won't tolerate someone like you. Why, look how your Führer reveres women, wants them to have lots of babies for the Reich. Can you imagine—?'

Willi was astonished that Reinhard had allowed him to go on this long. But now, finally, Reinhard leapt from his chair and came for Willi. Before he could even reach his pistol, Willi had smashed the crystal pitcher against his head and pulled the pistol from its holster. Reinhard fell across the table. His jaw was broken; he was bleeding from cuts up and down his face.

Willi cocked the pistol and held it against Reinhard's temple. 'Take off your clothes,' said Willi. Willi had expected he might die in Dachau, might even die today in this room. But now he was imagining another possibility. He was alone with an SS colonel. The colonel's car was right outside the door, seconds from Dachau's entry gate.

'Take off your clothes,' Willi said again.

'Are you crazy?' Suddenly Reinhard couldn't remember Willi's

name. 'What are you doing? What are you going to do? You can't
. . . Geismeier.' There was the name; finding it seemed very important. Reinhard had not known helplessness for a very long time. He
was out of practice, but it all came rushing back and now he saw
helplessness all around him. He was drowning in it.

'If you don't take off your clothes by the time I count three,'
said Willi, 'I will shoot you. And don't imagine anyone will hear.
Look at those walls; no one will hear a thing.' Willi hoped this was
true – the stone walls were half a meter thick.

Reinhard seemed paralyzed.

'One . . . two . . . three,' Willi counted. Reinhard still did not
move. The explosion of the Luger being fired made both their ears
ring. Reinhard screamed and stared at his shattered hand. Tears
welled in his eyes and he started sobbing.

'I said take off your clothes,' said Willi. Reinhard hurried to do
as he was told, but having one hand out of commission slowed him
down.

Escape

Most successful escapes from Dachau, and they were few
and far between, were opportunistic, where a prisoner or
prisoners suddenly saw an opening and took it. That was
the situation Willi found himself in now as he stepped from the
building. He had committed. His decision to escape was irreversible
– either he would succeed, or he would be killed.

Willi was taller than Reinhard, and thinner, and the uniform was
a bad fit. But he was only six steps from the car, so it didn't matter.
Reinhard Pabst had sobbed and lain still as a baby while Willi tied
his hands behind his back and to his feet using Willi's prison clothes
twisted into makeshift ropes. Reinhard's disgrace was sudden and
total.

It was raining lightly, a cold rain. Willi pulled the hat brim low
over his eyes. A work party of twelve or so was marching past with
two kapos – one of them Neudeck – in charge. They were singing
as they marched.

Neudeck's eyes widened slightly as he recognized Willi. 'Good luck,' he whispered as he passed. He saluted and Willi returned his salute. The guards in the tower above were watching. Willi gave them a long stare and they looked away.

Willi started the car easily, put it in gear, and drove to the gate. At that moment another work party was about to march through. The guards had already swung the gate open. But now they held up the work party, and waved Willi through. They snapped to attention and saluted. He turned left through some SS barracks, then right on Friedenstraße. Peace Street. And just like that, he was out.

Later that evening the Bergemanns' phone rang. 'It's for you,' said Sofia.

'Who is it?' said Bergemann.

'He wouldn't say.'

Bergemann picked up the receiver. 'Yes?' he said.

'Come downstairs and walk south,' said a voice.

'Who is this?'

'Come downstairs, Hans, and walk south.' The line went dead.

'Who was it?' asked Sofia.

The voice was familiar, yet unfamiliar. Then he realized why and jumped up. 'I'm going out,' he said.

'Where?' she said.

'Willi,' he said. Before she could ask, he was out the door. She understood it might be a while before he came back.

Bergemann's heart was pounding as he hurried along the street. He had heard rumors more than once that Willi Geismeier was dead. Gruber had said so a while back. They were at lunch, and Gruber had raised a glass to celebrate. He had probably just been trying to goad Hans; Gruber always seemed suspicious of him, although he never came right out and said it. Even though Bergemann didn't believe the rumors, he had feared that Willi might die in Dachau.

'Keep walking,' said a voice, and there was Willi beside him, wraith thin and haggard, but it was Willi for sure. Bergemann couldn't help putting his arm around Willi's shoulder and hugging him to him. He could feel his ribs and thin arms through his coat.

'Me too,' said Willi, and he smiled. 'Can we sit somewhere?' he said.

'My sister lives nearby,' said Bergemann.

'Monika?' said Willi.

'That one,' said Bergemann.

It was another ten minutes to Monika Bergemann's, and they walked in silence.

There were five Bergemann siblings, two brothers, two sisters and Hans. Monika was the eldest, Hans the youngest. She had never married or had any desire to do so. She had once been in love with a pretty young woman, who had decided after some months that loving a woman was too difficult, and had left to marry a man.

Poetry was Monika's only love now. She wrote constantly, filling notebooks, and publishing occasionally in small journals or in editions of a hundred books. Half of those might sell, if she was lucky. She didn't care about that. Critics said she was a poet's poet, which meant that her poetry was difficult and obscure. It was a good thing too, because if she had been more readily understood by the powers that be, if they had understood her obscure allusions, she would almost certainly have been arrested.

Monika and Willi were both prickly characters. They liked each other well enough, in part because they had a love of books in common and in part because they saw one another so infrequently. She knew from Hans that Willi had been imprisoned in Dachau, and so she embraced him happily when they arrived.

She offered them beer and then announced she was going to bed. Bergemann wanted to hear everything, but Willi was exhausted, so he stuck to the necessities, which were marvelous enough. Willi explained that he had learned for certain that morning that Friedrich Grosz was SS colonel Reinhard Pabst. 'I laid a trap for him,' said Willi. Bergemann had to laugh at the sheer preposterousness of that proposition, and because it was true.

'I hit him with a crystal water pitcher, got his Luger' – Willi patted his side pocket – 'and left him tied up in the interrogation room.'

'You didn't kill him?'

'Not my job,' said Willi.

Lying on the stone floor trussed up like a pig about to be slaughtered, Reinhard sobbed, then raged, then cursed, vowing revenge one moment and despairing the next. His curses echoed off the stone walls and died a silent death in that room. This was a humiliation and a defeat he would not live down.

Still, eventually he wriggled and writhed and worked himself free. He began pounding on the heavy door and shouting. A passing pair of SS guards finally heard his pounding and unbolted the door, and the lieutenant colonel, wearing only his underwear, came lurching out into the rain. His head was bloody, his hand too. 'I am Obersturmbannführer Reinhard Pabst!' he wailed. But, battered and dirty and in his underwear, he looked to the two SS guards like a berserk prisoner. They seized him by the arms.

'You fools – the prisoner has escaped! He shot me!' Reinhard screamed. Reinhard tried to show them his bloody hand, but they held him fast. They started walking him to the Juhrhaus where the duty officer would sort things out.

'My car! He stole my car!' Reinhard tried to shake free.

'Keep walking!' said one of the SS men.

'How dare you!' Reinhard screamed. 'Take your hands off me!' He tried to shake free again, kicked at them, struggled to get his hands free.

The SS men were uncertain about the situation. But they had been trained to respond to uncertainty with brutal resolve. One pulled Reinhard's two arms behind his back while the other began beating Reinhard with his fists. He punched his middle over and over again. Reinhard sagged in pain, but he was held upright and punched again. They maneuvered him in the direction of the Juhrhaus.

Once inside, someone went in search of the duty officer, an SS captain. He came running and quickly determined that Reinhard was who he said he was. The duty officer sounded the alarm that the prisoner Willi Geismeier had escaped. All work details were immediately herded back into camp. The guards and kapos were on edge and there was lots of pushing and hitting.

The prisoners were assembled on the Appelplatz for an emergency roll call. It was not announced that there had been an escape, but everyone had figured it out. And by that evening, they all knew it was Willi Geismeier and how he had done it.

'No one escapes for long. He'll be back.'

'No, he won't,' said Neudeck. He knew Willi. 'He's long gone.' The thought that Willi had succeeded and that he had played a small part in his escape made Neudeck happy. You had to hand it to that son of a bitch Geismeier.

SS Obersturmbannführer Reinhard Pabst had suffered a concussion, a broken jaw, some cuts to the face, and a gunshot wound to the hand, and that was just from the prisoner. Then he had suffered possible kidney damage, and other serious damage to his body from the two SS guards.

Reinhard filed a complaint against the guards that had beaten him up.

'But how were we supposed to know that guy was an SS colonel?' one guard said at his hearing.

'I mean, did you see him?' said the other guard. 'He was wearing prison clothes. He had shit his pants. He was bloody and filthy. He was fighting like crazy. What were we supposed to do?'

The captain conducting the hearing reduced both men in rank. SS Obersturmbannführer Pabst had insisted that they be punished, and that was the lightest punishment the captain could get away with. That's the way it went sometimes. You did what you were supposed to do, and still they punished you.

The Man Who Loved Women

According to the urgent bulletin tacked up on police notice boards all over Germany, the convicted criminal Willi Geismeier had attempted to murder a senior SS officer and had escaped from Dachau. Standartenführer Pabst (Reinhard had just been promoted to full colonel) had extracted a confession from the prisoner for various crimes when the prisoner had seized his weapon and grievously wounded him. The escaped prisoner was now also being sought as a suspect in the serial-killer case. He was considered armed and dangerous. A substantial reward was offered for information leading to his apprehension.

Gruber muttered as he read the notice. 'My God! That son of a bitch Geismeier. How does he do it?'

'No kidding,' said Bergemann.

'I didn't take him for a killer though,' said Gruber. 'Thirteen women? Jesus!' Gruber seemed unconcerned by the fact that Willi had been in Dachau when four of the murders had been committed. The official position was that Willi had done the murders, which meant that Willi had done the murders. Truth was a matter of policy, not a matter of fact. And it followed therefore that Willi would be sought for the serial killing of thirteen women. The police, the Gestapo and the SS were so notified.

After a week in the hospital and eight weeks at home recovering from his injuries, Reinhard Pabst went back to work. His subordinates and coworkers lined the hall and applauded as he arrived on his first day back. 'Thank you for your good wishes,' he said to them. 'Now, let's get back to the serious and important tasks at hand. We have a killer to catch.'

Reinhard's first task, as he saw it, was to take over the serial-killer case again. His deputy, an ambitious young Gestapo man and SS lieutenant, had taken over in his absence and had been a little too conscientious for Reinhard's taste. The deputy had fortunately not discovered the connection between the murders and the streetcar lines. But he had been going around to city hospitals trying to find out exactly what sort of wound the killer had sustained in his attack on Suzanna Merkl, and, having failed to do so, was about to begin questioning at smaller clinics.

Reinhard was eager to steer the investigation toward Willi Geismeier. This might require manufacturing some evidence, but that would be simple enough. He had already found a report filed by a man named Schleiffer, a neighbor of Geismeier's, that Geismeier, living under an assumed name, had left home late on the night of the Suzanna Merkl murder. Then there was also the fact that Geismeier had used a different false identity to impersonate a detective asking questions about the very murders he had himself committed.

In any case, Reinhard wouldn't have to convince a judge or a jury of Willi's guilt. The case was never going to reach a court of law. Geismeier's guilt was less a question of culpability than of utility. He had only to demonstrate that naming Geismeier as the killer would be useful to the Führer and his Reich.

With his recent promotion, Reinhard now reported directly to Heinrich Himmler. So he had only Himmler to persuade of Geismeier's guilt, or rather of the *utility* of Geismeier's being made the scapegoat. Himmler would dutifully report to the Führer that Willi was the killer. Then the full wrath of the Third Reich would come down on him.

Reinhard could not know the extent to which SS Hauptsturmführer Albrecht Altdorfer was a danger to him. After all, Altdorfer was merely a low-level SS thug, of prodigious size perhaps, but also of minimal intelligence. And he had himself punished Willi Geismeier mercilessly. But Altdorfer was also a man who loved women. He was kind and solicitous to his aging aunts, and tender and loving to his wife, to his daughters, to his mistresses, to all women. He never hit them, never even thought of doing so. He believed that women should be stood up on a pedestal, should be worshipped, should be wrapped in lace and veils and great swaths of pink silk, should be cherished for their innocence and innate virtues. He secretly wrote poetry in praise of women, all of it dreadful but at the same time entirely heartfelt.

After he had stormed out of his interrogation with Willi Geismeier those many weeks ago, Altdorfer had brooded for the rest of the day. And it had gotten even worse once he was at home with his women. The unbidden thought of some man savagely stabbing one of them over and over until she was dead kept entering his mind. A vivid dream of a blood-covered stabbing man woke him with a start in the middle of the night. He cried out and sat up in bed.

'Are you all right, Albrecht?' said his wife.

'I'm sorry, *Liebchen*,' he said. 'A bad dream. Go back to sleep.' By morning he had decided he had to search out Friedrich Grosz at least and take his measure.

It was not too difficult for an SS captain to find out that Friedrich Grosz was Reinhard Pabst, and so he made an appointment and called in at Reinhard's office. He was shown in, they exchanged salutes and shook hands. Pabst seemed a perfectly pleasant young man. He had a soft handshake, but then so did a lot of men. He was surprisingly young for an SS lieutenant colonel. Altdorfer was older by ten years and still a captain. He had been passed over for promotion several times and was likely to remain a captain for the rest of his career. Altdorfer didn't mind; he felt like a fortunate man. Rank wasn't everything. He liked his work, and he was as happy at home as any man could ever hope to be.

After some preliminary small talk, he told Reinhard about interrogating Geismeier at Dachau and about Geismeier's accusations. Reinhard was startled; he had never heard of Willi Geismeier, but he wrote down his name. Altdorfer told him what he knew about Willi, that he was a good cop gone bad and had been finally driven from the force for his malfeasance. Geismeier had turned to illegal activities, undermining the regime when he could, going so far as to impersonate a police detective. Altdorfer assured Reinhard that he didn't believe a word of Geismeier's accusations. Willi had long been known for his outrageous accusations and ridiculous charges concocted out of whole cloth. He just thought Reinhard should know.

Reinhard listened with his hands folded in front of him, a half smile on his face. Finally he had laughed and waved it all off as though it were nothing. 'Thank you, Captain, for telling me,' he said. They chatted a little longer about this and that. Altdorfer had asked Reinhard about his family and Reinhard had told Altdorfer he lived alone. Altdorfer had spoken a bit about the joys of family life. Then they said their pleasant goodbyes, and Altdorfer had gone on his way.

Geismeier had to be lying, didn't he? Making the whole story up for some reason? Geismeier was a known liar. And the lieutenant colonel had been very pleasant and relaxed about the whole thing. But that was a bit strange, wasn't it? How could he be so relaxed about such a terrible accusation? Wouldn't you at least be shocked or angry or disgusted to learn that somebody, even a criminal and a liar, had said something like that about you? And now that Altdorfer thought about it, when he had spoken of his own happiness in the bosom of his family, had named his women one by one in glowing terms, the lieutenant colonel's face had turned to stone.

Altdorfer had to be careful. The lieutenant colonel was Gestapo, after all. Still, Altdorfer decided he would make a few discreet inquiries to see whether there might be any reason to take Geismeier's accusation more seriously.

Altdorfer Investigates

Nobody had anything bad to say about SS Lieutenant Colonel Reinhard Pabst. He was well educated, thoughtful, dedicated to his work, a gifted interrogator. He was a little aloof, moody sometimes, a loner, but a good man.

On the other hand, almost everybody Altdorfer asked – former colleagues from his time in the police – spoke ill of Willi Geismeier. Captain Altdorfer decided again there was nothing to Geismeier's accusations. It was just more of the same troublemaking mischief that had always been his way.

After several weeks of asking around and several more of hesitating, Altdorfer called Dachau and asked to speak to the duty officer. He wanted to arrange to interrogate the prisoner Willi Geismeier one more time. 'That son of a bitch needs to be taught a lesson,' he said.

There was a moment of silence. Then the duty officer said, 'I'm sorry, Captain, but that isn't possible.'

'Isn't possible? Why isn't it possible?'

'I'm afraid, Captain, the prisoner has escaped.'

'What? Escaped?' said Altdorfer. 'Nobody escapes from Dachau.'

'Yes, sir, I know. But . . . well, Geismeier did.' Altdorfer wondered how it had happened. 'He was being interrogated. He somehow overcame his interrogator and fled in his car.'

'When did this happen?'

'Yesterday.'

Altdorfer thought for a moment. 'Who was his interrogator?'

'I am not allowed to say, Captain. The case is still being investigated.'

'Was it SS Lieutenant Colonel Pabst?' said Altdorfer.

There was a pause. 'I'm not allowed to say, Captain.'

So it was Pabst. That changed everything.

Captain Altdorfer thought about visiting Pabst again but decided against it. The only thing he could ask, that he hadn't asked the first time, would be about Geismeier's interrogation and his escape. And since the lieutenant colonel was responsible for Geismeier's escape, anything he would say would be self-serving and of little use. The one person he really needed to talk to was Geismeier, and that wasn't going to happen.

Bergemann was at his desk one morning, typing up reports that were due – actually they had been due the Friday before – when a very large SS captain, his hat at a cocky angle, came into the office. He ducked his head as he came through the door.

'Detective Sergeant Gruber?' he said.

'In the office, sir,' said Bergemann, and pointed at the door. The large captain nodded, stepped to the door and knocked. Gruber looked up, seemed to recognize his visitor, and got up to let him in. The two men seemed on friendly terms. They spoke for a while and then came out of the office together.

'Bergemann,' said Gruber, 'Hauptsturmführer Altdorfer is looking into Geismeier's escape. I told him you were here when Geismeier was still with us and that you knew him. He'd like to ask you a few questions.' He turned to Altdorfer. 'Geismeier and Bergemann were friends back then. Sometimes I think they still are.' He laughed. 'A little joke,' he said.

Altdorfer stuck out his enormous hand. 'Albrecht Altdorfer,' he said.

Bergemann took his hand. 'Bergemann, Hans.'

Altdorfer looked around the office. 'Is there somewhere we can talk, Hans?'

Bergemann took the captain into an interview room. 'How can I help you, Captain?'

'So, what did your sergeant mean about you and Geismeier?'

Bergemann gave an exasperated shrug. 'His favorite joke, Captain. He hates Geismeier.'

'And you?'

'I liked Willi. But I haven't seen him for years.'

Captain Altdorfer studied Bergemann for a moment, then seemed to decide to believe him. 'You know about Geismeier's escape . . .'

'Everybody does,' said Bergemann.

'I interrogated Geismeier twice at Dachau myself,' said Altdorfer.

'Really?' said Bergemann.

'And he accused an SS Gestapo officer of being the serial killer.'

'Really. Did he name somebody?'

'Your Sergeant Gruber tells me you briefly worked on the serial-killer case yourself. I wonder whether you discovered anything that would substantiate Geismeier's accusation. Anything at all . . .'

'No, I didn't.'

'So Geismeier is making it up?'

'I didn't say that. I just didn't find anything conclusive. Excuse me, Captain. I think I should get my case notes.' He went to his desk, got the folder, and came back. He looked through his notes for a minute, then told the captain about the streetcar connection, that all the women had been killed along three streetcar lines. He led him back out to the bullpen where there was a large map of Munich and put his finger on Gestapo headquarters at Briennerstraße, where the three streetcar lines intersected. 'This is as far as I got.'

The captain stared at the map, then at Bergemann, then back at the map, at Briennerstraße, where a few days ago he had been sitting in SS Gestapo Major Reinhard Pabst's office chatting about his wife and daughters. 'Hans,' he said, 'can I take you to lunch?'

The two men walked around the corner to the Gasthaus Zum Schwabinger Bach.

'Gentlemen,' said Elsa. 'What'll it be?'

Bergemann was hungry. '*Gulaschsuppe* and *Weißwurst* and a half liter of Hofbräu dark,' he said.

'I'll have the same, Fräulein, thank you,' said the captain.

Bergemann and the captain touched glasses – 'Prosit!' – and drank.

'Hans, are you in touch with Willi Geismeier?' said the captain.

'No, I'm not. If I saw him, I'd have to arrest him,' said Bergemann. 'I have no idea where he is.' That last statement was actually true. Bergemann had helped Willi to a safe house after his escape. And Willi had disappeared from there.

'OK,' said the captain. 'OK, Hans, I believe you. Do you think Geismeier knows more about the case than you do?'

'He probably does. Here's what I do know, Captain. The Detective Geismeier I knew never made accusations without evidence, he never made arrests without evidence. He had the best arrest record in the department, and his arrests usually ended in convictions because he always had the evidence. Always.'

'Really? Every other policeman I've ever heard talk about Geismeier says he was a serious troublemaker.'

'That's true, Captain. He was a troublemaker. But it's also true he was a good cop whose arrests led to convictions. He always had good evidence. Always. Whether that's still true, I couldn't say.'

'Fair enough. So, going back to your own investigation, having discovered the connection to the streetcar lines and the intersection of the three lines and all that, what would have been your next step?'

'I was taken off the case.'

'If you hadn't been taken off the case.'

Bergemann opened the case notes folder once again. 'It was kept out of the papers, but there was evidence that one of the victims had seriously injured the killer with a knife of her own. I would have looked to see whether he had been treated at a hospital or clinic. That would have been my next step.'

Altdorfer was making notes. 'How would you have looked? Where would you have looked?'

'Well, she was killed . . . here!' Bergemann pointed at the map.

'So I would have started looking at hospitals and clinics along that streetcar line between here and Briennerstraße.'

'What else would you have done as a next step, Hans?'

'Captain, I'm a little uncomfortable here. I'm supposed to be off the case; I don't want to get in trouble.'

'Hans, this isn't the serial-killer case I'm investigating. I'm investigating the Geismeier escape from Dachau. Think of it that way.'

The Bavarian Forest

Bergemann and Willi rarely met these days. Meetings were dangerous for both men. When it became urgent that Bergemann talk to Willi, he called Edvin Lindstrom at the Swedish consulate. Bergemann left a coded message, and Lindstrom got back to him with a meeting time and place Willi had chosen. It had been easier when Willi was in Munich, but now, because the hunt for Willi had gotten broader and more intense, they met in the Bavarian Forest, two hours northeast of Munich, not far from Schloß Barzelhof where Willi had been in school, and not far from the Czech border.

Eberhardt von Hohenstein, Willi's schoolboy nemesis, had outgrown his cruelty during his final years at Barzelhof and had become an exemplary university student. He was ashamed of his earlier behavior toward Willi and Andrea Welke, and eventually sought both of them out to ask for their forgiveness.

After serving in the trenches in the Great War, Eberhardt became a diplomat, as his father had been before him. He was a devout democrat, served throughout the Weimar time in various foreign outposts, and then left the government when Hitler became chancellor. Germany's interests at home and abroad were no longer interests he could represent.

Eberhardt retired with his wife, his daughter-in-law and a four-year-old grandson (Eberhardt's son was away in the army) to the estate that had been in the von Hohenstein family since the middle ages. They lived in one wing of the gigantic stone and timber manor house. Eberhardt oversaw five thousand hectares of farm and forest. His staff of foresters and farmers lived, along with the small household staff, in the dependencies built around a courtyard in front of the house. A flock of chickens pecked in the dust and six or eight dogs lay about, getting up only to move when the sun had shifted and left them in the shade.

Willi was staying in one of the logging huts that were scattered throughout the vast forest. 'Stay as long as you need to, Geismeier,' Eberhardt had said. 'You'll be safe here.' The hut was four kilometers from the house on a narrow, straight two-track road, which then went on for many more kilometers through endless pine forest. Eberhardt had used this particular hut himself as a sort of retreat, and Willi had stayed there during his first flight from Munich. There was a cot, a table, two chairs, a cast-iron cook stove, cookware, tableware, lanterns, and other necessities. There was a radio that worked with a crank and had a wire antenna strung between two ancient pines. Eberhardt would drive out to the cabin every so often with a basket of food and a bottle of wine or some bottles of beer. It was summer and Eberhardt and Willi would sit outside and talk.

Willi worked for Eberhardt as a woodcutter, not because he had to, but because he wanted to. Eberhardt had lost several young woodcutters to the army. Willi wanted to get his strength back, and pulling the crosscut saw helped him do that.

Eberhardt was a reader like Willi, but he read mostly German literature. He brought Willi books Willi knew of but hadn't read. In turn, Willi suggested some Shakespearean plays Eberhardt didn't know.

Willi hadn't read Kafka before. He had the sense when he read *The Metamorphosis* and then *The Trial* that he was reading about his own life. 'You know, Willi, in a sense Kafka's stories are all crime stories. Perfect for an ex-cop. They're about crime and punishment. For Kafka, of course, human existence seems to be both the crime and the punishment.'

Bergemann had driven east for two hours. He had stopped twice to make sure he wasn't being followed. Willi's was the shorter trip. He had to walk the four kilometers to the house, and then drive one of Eberhardt's farm trucks to a rendezvous point some distance from the estate. Reinhard was now obsessed with killing Willi, and he had let the Gestapo and SS know that Geismeier was public enemy number one. There were several teams of Gestapo on Willi's trail. They knew Willi would probably be somewhere where he had connections or knew his way around, and one such place was the Bavarian Forest near Schloß Barzelhof. Eberhardt had learned there was a Gestapo team in Passau asking questions.

Willi and Bergemann met just inside an abandoned train tunnel near Spiegelau. Willi looked better than he had the last time Bergemann had seen him. His body had thickened up again. His hair had grown back, although now it was white. He still carried a haunted look in his eyes.

Willi had already heard about Altdorfer's interest in Reinhard. 'He's been asking anyone and everyone questions,' said Willi.

'He's pretty clueless as a detective, but he's not stupid. I think he's serious about finding the killer. And Reinhard looks like his leading candidate.'

'Does he have the nerve?' said Willi. 'He's a washed-up captain up against one of Himmler's disciples.'

'Actually, I think he does have the nerve. But there's only one way to know. So do we keep feeding him "suggestions" that will lead him to Reinhard?'

'We could,' said Willi, 'but in the time it might take, Reinhard could kill again.'

'What if we just feed him the information?'

'He'd trace it right back to you, Hans,' said Willi.

'Well, what about someone not connected to either of us?'

'That's a good idea.' Willi considered for a moment. 'I think I know just the person.'

Heinz Schleiffer Gets a Letter

It was Friday. Trude Heinemann, the mail lady, was worn out. Not just today either. Every day her knees hurt and were swollen by day's end. She needed aspirin at night just to be able to sleep. The mail bag she carried six days a week seemed heavier than ever. She had asked for an inside job, but those jobs – sorting the mail or selling stamps – were all held by men, and none of them was about to leave. So she had decided to retire from the postal service. Dieter, her son, was grown and recently married. He had a decent job in a bank, so she didn't have to worry about him. He talked about finding a bigger apartment and having her move in with them, but Trude liked her independence. She thought she'd stay where she was.

She would miss her people, the people whose mail she delivered. She thought of them almost as family. She had gotten to know them over the years, knew their stories, their sorrows and their joys. Some would give her little treats from time to time, chocolates or a bottle of schnapps. Of course, then she had to carry whatever it was around for the rest of the day, which didn't help her knees.

There were a few sourpusses on her route. Like Heinz Schleiffer, for instance. His building was next, and she used to dread even seeing him. He had been one of the worst, an obnoxious, nasty little Nazi. But then a while back something had happened and he had changed, had gotten nicer. It had been around the time that Frau Schimmel had died. Now, there was a *really* nice person. She had been sick for a while with cancer. Trude had decided then that she didn't want to wait until she was old and sick to retire. Anyway, Heinz Schleiffer had gotten nicer. He had dropped the 'Heil Hitler' stuff. He never strutted around in his uniform these days. And he had learned to smile. Sometimes on a nice day he would offer her a glass of lemonade or beer. He'd ask how she was, ask after her family.

Trude rang Schleiffer's bell. He opened the door. '*Grüß Gott*, Frau Heinemann,' he said. 'How are you?'

'Fine, Herr Schleiffer. How are you?'

'Fine, thanks,' he said.

'I've got a registered package for you,' she said.

'Really?' He looked worried. 'I hope it's not bad news.'

'I hope not,' she said. 'Sign right here.' Heinz signed and she handed him the package.

He looked at it, turned it over a few times. 'Who's it from, I wonder?' he said. 'There's no return address.'

Trude looked at it. 'I don't know,' she said. 'It looks important. They do that sometimes. Maybe the return address is inside.'

'Well, I better look into this then. Thank you.'

Once inside he got scissors and cut the brown tape sealing the flat, brown cardboard envelope. Inside was another smaller envelope with a handwritten letter attached. Still no return address. He looked at the signature: Karl Juncker. The small hairs on the back of his neck stood on end.

Herr Schleiffer,

I was very sorry to learn of Frau Schimmel's death. I know
that you and she were close and that she valued your friend-
ship. That is why I am asking you for a favor.

An SS Officer investigating the Munich serial killings is going
to show up at Tullemannstraße, probably on Monday. He
will be looking for me, but I would like him to find the
contents of this envelope instead. If you would be so kind
as to put the enclosed envelope inside the top desk drawer
in my apartment, and then, for your own safety, destroy this
letter to you, it will go a long way toward bringing the serial
killer to justice.

Thank you for your help in this matter.

> *Respectfully,*
> *Karl Juncker*

Heinz Schleiffer had the entire weekend to think about what he
should do. But the answer was obvious. If he decided to follow
his own course and, say, take the packet to Ortsgruppenleiter
Mecklinger, who was still in charge of the neighborhood, he would
himself be implicated in whatever Juncker was up to. In fact, if he
was connected to this plot in any way, he would be in trouble. He
would be hauled in and questioned, and he knew where that would
lead.

Karl Juncker had trusted him and had given him an out. And
there was the fact, which he could not easily forget, that he had
reported Juncker multiple times for something he had not done.
Heinz sometimes even wondered whether he had perhaps caused
Karl Juncker to be incarcerated. Of course, he had not, but the
thought still weighed on him. Now all he had to do to make amends
was put the envelope in Juncker's desk and say nothing.

The inside envelope was unsealed, almost as though Juncker
wanted him to look at the contents. And Heinz went so far as to
slide the papers halfway out. But the first word that caught his eye
was 'Gestapo,' and he quickly slid the papers back into the envelope
and closed it up.

Heinz got his keys and went up to the apartment. It had not been
opened for many months. There were cobwebs, dust and dead flies
everywhere. One of the pictures was hanging crooked. How did that
happen in an empty apartment? he wondered.

He opened the desk drawer. There was the box of medals. He looked at the medals again and was encouraged that he was doing the right thing. He debated whether he should put the medals on top of the envelope, but decided then he should do exactly as instructed. He tiptoed out of the apartment and carefully turned the lock. He could almost have believed that Karl Juncker was watching him.

The Evidence

Hauptsturmführer Altdorfer had called hospital after hospital, clinic after clinic, before he had finally come up with the clinic that had sewed up Friedrich Grosz's hand. The nurse and the doctor there both wondered that, with so many different authorities coming with all their questions, why this killer had not been caught. Four more women had been killed in the meantime. How could it take this long?

'What authorities?' Altdorfer demanded. Nurse Grosz said he was the third one. One he recognized from her description as Willi Geismeier. It made the Hauptsturmführer want to go after Geismeier all over again. Then he reminded himself who was killing women, and it wasn't Geismeier. It occurred to him then to ask Nurse Grosz and Doctor Rosenberg if they could remember the questions Willi had asked them. Whatever else he was, Geismeier was smart. Maybe he could use Geismeier's questions to speed up his own investigation.

It had been a long time, so neither one could remember much. Doctor Rosenberg remembered Willi asking about drugs. Nurse Grosz remembered that she had described Friedrich Grosz to the detective's satisfaction, but she didn't think she could come up with the description again. However, Altdorfer had thought to find a photo of Reinhard Pabst. 'Is this the man?' he asked. Doctor Rosenberg couldn't be sure, but Nurse Grosz was certain. 'That's him. For sure. I remember those eyes,' she said.

The following Monday, Altdorfer was about to begin canvasing pharmacies when he got an urgent call from Detective Sergeant Gruber. Gruber had received an anonymous tip that Willi Geismeier had been spotted in his old neighborhood. It seemed like a long shot, but every criminal slipped up at some point. Gruber had caught Geismeier once. Maybe he could do it again.

'Where are you off to, Sarge?' said Bergemann.

'Never mind,' said Gruber as he was strapping on his Luger.

'You don't want back-up, Sergeant?'

'No,' said Gruber. 'Not necessary.' He hurried out of the office.

Hauptsturmführer Altdorfer was waiting at the corner of Tullemannstraße when Gruber arrived. They walked to number fifty-four and rang the bell. Heinz Schleiffer let them in. They showed him a search warrant to get into Karl Juncker's apartment.

Heinz blinked. 'It's no longer Juncker's apartment,' he said. 'It's unoccupied, but his furniture is still there.'

'Have you seen anybody go in or out?' said Gruber again.

'I haven't, no. As far as I know, nobody has gone in or out for a long time. I tried to put the place up for rent, but I haven't . . .'

'So, you haven't seen Juncker around?'

Schleiffer swore he hadn't.

'Just open the apartment,' said Gruber. 'And do it quietly.' He pulled his gun, although he already knew they were on a wild goose chase. Geismeier wasn't stupid enough to show up at his old apartment in broad daylight.

The blinds were pulled, there was dust everywhere. They searched the apartment, first the bedroom, the closets and dressers. Heinz was afraid they'd skip the desk, so he stood beside it. Eventually, though, Hauptsturmführer Altdorfer came over and opened the top drawer. He took out the envelope.

'What's this?' said Gruber, taking out the small metal box.

'Those are his medals,' said Schleiffer. Gruber and Altdorfer both gave Schleiffer a look. 'He showed them to me once,' said Schleiffer.

Back at his office, Altdorfer went through Willi's notes. They had been written recently and presented a damning case against Reinhard Pabst. It began with the prostitute Pabst had abused those many years earlier. She had not died after all, but had recovered and had eventually returned to her trade, telling everyone who would listen, including the police at one point, that the Pope had raped her. It turned out on further research that Reinhard had abused other women in a similarly frenzied manner. Willi had also included an account of the attack on Lola without mentioning her name.

Once Reinhard started killing, there were the muddy footprints, the all-night streetcar lines, the focus on Briennerstraße. There was Erna and Horst Raczynski's accounts of the attack, their description of the assailant, including the sound of his voice. Then there was the chronology after Suzanna Merkl had stabbed him, the streetcar driver's description of Pabst and his wound, his arrival at the clinic, with Nurse Grosz and Doctor Rosenberg's descriptions, his cold demeanor, his bitten fingernails, the bloody rag he kept, the jagged cut around his hand, then the pharmacy with its registry and the SS number and the signature. Willi had even found witnesses who saw Pabst go in and out of Briennerstraße 20. Despite the late hour, two witnesses – one a streetcar monitor stationed near the building, the other a newspaper vendor at the train station – had seen someone fitting his description. And his arm was in a sling. The streetcar monitor had noticed his 'ruined, bloody coat sleeve.'

'Did you think to call the police?' Willi had asked.

'Are you joking?' said the man. 'It was Gestapo headquarters. No, thank you.'

'Did you see him again?' said Willi.

'Well, not right away. But then, after a while, I watched for him and thought I saw him again, also late at night.'

'Why would you notice this particular man?' said Willi.

'Well, at first his arm was still in a sling, then his hand was bandaged. Anyway, it's my job to monitor the streetcars to make sure they're on schedule. There's lots of time between streetcars. Watching people come and go helps pass the time.'

Willi had written finally that, while in Dachau, he had been interrogated by SS Standartenführer Reinhard Pabst, who had become aware of Willi's suspicions about him. The peculiar and savage scar circling Pabst's right hand had confirmed Willi's suspicions that Pabst was the killer, and when confronted with Willi's accusations, Pabst had all but admitted that he was the killer.

Hauptsturmführer Altdorfer sat for a long time contemplating what he had just read. Geismeier presented a convincing case. There could be little doubt that Colonel Pabst was the perpetrator of multiple brutal attacks and these thirteen perverted and heinous murders of innocent women. Altdorfer also knew, however, that Pabst was a close disciple of SS Reichsführer Heinrich Himmler, and Himmler was not likely to accept the testimony of a renegade police detective, an enemy of the Reich and a Dachau escapee, against the word of his fair-haired boy.

Heinrich Himmler was in Berlin at the Prinz Albrecht Straße SS headquarters these days, occupied with other far more important matters. The Führer was finalizing war preparations, so messages were flying back and forth between the two men. Himmler had three aides whose job it was to arrange and oversee his communiqués and meetings with the Führer. A junior aide, an SS lieutenant, was responsible for monitoring all incoming messages and mail. He opened everything to make certain it was worthy of Reichsführer Himmler's time and attention. He made certain no mail from cranks slipped in, no dangerous packages, and then delivered the appropriate pieces to Himmler's desk.

Himmler leafed through the stack – starting with the Führer's messages – to see whether anything required immediate attention. Everything else went back in the inbox where it sat until the end of the day. There were always messages from various politicians or other interested parties offering suggestions or asking for support for this or that project. These messages usually commenced with flattering phrases, praising the Reichsführer's perspicacity or expressing gratitude for his kind attention on this matter or that.

Today the Gleiwitz matter was at the top of his agenda. Himmler's minions had staged a false flag incident, an attack on a German radio station by 'Polish soldiers,' who were, in fact, German prisoners forced to dress in Polish uniforms and then killed. Hitler feigned fury. 'This night for the first time Polish regular soldiers fired on our territory. Since five forty-five a.m. we have been returning the fire, and from now on bombs will be met by bombs.'

By the time Himmler had finished dealing with Gleiwitz, it was almost ten in the evening. A manila envelope without return address was the last thing left in his inbox. Himmler thought he would leave it for another time. He turned the envelope over a few times, trying to see whether there were some identifying marks. Seeing none, he slid the papers out. It was a handwritten document on ordinary letter paper, but it had a business format.

TO: SS Reichsführer Heinrich Himmler
SUBJECT: SS Standartenführer Reinhard Pabst: Serial Killer.

'What the devil . . .!' Himmler said aloud. He sat up straight and started reading.

The material in Himmler's hands had not come from Hauptsturmführer Altdorfer. It had come directly from Willi.

The Arrest

R einhard Pabst was dressing for work. He had ceremonial duties today, so he was wearing his uniform. There was a knock at his door. When he opened it, two SS men stepped inside, followed by an SS Hauptsturmführer he did not recognize. 'Reinhard Pabst,' the captain said, 'you are under arrest.'

Reinhard was put in handcuffs. All rank and decorations were torn from his uniform, and he was taken by car straight to Gestapo headquarters. He was led to an interrogation room where he sat alone and waited.

Recently promoted, thinking himself at the top of his game, Reinhard was stunned by this turn of events. He could only believe that someone had made a terrible error and would have to pay grievously for this. Two Gestapo interrogators came into the room.

Before either man could speak, Reinhard said, 'I hope you know who I am, and that I report directly to Reichsführer Himmler. I warn you now, before it is too late, before this foolishness goes any further.'

The two men did not look as if they had even heard him. They studied the sheaf of papers they had brought in with them. They pointed at text and nodded at one another.

'I have to warn you again, gentlemen . . .'

'Reichsführer Himmler ordered your arrest,' said one of the interrogators, looking up finally.'

'That is not possible,' said Reinhard.

One held up the order with Himmler's signature for Reinhard to see.

'That is a mistake,' said Reinhard just as firmly. One could almost imagine that he did not even remember having murdered thirteen women, or, if he did remember, could not conceive of it as a punishable offense.

The two interrogators looked at him with blank faces. One man said, 'The time is ten twenty-five,' and wrote it on the blank page in front of him. The two men began questioning Reinhard, which consisted of going through the murders one by one in detail, turning what they now knew to be true into a question. Each question began, 'And did you on such and such a date . . .' and ended with Reinhard saying, 'I did not.'

It was a measure of the depth of Reinhard Pabst's insanity that in response to every question he was asked by his interrogators, he protested his innocence. When he saw that wasn't working, he rambled on about the superiority of men, the uncleanness and deceitfulness of women. To become the superman we were all capable of, he had to quash the darkness within, to kill his feminine side. 'I am following the Führer's own foundations. The sacred soil on which we stand. We are all baptized in blood.' He went on and on in that vein, straying further and further into hysteria and madness. After three exhausting hours of unproductive questioning, Reinhard was handcuffed and driven to Dachau where he would stay until a final judgment was rendered.

Reichsführer Heinrich Himmler was not squeamish about violence. After all, an SS man was supposed to be violent. And even an SS man *enjoying* violence was not a problem as far as Himmler was concerned. That was to be expected, given their training, and it was even to be encouraged. Still, the Reichsführer was shocked, he had to admit, at the wanton brutality the killer of these thirteen women had exhibited. This was somehow killing on a different level, although he would have been hard pressed to explain the difference between what Reinhard had done and the killings that were done every day on his orders. Maybe it was that the perversion was so blatantly on display here. There was no rational ideology behind the killing, no societal objective, no larger good. It was just violence for the sake of violence. Himmler wondered what had driven Reinhard Pabst to do it, while never once wondering what drove him, Heinrich Himmler, to do what *he* did. He liked Pabst and had thought of him as the ideal SS man.

Himmler saw that a criminal of Pabst's sort probably had to be executed. But he considered briefly whether there might be a way to paper over the 'inconvenience' of his killings of these women. He decided there wasn't. Whoever had sent this document to him was still out there and had almost certainly sent the same information to others.

Hauptsturmführer Altdorfer had delayed for two days before deciding that he had no choice but to get the evidence into Himmler's hands. After all, he had much to lose – Pabst was known to be Himmler's favorite, and he was a senior member of the Gestapo. On the other hand, if Altdorfer didn't report what he knew to be criminal activity and it was later discovered, he could be seen as an accessory to the crime.

By the time Himmler received the phone call from Munich that Hauptsturmführer Altdorfer had brought a packet of documents to SS headquarters concerning criminality in the upper ranks of the SS, Himmler had all but decided Pabst had to pay the price.

'Is it Pabst?' he asked.

'It is,' said the officer who had called.

'How did this Altdorfer come by the information?' Himmler asked.

'He found it in the apartment of a former police detective.'

'Have you questioned the detective?'

'His name is Geismeier, Herr Reichsführer. He is himself a wanted man.'

'Wanted? For what?'

'A number of things, most recently escaping from Dachau after shooting Pabst with his own pistol.'

'I thought that name sounded familiar. So we have no idea where he is?'

'We're working on it, Herr Reichsführer.'

'Well, it doesn't really matter, does it?' He hung up the phone.

Himmler realized that Reinhard Pabst, by indulging his own perverted passions, had grievously betrayed the SS Reichsführer's trust. That was unforgivable. He hoped the Pabst story could be handled without ever having to explain to the Führer, who, if he learned of it, would go through the roof. Himmler had called Munich back and ordered Pabst's arrest.

The Führer was busy overseeing the delicate and secret non-aggression negotiations between Ambassador von der Schulenburg and the Soviet Union's Ambassador Molotov when Himmler had decided he better mention the Pabst affair, just to avoid having the Führer hear about it from somebody else.

Hitler did not want to even hear another word. 'Don't bring me this piddling shit, Himmler. You take care of it.'

*   *   *

At the *Juhrhaus* in Dachau, Reinhard was made to undress. He stepped out of what was left of his uniform. He was ordered to take off his underwear too. He had to squat and bend over to be inspected for contraband. He was given a thorough physical examination. The doctor was interested in the angry red scar that coiled around his right wrist.

Word of Reinhard's arrest had preceded his arrival. Every SS man at Dachau knew by now who Reinhard was. Reinhard got a striped jacket and striped pants. The shoes he got fit, although that was a lucky accident. By the time he was escorted to his barracks, most of the prisoners knew who he was as well.

Marching to the evening roll call, they sang 'Holy Fire.' No one sang more loudly than Reinhard Pabst.

> *Holy fire burns through the land,*
> *The people wake out of their sleep.*
> *Brothers, unite and join hands,*
> *We want honor instead of pain.*
> *Work will make our deeds noble,*
> *And we are all soldiers of work.*

He marched joyfully. He stopped at one point and looked around, as though he were having trouble understanding where he was and what had happened to him. Two SS men ran up to him. But instead of punching or beating him, they gently walked him back into formation. Despite the crimes he was accused of, for the SS officers and men of Dachau, Reinhard was someone to be reckoned with. He was one of their own, an SS colonel and a Gestapo man. He was also a killer of epic reputation.

The Woodcutter

The two-man crosscut saw is a brilliant tool. Each man cuts on the pull and rests on the push and it slices through the largest trunks like a hot knife through butter, showering their feet and legs with sawdust. Sometimes Willi forgot everything but the rhythm of the work. The two men – often his partner was

Eberhardt's teenage son – paused their work to sharpen the saw teeth or just to look to the sky when the Stukas came flying overhead on their way to Poland.

Poland was being bombed into ruin. Warsaw was destroyed, Krakow too. There was courageous resistance by Polish irregulars, but they wouldn't last long. Danzig was occupied, and safe enough for the Führer to visit and make a speech, which he did. Russia invaded Poland from the east to get their share before Germany took it all.

Interest within the Gestapo in catching Willi had flared up after Reinhard Pabst's arrest, but it had died down again just as quickly. The sooner the Pabst affair was forgotten the better. Besides, the Gestapo had their hands full with Poland, and now everyone was getting ready for Russia. Russia was next, and Russia would be a different story. Likewise, Gruber's pursuit of Willi had not worked out to Gruber's advantage. He had wasted time on a wild goose chase. His squad's case closure rate remained pathetic, and Captain Wendt was threatening to take the squad away from him and reduce him in rank.

Willi had the sense that he could begin looking for Lola, as long as he was careful. Even without the Gestapo on his tail or Gruber to worry about, it wouldn't be easy.

'Where do you want to start?' asked Bergemann. Willi, Bergemann, and Eberhardt von Hohenstein sat in front of Willi's hut eating black bread and ham and drinking cold, foamy beer. It was the last day of September. The sun was brilliant and hot as a few stray birch leaves – birch leaves were always the first – drifted to the ground.

'I'll start in Munich,' said Willi. To his surprise, Bergemann did not object.

'I can drive you,' said Eberhardt.

It was late evening. Eberhardt drove fast. He pulled up at Tullemannstraße and parked. They watched the building for a while. Heinz Schleiffer stepped outside. He looked up at the sky and stretched his arms in a yawn. He had put on weight.

Willi got out of the car and walked up the steps as Heinz turned to go inside. 'Good evening, Herr Schleiffer,' he said.

Heinz turned and stepped back in surprise. 'Herr Juncker!'

'Let's go inside,' said Willi. Heinz tried to see Willi's hands, but they were in his jacket pockets. He backed into the building.

Willi emerged after half an hour. 'What did you learn?' Eberhardt said as they sped off. Willi shook his head and laughed. 'What a piece of work is man.'

Schleiffer had been incoherent, ricocheting between terror, remorse, giddiness, and rage. He had rambled on about Frau Schimmel. Willi had thanked him for looking after her. 'Why thank me?' said Heinz. 'I did what any human being would have done.' By which he seemed to mean he had been very brave and noble.

Willi thanked him too for placing the package in his desk drawer, and praised him for helping stop a murderer. Heinz seemed unable to accept Willi's thanks or praise without lapsing into meandering, sometimes abject, sometimes angry apology. One minute it was, 'Please, don't hurt me,' the next it was, 'How dare you undermine the Führer's great work.'

Schleiffer knew nothing of Lola's whereabouts, although he said Bertha Schimmel had been in touch with her until her death. He had found Bertha's letters and burned them after she died. 'I didn't want them to fall into the wrong hands.' He gave Willi a meaningful look. Heinz was still inclined to ascribe heroic motives to his own decent behavior.

Lola had moved several times since Frau Schimmel had died. Fedor Blaskowitz had learned the Gestapo was snooping around Murnau. He didn't know whether they were there for Lola, but he and Lola had agreed it was no longer safe for her to remain in the green house by the Riegsee.

A car arrived one morning and drove Lola west to Bad Aibling where Fedor knew a young farm couple – the husband was a former pupil – willing to help out in exchange for a little money and some help with the farm chores. For several weeks Lola got up early each morning, fed the animals, gathered eggs and helped out in other ways. There was a dog too, and a large family of cats.

One morning the couple and Lola were having breakfast together, as they did each morning, when Hitler came on the radio and declared war on Poland. The young couple looked at one another and then went silent. Lola overheard them whispering later that morning about the danger of harboring a fugitive. The war changed everything, made everything more dangerous.

'What can we do?' said the husband.

'We have to . . .' Lola didn't hear the rest of the conversation, but at lunch that day neither one of them spoke to her or met her eyes. And that afternoon the wife kept looking out the window as though she might be expecting someone. Probably it was nothing, but Lola couldn't take the chance. She packed her small suitcase.

Early the next morning she left the house without telling anyone and walked to the train station. She took the first train to Salzburg where she changed to a train to Vienna. She had a cousin there who had offered a place to stay if Lola ever needed it.

She would be safe there. But at the same time, the chain of connections that would allow Willi to find her was now broken. How could he look for her? He wouldn't even think to look for her in Vienna. And where should she look for him? She knew he was out of Dachau, but she had no idea where he might have gone.

Eberhardt drove Willi to Lola's parents' house. The two men watched for a while before Willi went to the door. Lola's father didn't recognize Willi at first, but once he did, he pulled him inside and embraced him.

'We don't know where she is, Willi, but a card came last week. She's safe, I think.'

'Can I see the card?' said Willi.

'Having a wonderful time,' was all she had written. She hadn't signed it. The stamp was Austrian, the postmark was Vienna, the picture was vineyards.

'Our niece is there.'

'You should destroy the card,' said Willi.

The niece was in Vienna, and Lola was living in a hut in the vineyards above Grinzing. You could get there by streetcar from Vienna. It was as though she had been expecting him. When he knocked and she opened the door, she was wearing the green dress.

The Holy Fire

Willi read in the Nazi paper about Standartenführer Reinhard Pabst's 'martyrdom.' A German hero, he had been brutally assassinated by a conspiracy of enemies of the German people. Pabst was given a state funeral, with a mounted guard and goose-stepping legions of SS men. And, in a fiery oration, the Führer himself warned Germany's enemies to take note. The resolve Reinhard Pabst had shown in his devoted and relentless pursuit of Germany's enemies would be repeated in the Reich's pursuit of its enemies. The Führer promised that the despicable assassins of this great German hero would soon know the full fury of German justice. Hauptsturmführer Altdorfer, at home in the loving collective bosom of his women, read the same account. His youngest daughter had just brought his morning chocolate and a sweet roll. Altdorfer was not surprised to learn that Goebbels' Propaganda Ministry had turned the murderer Reinhard Pabst into a symbol of German victimhood, a fallen hero of the Fatherland. The Führer and Goebbels always understood how to make full use of whatever cards they were dealt.

It did briefly give Altdorfer pause that such cynical use could be made of such a stone-cold killer's deserved demise. But mainly Altdorfer felt grateful that Reinhard was dead and that German women no longer needed to fear for their lives when they left home. He was grateful also, and more than a little proud, that he had managed to bring that particular crime spree to an end while staying clear of the whole affair. He thought he could take some small credit for how it had turned out, although he had to admit that the real hero in the matter was Geismeier. Somehow Willi Geismeier, an imprisoned and then a hunted man, had caught a vicious killer. You had to admire that. He found himself hoping Geismeier would get away scot-free, though he doubted that would happen.

Neither Gruber nor Bergemann knew anything of what had actually happened to the serial killer until Altdorfer showed up one morning to give them the details. Gruber was amazed, Bergemann less so, although he put on a good act. But then Altdorfer astonished both men when he said, 'The credit actually belongs to Geismeier.'

'What?' said Gruber. 'That's ridiculous! What are you talking about . . . Herr Hauptsturmführer?' Gruber's incredulity had caused him to momentarily forget his place.

Altdorfer didn't seem to notice or care. He explained that Geismeier had not only assembled a compelling and irrefutable case, but had then managed to get the evidence before Himmler. 'It wouldn't surprise me to learn that he got it to Goering, Goebbels, and all the rest as well. Anyway, justice was done.'

Justice? Well, not exactly, thought Bergemann.

Heinz Schleiffer was surprised to find Hauptsturmführer Altdorfer looming at his door one morning as well. 'You have done the Führer a great service, Herr Schleiffer, by helping rid Munich of a dangerous serial killer. You can be proud of that. And if you should see Geismeier again' – Altdorfer winked – 'thank him for me as well.'

Heinz didn't know what to say. He didn't expect he would ever see Geismeier or Juncker or whoever he was again. At least he hoped he wouldn't. He stammered a bit, and took the captain's huge hand when it was offered.

'Justice was done,' said Altdorfer again.

Reinhard had received special treatment when he first arrived in Dachau. But that had lasted about twenty-four hours. It took that length of time for the camp administration and the guards to make the mental adjustments they needed to make. By the next afternoon, when he was part of a road building crew and stood looking at the sky, having disappeared into his own thoughts, an SS man came up behind him and hit him hard in the side, knocking him to the ground. Reinhard tried to stand and the SS man knocked him down again. When he cried out that he was SS Standartenführer Pabst and demanded to see the officer in charge, the SS man hit him with his club, this time in the face. Reinhard's nose was crushed and bleeding, his cheekbone was broken, and he spit out several teeth. The SS man told him to get up and start working, but Reinhard lay there bewildered and confused. When he finally struggled to his feet, the SS man hit him again and this time Reinhard remained lying on the ground. He stayed there the entire afternoon. Sometimes he would speak or whimper, but he didn't move and no one tried to move him.

Soon enough it was time for the crew to move to a different part of the road. They got into formation. Reinhard stood up then. He was unsteady on his feet. He got in line at the back of the formation. As they started to march, Reinhard spun around suddenly and started running. He charged with surprising speed, given his injuries, toward the death zone and the fence beyond it, screaming incoherently as he ran. By the time the guards in the tower could swivel their machine gun around and point it in his direction, he had reached the zone and was only steps from the fence. They began shooting, splattering the ground with raking fire. Reinhard was hit several times, but somehow kept moving forward, jerking and convulsing with each step, almost as though the bullets were carrying him to his destination. His arms were stretched out in front of him as though he wanted to, he *had to* reach that fence. No one knew whether he was still alive when he did. The fence's barbs caught his clothes and his flesh and held him upright while the electricity crackled and flamed around him.

There was a hum from the west that grew into a roar as a squadron of Stuka dive bombers passed overhead on their way to Warsaw. There seemed to be hundreds of them. Reinhard's body smoked and smoldered. It remained hanging there on the fence until the prisoners were back in their barracks and the electricity running through the fence could be turned off.